THE
FELONS'
BALL

ALSO BY POLLY STEWART

The Good Ones

THE FELONS' BALL

A Novel

POLLY STEWART

HARPER

An Imprint of HarperCollinsPublishers

THE FELONS' BALL. Copyright © 2025 by Mary Stewart Atwell Schultz. All rights reserved. Printed in the United States of America. No part of this book may be used or reproduced in any manner whatsoever without written permission except in the case of brief quotations embodied in critical articles and reviews. For information, address HarperCollins Publishers, 195 Broadway, New York, NY 10007. In Europe, HarperCollins Publishers, Macken House, 39/40 Mayor Street Upper, Dublin 1, D01 C9W8, Ireland.

HarperCollins books may be purchased for educational, business, or sales promotional use. For information, please email the Special Markets Department at SPsales@harpercollins.com.

hc.com

FIRST EDITION

Library of Congress Cataloging-in-Publication Data has been applied for.

ISBN 978-0-06-341206-4

25 26 27 28 29 LBC 5 4 3 2 1

For my mother, Mary Welek Atwell,

and for Sarah, Diane, Sabrina, and Norm,
my sisters from another mister

THE FELONS' BALL

1.

Natalie walked through the blood, leaving a trail of red footprints across the laminate before she realized what she'd done.

She always left the overhead lights on dim, preferring the illumination of the battery-operated candles along the mantelpiece, and she'd turned the lights down another notch as they began the cooldown. After helping a woman in the back row lengthen into a side bend, she'd come back to the front, ready to move them through a final sun salutation and then to the floor for seated poses.

"Raise your arms over your heads, bringing the hands together," Natalie said in her softest and most gentle voice, and all the students obeyed. Then suddenly Amanda Vergotti sat down on the floor, face gray as a gym towel.

Natalie stared at the footprints leading back from her place at the front of the room to Amanda's black rubber mat. *She's peeing blood,* she thought. Then somebody started screaming.

Later she would wonder if maybe the whole thing was her fault. Afterward Natalie would think that perhaps she'd been in too big a hurry, rushing the students along, her mind already moving on to her plans for later that night. Cassie's voice echoed in her head, reminding her that yoga was more than a physical practice and that the people who came to her studio were entrusting her with their entire selves, not just their bodies. *That's why we always say that it's not an exercise program,* Cassie would surely tell her tomorrow. *You can't put people into poses without any awareness of what's going on with them on the inside.*

But that was exactly what Natalie had done, and now a woman she'd known her entire life might be dying on the floor of her studio.

She prayed for the first time in years. *God, don't let her die. God, please don't let it be something I did.* When Natalie was a child, Amanda—an unruly girl with long curly hair and a raspy laugh that made her sound several decades older than the rest of them—had been a friend of her sister Kaitlyn's, but a few years ago she'd moved back to town, transformed from a wild teen to a sleek beauty with a rich husband in tow, and though Natalie was bemused by the change, she was glad to have Amanda as a client. She was the kind of yoga student who threw herself into the practice, insisting on the most advanced version of the pose as if she expected a gold star for her efforts, and Natalie had mostly allowed it, afraid that if she pushed back, Amanda might switch her allegiance to the Pilates studio two towns over.

Kaitlyn appeared at her side, phone to her ear. "I'm talking to emergency dispatch," she whispered. "The EMTs want to know if she might be pregnant."

"Could you be pregnant?" Natalie said, speaking as quietly as she could, hoping her voice wouldn't reach the students still clustered behind her.

"No," Amanda whispered, shaking her head as tears ran down her cheeks. "We're not . . . I know that's not it."

But there was so much blood. Natalie snapped her fingers at the woman beside her and pointed at the cabinet along the back wall. "Towels," she barked, and the woman, whose name she couldn't remember, sprang into action, throwing open the doors of the cupboard, revealing half a dozen cheap loaner mats, blocks, straps, but no towels. "Locker room!" Natalie shouted. On her way to the door, the woman thrust a tote bag at her chest. Natalie pulled out a wadded pair of jeans and a white sweater and pressed them between Amanda's legs. Amanda's eyes fluttered and she vomited, quietly, as if she didn't want to make a fuss.

Someone handed Natalie a trash can, and she moved the towels to position the can by Amanda's chin. The reek of the air freshener she'd sprayed in the can that morning turned her stomach. Amanda's expression had gone from puzzled to astonished, as if she was looking at something the rest of them couldn't see. Natalie found herself wondering whose sweater was turning red under her hands, and whether she'd want the studio to reimburse her for the damage.

Natalie didn't hear the EMTs come in, but then a man in a uniform took her by the shoulders, gently tugging her away. They had their shoes on, Natalie realized, black sneakers making scuff marks across the floor. No one was supposed to wear shoes in the studio, but she couldn't very well ask them to take them off, not at a moment like this. The EMTs wheeled the gurney out into the lobby, bumping the wheels over the plastic transition strip with more force than seemed necessary.

Then they were gone. The other women gathered their things from the locker room and left in small groups, murmuring to each other. Natalie could hear Kaitlyn, at the front desk, apologizing and promising each of them a complimentary five-class pass. The gesture seemed both tactless and excessive, but Natalie didn't have the energy to interfere. She grabbed the disinfectant spray and mopped up the blood and bile in the studio. The strangers' shoes had tracked it all over the bamboo flooring, and she used up nearly a whole roll of paper towels.

She tried to go back to her prayer, but she couldn't stop picturing Amanda's white face, her terror so palpable that Natalie might as well have absorbed it into her body. No matter how many deep breaths she made herself take, her heart galloped as if she'd just finished a five-mile run.

After turning off the lights in the studio, Natalie found Kaitlyn saying goodbye to the last of the students. The skin around her eyes was red, as if she'd been scrubbing them with her knuckles. "I called her husband," Kaitlyn said to Natalie as she closed the door and locked it. "He's meeting them at the hospital."

Natalie leaned against the wall, trying to remember exactly what they'd been doing—what cues she'd given or hadn't given—in the moments before Amanda collapsed. "What do you think is wrong with her?" she asked. "She said she wasn't pregnant, but what else could make you bleed like that?" What had come from inside Amanda had looked vital, the body turned inside out.

"They don't want kids," Kaitlyn said. "I know this sounds crazy, but my first thought when I came in was that someone had hurt her, like she'd been shot or something. It was like a movie, where the police come in and draw the outline around the body on the floor."

Natalie shuddered. "How do you know they don't want kids?"

Kaitlyn lowered herself into the desk chair, propping her elbows on the ledge by the computer. "Amanda told me," she said. "I was complaining about morning sickness, and she said that Matt had a vasectomy. She said she'd always known she didn't want to be a mother."

"That's pretty personal," Natalie said, but Kaitlyn just shrugged. It was true that for many of the women who came through their doors, the studio was like the hair salon, a place to air secrets and grievances. Then, too, Amanda and Kaitlyn had been friends in high school, though as far as Natalie knew, they hadn't spent much time together since Amanda moved home.

Kaitlyn coughed and touched a finger to the corner of her eye, and Natalie wondered if her sister was more upset by what had happened to Amanda than she'd realized. "Did seeing that stress you out?" she asked. "Even though Amanda isn't pregnant?"

Kaitlyn shook her head. "No, it's not that," she said. "I was just wondering if one of us should have gone with her in the ambulance. I didn't want to leave you alone to deal with the other students, but it must have been so scary for her." She sighed and knitted her fingers behind her back, stretching out her shoulders. "Let me shut everything down here, and I'll meet you out back in five."

Natalie nodded and pushed open the door to the locker room, which was a mess as usual. She picked up the towels and dumped them in the basket under the counter. The soap scum and scuff marks on the tile would have to wait for the cleaners. The sink was leaking again, and what should have been a minor irritation suddenly made her feel like screaming. Her father had designed Ewald Yoga to Natalie's specifications—stucco walls painted butter yellow, a mirror wall in each practice room, and even the outline of the Blue Ridge Mountains stenciled above the front desk—but it seemed to her now that he'd also built in a series of little quirks and mistakes that kept the space from being quite perfect. Anyone who knew Trey Macready knew that no gift from him ever came without conditions, fine print you wouldn't bother to read until it was too late. Sometimes Natalie wondered if he really wanted her to succeed, or if it would have given him more satisfaction to see her lose interest in running a business and go back to school for something practical, like radiology.

She knew her parents thought she'd only gotten into yoga because of Cassie, and maybe that was true, but Natalie resented the skepticism that her family still seemed to have about her staying power when the studio had been open for over a year and they were actually making a profit now. Kaitlyn taught the beginner classes while Natalie took the intermediates, the rooms filling to capacity with a motley assortment of regulars: blue-haired ladies from church; dazed new moms rushing through a workout during play group; a clique of Natalie's old volleyball teammates; friends of her mother who worked part-time at the bank or the school board; the Garrett twins, who sometimes dressed alike even though they were nearly fifty. Still, there had been moments when Natalie wondered whether Ewald County wasn't ready for enlightenment. Occasionally a high school classmate or old neighbor approached her in a store to tell her they were concerned about her; didn't she know that yoga was satanic? Sometimes a student took her aside to say that chanting "Om shanti" made her uncomfortable because she didn't want to pray to anyone but her Heavenly Father.

And now Amanda Vergotti had almost died in her studio the day before Cassie arrived to spend a month at the lake. Natalie could already imagine the look of poorly concealed exasperation on her sister's face when she found out what happened—as if Natalie's failure to manage the situation was just another example of her general failure to adult.

Natalie braced the basket of towels against her hip and carried it to the back door, where the red glow of the exit sign showed Kaitlyn sitting at the picnic table, facing the thin line of woods that separated them from the back lot of Macready Contracting. Natalie set the basket on the table and took out her cigarettes. A reddish-brown dog trotted by without acknowledging them, its brushy tail sticking up like a feather duster.

"Jay and Cassie are supposed to get in around noon," Natalie said. "If you see them before I do, don't say anything about Amanda, okay?"

"I won't." A pickup blasting Top 40 country rolled over the tracks at the crossing, and Kaitlyn waited until the noise had faded before adding, "I finished that photo album for Daddy last night."

Natalie took another drag, not wanting to admit that she had no idea what Kaitlyn was talking about. At least she hadn't forgotten that tomorrow was their father's fiftieth birthday as well as their family's annual fall bash, nicknamed the Felons' Ball. The Felons' Ball was always held on the Saturday before Thanksgiving, but when their mother had realized that this year's date happened to coincide with Trey Macready's half century, she'd gone all out, hiring a whole team of caterers and ordering enough monogrammed linens to wrap the county courthouse. "I found a box of old pictures in the attic," Kaitlyn went on. "Mama and Daddy were so cute. They're holding hands in almost every one."

The phone in Natalie's hand buzzed, and she pressed decline before stuffing it back in her pocket. "I have to go," she said, leaning forward to kiss Kaitlyn's cheek. "If Luke smells cigarettes on you, tell him it was my fault. Tell him I held you down and forced you to inhale my secondhand smoke."

"That's what he'll think anyway," Kaitlyn said.

2.

Natalie took the shortcut around downtown, speeding past the rows of look-alike ranch houses behind Ewald Community Hospital. She looked up at the lighted windows and thought of Amanda in one of those white-walled rooms, waiting to find out what was wrong with her. Exercise and stretching were supposed to keep you healthy, but there were always so many ways the female body could betray itself.

Stuck in the stuffy car, Natalie could smell her own sweat. They kept the studio at a sweltering eighty-eight degrees, but this wasn't the good clean perspiration that came after a hard workout. When she pulled her tank top up over her nose, it was rank as old socks. Fear, she thought. Maybe she'd gone too fast, pushed too hard. Maybe Cassie's unstated judgment was correct, and Natalie had no business taking on the health and well-being of others when she could barely manage her own.

Her heart beat faster, and with it came something she had no words for—less an image than a feeling of cold, heaviness, her body being pulled down even as she fought to rise. For a moment she felt her lungs constrict. Gasping, she took her foot off the gas, and the guy behind her laid on his horn.

Cassie and Jay called these intrusive memories, and said that yoga could sometimes trigger them but could also decrease their power. On their podcast, *Hashtag Yoga*, they talked a lot about a trauma-informed practice and how deep breathing and mindfulness could heal a dysregulated mind. Natalie had yet to experience the healing part, but then again, she'd never taken deep breathing and mindfulness very seriously, even after she started teaching. She'd majored in marketing in college, and she'd known that the only way to sell yoga in Ewald County was to take the woo-woo out of it and tell women it would make their butts look tight.

She pulled up her podcast app and switched on an episode she'd paused in the middle, coming in just in time to hear Jay describe the day he'd first seen Cassie popping into a handstand on Venice Beach. "She was stunning, but that wasn't what got my attention," Jay said, with a lift in his voice that made it sound as if he were smiling. "There was just this joy in her. I don't know how else to describe it. It was like she was lit from within."

Natalie rolled her eyes and pretended to gag. She loved her sister, but Cassie was not the woman Jay described—this fey, mischievous sprite who sprinkled love and light wherever she trod. Natalie sometimes wondered if Cassie had genuinely fooled him, or if Jay was fully aware that he was describing her brand rather than her personality. Their courtship and marriage had been chronicled exhaustively on Instagram, from the joint selfies on Zuma Beach to the vacation in Bali to the destination wedding in Cozumel. Jay Desai had first become known in the yoga world for doing impossible poses in daring locations, but his fame had exploded once he'd added Cassie, whose wholesome prettiness made her a natural on social media. Natalie still remembered the way her breath had stopped when she first saw the photo of the two of them in scorpion pose on the rim of the Grand Canyon, their feet touching to form a heart.

It still seemed strange to Natalie that her sister was famous, at least in the nichey way of influencer fame. Then again, Cassie had always believed that she was meant for someplace better than Ewald County. After high school, she wangled a scholarship to a small college in northern California where she majored in English and minored in gender studies, or, as their father chose to remember it, "underwater basket weaving." After graduation she moved to LA, where she got her certification to teach yoga and met Jay. Now they went from one guest-teaching gig to another, crisscrossing the globe with their six-month-old daughter, Anjali, in tow. From something Cassie had said once, Natalie knew that they'd also been approached about sponsorships, but Cassie had turned them down, insisting that they didn't want to commodify the practice. On the podcast, she gently steered the conversation from Jay's reminiscences about their meet-cute into how love, like yoga, should make you a better person—more peaceful, more caring, more compassionate.

"It's not just that we don't want to hurt anybody, although of course that's part of it," she said in her teacher voice, the one that made it sound as if she was dispensing wisdom from a mountaintop in the Himalayas. "It also means being careful about our own words, thoughts, and actions so we can keep ourselves in a space of loving-kindness."

Natalie sighed and switched back to music, belting out the first words of "Strawberry Wine" in time with Deana Carter.

As she turned onto Southridge Road, she caught a glimpse of the lake glimmering through a thin line of pines to her right. She was taking the same route that she would have taken to her parents' house, but she wasn't headed home, at least not right away. When she got to Macready Cove, she took the back way around the family property, skirting her parents' driveway by turning onto a dirt two-track that led into the woods. The lights were on in the kitchen, which meant that her father was still up, probably smoking brisket and stocking the bar. Natalie had never asked her parents what they spent on the party, but she guessed that between food, liquor, and landscaping, the cost of the Felons' Ball ranged into the thousands, maybe more. Trey Macready loved to host; it was the essence of his nature—an expansive generosity that was probably the reason he'd been so successful in business once he turned his full attention to his legitimate career.

Two years ago her parents had done a complete remodel on the house, including building a new two-story boathouse set into the rocky cliffside above the dock. The new boathouse even had a covered porch where you could sit and look out at the lake, but Natalie still kept what she thought of as her spare kayak in an old tumbledown boatshed near the back way into the Hazel Valley dam.

She parked in a gravel lot near a rocky, overgrown beach and pulled her kayak out of the shed and into the shallows. She paddled out to the first blue buoy, and now she could see the lights of the TVA dam more than a mile away on the other side of the lake. On her left, she came up on an abandoned houseboat that her sisters and their friends had used as a party boat back in high school. Out of long habit, she took a wide circle around it, as if something might reach out and pull her onto the rotting deck.

Now she glimpsed the lights of Ben's boat. He was moving behind the windows, and as she got closer, she could hear the music pulsing from the speakers he'd installed in the galley kitchen. She was tying the kayak to the cleats on the dock when the door banged open and he barked, "On the ground, motherfucker, hands where I can see them."

Natalie crouched in the shadows, blood thrumming in her ears. "Ben," she said, and she heard the gun clatter to the deck.

"Holy shit, Natalie," he said as he raised her to her feet and drew her into his arms. "I didn't know you were coming. Why didn't you call me back?"

"I was teaching," she said, wondering if she should tell him that the orders he'd barked at her just now sounded like dialogue from a second-rate action movie. "Did you drop your gun?"

He bent to retrieve the pistol, a 9mm that he usually kept in the drawer beside his bed. "The safety was on," he said, looking embarrassed. "Are you hungry? I was making fajitas."

He put his arm around her and led her into the boat's cabin, where the smell of roasted meat and peppers rose in a cloud of steam from an iron skillet on the two-burner stove. He opened a seltzer for her, and she sat in the little cedarwood booth built into the curve of the stern. A small bookshelf stocked with Stephen King and Michael Connelly novels separated the kitchen from the bedroom, with its surprisingly spacious double bed, neatly made with pale-blue sheets and a patchwork quilt. Beside it was a mini dresser, with two drawers containing clothes and a third where he kept the postcards and letters he received from his son, Lanny, who'd joined the merchant marines after high school.

She watched Ben nudge the spatula across the skillet. He wasn't exactly handsome, but there was something appealing about him—the tall, lanky body and longish hair that made him look much younger than his forty-nine years. He smelled good too, like the smoky cologne with hickory undertones that always made her think of barbecue. Most of the guys she knew around the lake dressed like frat boys, in khakis, boat shoes, and pastel polos, but Ben had always had a bit of a hippie vibe that made him stand out in their rural county. When she was a child, he'd always taken the more liberal position in drunken arguments with her father, though she'd never been sure if he really believed what he was saying or it was just to get a rise out of her dad. They still argued about everything from zoning laws to assault weapons bans, but Ben had been in recovery for twelve years now, and these days he drank peach seltzers instead of bourbon. "Did you park at your dad's?" he asked, grinning at her over his shoulder.

She knew what he was really asking: Did her dad know she was here? "I parked in the woods," she said. "I was hoping I could stay the night, if it's all right with you."

She could tell he was still smiling as he shook hot sauce into the skillet and slid it off the burner. " 'If it's all right with me,' " he repeated mockingly. "Like you have to ask."

The phone in her pocket buzzed, and she slid it out to find a text from Kaitlyn. *Amanda has fibroids*, she said. *I just got a call from her mom. They might have to do surgery but it sounds like it's nothing life-threatening. See you tomorrow xoxo.*

Natalie closed her eyes and exhaled.

"What?" Ben asked, but she shook her head.

"Just tired," she said. "Long day."

He took her hand and pulled her to her feet. "I know what you need," he said, and though she would have rolled her eyes at a line like that from a younger man—maybe from any man—there was something about Ben that made her turn to jelly, her body responding as if it were no longer receiving commands from her brain. She stood passive while he pulled her shirt over her head and peeled her jeans to her ankles, where she kicked them to the side. Rising again, he slid one hand between her legs and used the other to tilt her chin up until she met his gaze. "You know I always take care of you," he said, and she moaned because he was right, he was so right, he always did.

3.

The text woke her, the phone on the nightstand lighting up with an audible buzz. *Croaker Farber is back in town.*

Natalie rolled over and folded a pillow behind her head. Ben lay naked on top of the sheets, light snores issuing from his mouth. The text was from her brother-in-law Luke, and he was still typing: *He came up to me outside Tractor Supply. Think maybe he was drunk. I let your dad know but I wanted to warn you and Cassie to keep an eye out for him.*

"For fuck's sake," Natalie murmured. She hadn't spoken to Croaker Farber since the fall of 2011, when she and her sisters had nearly died in a boat accident after attending a party with Croaker, Luke, and Lanny Marsh. After being convicted of inflicting bodily injury while operating a watercraft, Croaker had spent two years in a juvenile facility and then been released into the custody of relatives in the eastern part of the state.

Before that, back in high school, Croaker and Luke and Ben's son, Lanny, had been teammates and best friends, all of them good-looking and likable enough to get girls without trying that hard. The Farbers lived in a trailer park where lazy long-eared hounds of an indeterminate breed milled around the packed-dirt lot, but that hadn't mattered when Croaker threw the winning touchdown against Tyndall County, when the boosters were falling all over themselves to introduce him to scouts from Tech and UVA. Natalie had assumed that even after he got out of juvie, he'd be too painfully aware of what he'd lost to ever want to come back home. *What's he doing here?* she wrote. *And why are you warning me? I never did anything to him.*

I know but he doesn't see it that way. He thinks Trey ruined his life.

She tossed her phone onto the built-in shelf and lay down again, planting kisses on Ben's neck until he moaned and reached for her. "I have to go," she said, pulling away. "Dad wants me there when the guests start showing up."

She didn't want to tell Ben what Luke had said about Croaker Farber. She didn't want to validate Luke's concerns by repeating them. No matter how crazy he was, Croaker couldn't possibly convince himself that it was a good idea to show up at the Felons' Ball uninvited.

Natalie shivered as Ben's hand moved down her body. "I want to see you tonight," he said without opening his eyes. "Maybe we can meet up back here after the tournament."

She slapped his shoulder. "You just can't get enough, can you?"

He smiled drowsily. "I didn't mean it like that," he said. "We need to talk."

Natalie felt her palms begin to sweat. She'd managed to avoid any hint of seriousness or planning for the future in their relationship so far, but everyone knew that it was never a good thing when a man said he wanted to talk. "What's wrong with right now?" she said. "I might be busy tonight."

But Ben shook his head. "I need coffee. I'll find you at the party."

There was no way to press the issue without betraying more alarm than his casual tone had warranted. "I wish I had clean clothes," she said, fishing her discarded panties out of the sheets and wrinkling her nose at them. "I didn't think to pack a bag last night."

Ben yawned. "You left clothes here last time, remember?"

They'd spent a weekend on the houseboat back in August, when her parents were out of town. "I did?" Natalie said. "But they'd be dirty."

"I took them to the laundromat with my stuff."

He looked so proud of himself that she felt a sudden wave of tenderness, and to keep him from seeing it, she turned her head away. "Shut up, you did not."

He sighed and lifted himself out of bed, bending over the tiny dresser and pulling out a pair of jeans and a pink tank top. "See?" Ben said. "Who's looking out for you, girl?" He held out the stack of folded clothes, smiling as if he'd just made her come for the first time.

4.

The shape of the cove made it possible for Natalie to return the kayak to the old boatshed without fear of being seen from the house. Macready Cove was on the east end of the lake, invisible from the marina and nearly two miles away from Lake Monroe Resort and the hydroelectric dam that had called the lake into being back in the thirties. Tucked in their little corner of paradise on the back end of nowhere, the Macreadys were inaccessible to the world unless they chose to invite the world to visit, and she knew that was just how her father liked it.

But Natalie wasn't thinking about her father or the Felons' Ball, the one day a year when he opened his doors to the movers and shakers within driving distance of Ewald County. She couldn't get her mind off how different Ben had been that morning—the solemnity of *We need to talk*, and then the tender, almost sentimental way he'd touched her cheek after she took her clothes from his arms. Did he want to break up, or to make some kind of commitment, or even tell her parents? Natalie didn't want to do any of those things, and she saw no reason why she and Ben couldn't go on the way they were for a while longer, having great sex and then talking in the dark as the boat rocked them to sleep. She'd always thought they agreed on living in the moment, and his unexpected gravity had spooked her.

She dipped her hand into the lake and splashed water on both cheeks. Today wasn't just about her father, and it certainly wasn't about her and Ben. Today would be the first time that she, Kaitlyn, and Cassie had been together since last Christmas, and Natalie had vowed to be a better sister starting today. She would not snap at Cassie for being condescending or roll her eyes if Kaitlyn said something naive. She would be mindful of her conditioned patterns and take care not to fall back into her role as the spoiled brat who would never grow up or step out of her family's long shadow. She would show her family, and Cassie in particular, that she wasn't that person anymore.

She retrieved her car, followed the dirt track to Southridge Road, and circled back as if she'd come from town. The extra steps took more time than she'd anticipated, and a steady stream of cars was already turning in at the gate. The guests who had settled in were lounging around the firepit or on the wide wraparound porch, staring out at the clear water and the autumn-fired foliage on the far shore. Some browsed the bagel bar set up by the outdoor kitchen cabana, while others lined up at the bar to give their orders to a blond girl with a pixie cut whose smile never wavered, not even when a loud man in a pink golf shirt spilled his drink into a jar of sliced oranges. Only the bocce court was untouched, roped off until after lunch.

She found her father on the porch, wearing red suspenders and a fedora and reading the list of names on the whiteboard mounted on the wall. "Happy birthday," Natalie said, kissing him on the cheek. "You're going to let all those losers go first?" She gestured at the whiteboard, where her father and Jay were number eight on the rota.

"Strategy," her father said, rocking back on his heels. "You get the opening acts out of the way in the early afternoon, when nobody's paying attention. Then about the time they get bored with socializing and looking at the lake, it's time for the big dogs." He slipped his arm around her shoulder. "Why, you thinking of playing this year?"

"Wouldn't do you much good," Natalie said. She hesitated. "Are Cassie and Jay here yet?"

He shook his head. "Ran into some kind of issue with the rental car." Dropping his arm, he fixed his gaze on her for the first time, and she felt the same sensation she'd felt when he scolded her as a child, as if the bottom had just dropped out of her stomach. "Matt Vergotti called me this morning," he said. "Doesn't sound to me as if they're feeling litigious, but you got to think about how something like this can affect your reputation."

Her father had never presumed to give her advice about the studio before. She knew he thought it was funny that she and her sisters were making a living from yoga, which he'd persisted in calling "yogurt" for at least the first year after Cassie got her certification. She knew he thought of them as soft where he was hard, taking it easy after he had put in the work to move their family up in the world. "I don't know why Matt felt the need to call you," she said, trying to keep the frustration out of her voice. "I'm sorry for Amanda, but it's not my fault."

"Well, you don't know really that," he said. "You don't know how those movements might place stress on a woman's system."

"Daddy, I do know," Natalie insisted, but now, surprisingly, she found herself on the verge of tears. To stop them from spilling over, she had to swallow her words, biting her lip and balling her hands into fists. "Ask Cassie if you don't believe me. There's no universe where practicing yoga makes you bleed uncontrollably out of your vagina."

Her father put up his hands, as if the word *vagina* was a charm to make a middle-aged man absent himself from any given situation. "Kaitlyn's talking to the caterers," he said. "Why don't you go on in and see if she needs help?" A red Buick had just turned into the parking area, and he waved and walked toward the car, calling back over his shoulder, "I know she'd appreciate it."

It was a petty kind of revenge not to listen, since Natalie knew he was right and Kaitlyn could use all the help she could get. The Felons' Ball was a massive undertaking, bringing together nearly a hundred guests from all over the state. From her father's perspective, it was less of a social occasion than a business opportunity, where locals mingled with the politicians, lobbyists, and entrepreneurs he hoped to convince to invest in Ewald County. He'd told Natalie more than once that the party had the same kind of potential for her. He thought she should be handing out business cards, touting the benefits of yoga over pimento cheese and deviled eggs, and maybe she would have been thinking along those lines if she hadn't been so annoyed. Her sisters had always joked that Natalie was the favorite child, and though she'd sometimes felt guilty about it, she'd always counted on her father's preference for her, his desire to keep her happy. Apparently that didn't count for much when he decided that he knew better than she did about the female reproductive system.

Her mother was downstairs by the front steps, a wide smile plastered to her face as she waited to greet the arriving guests. Rosemary Macready wore a black puffer jacket over a calf-length sequined dress, and she cast a critical eye over Natalie's tank top and jeans. "Couldn't you at least put on a boa?" she said. "Just to make your father happy?"

"No, I don't want a boa," Natalie snapped. "Did you know that Matt Vergotti called Daddy this morning? Because I guess if someone is concerned about what happens at my place of business, they automatically call my father instead of talking to me?"

Her mother blinked, and Natalie could tell that she hadn't known. "Now don't make a fuss," she said, light glinting off her diamond rings as she raised her hands in warning. "You know Matt and your father are in that men's group at church. You don't have to take everything so personally."

It was an old refrain, the fatal flaw that the family had agreed on when she was a little girl: Cassie was hotheaded, Kaitlyn was indecisive, and Natalie, everyone agreed, took things far too personally. She wanted to prove her mother wrong, but how could she make a rational argument when, once again, she found herself blinking back angry tears? "I feel like everything's ruined," she said. "I was so excited to have Cassie and Jay in the studio, and now the first thing they're going to hear about is what happened to Amanda and how it's all my fault."

Her mother looked down at the clipboard in her hand. She said, "I think you're being a bit dramatic. Why don't you get a drink and try to enjoy yourself? Remember, this is for Daddy."

Before Natalie could point out that it was only eleven a.m., her mother was distracted by a fat man in a black suit and white suspenders waddling toward her, hand outstretched. Natalie took advantage and slipped away toward the lake, scanning the crowd for Ben, who seemed at the moment like the only person who could make her feel better.

No one else looked like him. There were twenty men on the cliff steps and on the beach that might have passed for her father if you saw them from the right angle: gray-haired men in suspenders and fedoras, all a bit heavier than they should have been, their faces a bit too red, while Ben still looked more or less the same as when she was a teenager and used to watch him dive from the floating dock. Now and always, he looked like a man whose life found its truest form on vacation, who lived for blue skies and tailwinds and a Jimmy Buffett cover band on the hotel patio. Over the summer, he'd taken her with him on one of those trips. Natalie told everyone at home she was going to a yoga conference, and she and Ben spent three days lounging in their underwear at his condo in Big Pine Key.

She was gazing toward the bend in the bank that hid the view of his houseboat when she heard a series of familiar yips and looked down to see Uncle Leo's dog, Capone, nipping at the knee of her jeans. Behind him, her uncle came toward her with his arms outstretched. "Luke just got here with the cake for your daddy," he said. "Three layers of double dutch fudge. Just promise you'll save a piece for the rest of us."

It was an old joke, and Natalie grimaced despite her effort to smile as he drew her into a hug. "I gave up sugar," she said. "So you don't have to worry about me eating the whole cake this year, Uncle Leo."

He widened his eyes comically. "Well, why the goddamn didn't anybody tell me? I would have brought you a banana."

A group of men near them guffawed. Uncle Leo was ten years younger than her father, and tried to counteract his natural baby face with a thick blond beard and sunglasses that made him look like he belonged on *Miami Vice*. His personality was like his clothes, oversize and loud, his southern accent so thick that it sometimes seemed like a parody. When they were little, he'd been the one that she and her sisters went to when they were afraid to go to their parents. He'd palmed them twenties, forged their mother's signature on teachers' notes, slipped them Barbies and Bratz dolls and, later on, beer and cigarettes. He had always given the impression of being more tolerant, more understanding, and more lenient than her father, and Natalie couldn't entirely explain why she was still a little afraid of him.

He put his arm around her and led her away from the group of men, to the edge of the cliff looking down on their private beach. "I've got a question for you," he said, his fingers digging into her shoulder. "Have you seen our friend Mr. Marsh today? I need to have a word with him."

She met his eyes, willing herself not to blush. Was it a coincidence that they happened to be looking for the same person, or was Uncle Leo hinting that he knew something about her and Ben? "I haven't seen him today," she said. "Maybe he's still out on his boat."

"Well, shit," Uncle Leo said, dropping his arm and turning to look out at the lake. "It's been a long time since I tried to wedge my fat ass in one of those little kayaks. You think he has cell service out there?"

Again the question felt like a trap. "You could take the motorboat," she suggested.

Uncle Leo shook his head. "It's not important," he said, but the restless way his eyes swept the horizon made her wonder if he was telling the truth.

5.

Cassie and Jay had arrived in her absence, and when Natalie made her way to the front of the house, she spotted Jay to the side of a group clustered around her father, who was telling a story that had his guests in fits of laughter. She'd come too late to hear the specifics, but she knew that it would be one of his greatest hits—the time that he and Uncle Leo and Ben climbed a water tower to escape from the old sheriff, or the time they picked up a stripper at a Richmond club and convinced her to skinny-dip in the fountain in front of the governor's residence. The men were roaring, beating each other on the back, sounding more like a bunch of teenagers than middle-aged businessmen, thinning on top and soft around the middle.

Natalie felt the settling effect that always came over her when she saw her father with a group of his peers. Trey and Leo Macready had once been the wildest among them, but now they were accepted by their community, called friends by these decent men who liked pretending to be bad guys one day out of the year but had never been charged with so much as a misdemeanor in real life. If the worst rumors about her father were true, she thought, these men would not have accepted his invitation in the first place.

Jay had his daughter clasped to his shoulder while he chatted with her father's lawyer, Lester Singletary. Mr. Singletary was short and round, and he made Jay look even more handsome by contrast, with his athletic build and high, sharp cheekbones. Natalie always felt a little flutter in her lower stomach when she looked at him, and she couldn't help wondering if he looked at her the same way.

"Hey there," he said, breaking into a grin as he transferred the baby to Natalie's arms. "She's been fussy today."

But Anjali was all smiles now, patting her aunt's cheeks, her face scrunched in an expression of delight. Physically she was a miniature version of Cassie, with dark-brown hair, big eyes, and a button nose. "She recognizes me from FaceTime," Natalie sang, batting her eyelashes.

"Lester was just explaining why it's called the Felons' Ball," Jay said, gesturing with his tumbler. Natalie tensed, but Mr. Singletary wore a jovial expression as he repeated himself: "I told him that it used to be the Flappers and Felons' Ball, but you don't see as many flappers around these days. Except your mama over there—I'm glad to see that she's keeping up the tradition."

"It's a little cold to be a flapper today," Natalie said, trying to mirror his grin. Mr. Singletary must have known perfectly well why it was really called the Felons' Ball, but she was glad to know that he hadn't felt the need to trot out the old stories about the Macreadys for Jay's benefit. She had never been sure how much Cassie had told her husband about where their money came from, but Natalie thought she wouldn't blame her sister if she'd kept some of that information to herself.

A man walking by stuck out his hand for Mr. Singletary, who boomed, "Nice to see y'all," before moving away.

"You know, when Cassie first told me about the houseboats, I thought she meant like on the rivers in Europe," Jay said, turning to look out at the lake. "The ones that look like boats that somebody decided to live in. These are actual houses, though."

Natalie had never seen a European houseboat, not even in a picture, but she wasn't about to confess her ignorance to Jay. "Some of them are pretty fancy on the inside," she said. "I know one family who has a hot tub and a full bar. Daddy's friend Ben owns the one closest to the cove, if you ever wanted to see it."

Jay nodded, but absently, as if he wasn't really listening. "I can see why your family held on to this place," he said. "You've got a little piece of heaven right here."

She beamed. "When the TVA bought up all the property around here, my great-granddaddy negotiated a deal to move the national forest line a quarter of a mile to the west, so he got to keep his land when everybody else around here had to sell to the government."

As soon as the words were out of her mouth, she wished she hadn't spoken. It made her family sound like opportunists, she thought. It made her great-grandfather Macready, dead long before she was born, sound like the kind of man willing to sell out his friends and neighbors to gain an advantage for himself. She cringed a little, but Jay didn't seem to notice.

"You know what would be amazing here?" he said. "A retreat center. You could have a yoga pavilion right at the edge of the lake." He moved his hand over the long green lawn, and for a moment Natalie could see it—an open-air structure like she'd seen on the websites of yoga centers in California and Costa Rica, where reflected sunlight rippled over the peaceful faces of guests who'd paid three hundred dollars a night for the privilege.

The vision was so compelling that she didn't notice Cassie until her oldest sister stepped up to give her a quick side hug. Natalie wanted to hold on longer, but Cassie disentangled herself quickly, fingering the ends of Natalie's new chin-length hair. "You got it cut," Cassie said. "Doesn't it get in your face when you practice?"

Natalie knew from long experience that the neutrality of Cassie's voice meant disapproval. "I wear a headband," she said, still stung by the way Cassie had pulled away from her hug. The baby started to fuss when she saw her mother, and Natalie, with an unexpected pang of reluctance, transferred her into Cassie's arms.

She was relieved to see Kaitlyn walking toward them across the lawn, wearing a long cotton dress that clung to her frame and carrying a wrapped box that looked like it could have held a bathrobe. She gave Jay a one-armed hug and leaned toward Cassie for an air kiss, but Cassie pulled her in, the box sandwiched between them. "You're so *skinny*," Cassie said. "I wouldn't have even known you were pregnant."

Kaitlyn put a finger to her lips. "It's not public knowledge yet," she said. "Luke just told his mom, and I want to kill him. She's the biggest damn gossip in town."

Cassie kept one hand on Kaitlyn's arm, looking her up and down. "Seriously, though, are you okay? Mama said the doctor gave you medication for the vomiting."

"Yeah, I think I might just have to get through it," Kaitlyn said with a grimace. "Nat said that y'all might be willing to teach some of my classes while you're in town? That would help a lot, honestly. All I want to do is sleep."

"I remember those days." Cassie squeezed Kaitlyn's hand.

Anjali started fussing, and Kaitlyn took advantage of the distraction to take Natalie by the arm and turn her toward the house. "Let's go find Daddy," she said. "I want to give him this photo album before they're all too fucked up to recognize their own faces."

So that was what was in the box. "But it's from you, not me," Natalie said.

Kaitlyn gave her a look. "Well, I'm not going to tell him that, are you? I'll say it's from both of us."

"Let me carry it then," Natalie said, taking the box from her sister's arms. It was typical of Kaitlyn to share the credit even where no credit was due. She'd always been the quietest and sweetest of the sisters—the timid one, the homebody. After high school, she'd stayed in Ewald and gotten an associate's degree in accounting at the local community college. If Luke Caldwell hadn't made a play for her after he'd struck out with Cassie, she'd probably still be single.

"Have you heard anything about Amanda today?" Natalie asked.

Kaitlyn shook her head. "I'll probably stop by and visit tomorrow."

"Tell her we're all thinking about her," Natalie said. Kaitlyn didn't seem as emotional as she had the night before—no red eyes or air of distraction—and Natalie was relieved. Kaitlyn was the quiet one, but she was also the reliable one, the one they all counted on. After the boat crash, it had been Kaitlyn who got all of Natalie's assignments from her teachers and read *The Old Man and the Sea* out loud when Natalie's eyes blurred from pain. It had been Kaitlyn—never their mother or father—who came with Natalie to physical therapy, helping her through shoulder rotations and grip strength exercises to repair the muscles dependent on her fractured collarbone.

She was just about to tell Kaitlyn about Matt Vergotti calling their father when she spotted their mother coming toward them across the lawn. Natalie groaned softly.

"What are you girls planning?" their mother asked, gesturing to the box. "We were going to do family gifts tomorrow."

"But this is his actual birthday," Natalie said, shifting the box from one hip to the other. "And I feel like I'm carrying a box of rocks. Can I just give it to him so I can put it down?"

"Oh, I guess that's fine," her mother said, hands on her hips. "Just as long as it's not another bottle of bourbon."

On the porch, their father was again surrounded by a group of men, their chairs angled toward him. "What is this, a winter coat?" he asked as Natalie slid the gift onto the table. He was always excruciatingly slow about unwrapping presents, folding back the corners as if he might want to reuse the wrapping paper, and Natalie and her mother smiled at each other as he used his penknife to carefully slit the ribbon.

As soon as he lifted the lid of the box, Natalie could see his eyes get wet, and she felt herself tear up even before he began to page through. She and her mother shouldered closer, holding on to each other. There was Trey Macready as a young man, bare-chested on the dock. There were Uncle Leo and Ben, raising their Budweiser bottles in a toast. There was her mother, wearing a red halter-top sundress and holding a cigarette. There were Cassie, Kaitlyn, and Natalie as toddlers, Cassie clutching her sisters' hands and staring down the camera as if she wanted everyone to understand that she was in charge.

These were the best days of his life, Natalie thought—the time that her father would have lived over and over again if he could. His father, John Macready Jr., had owned a feedstore that had supplied sugar, rye, and plastic containers to moonshiners across six counties. He didn't run his own still, but he was friends with the men who did, and when Trey Macready was still in high school, he became their deliveryman, running truckfuls of plastic jugs up to the underground bars in Richmond and Norfolk, equipped with night-vision goggles and a two-way radio to stay one step ahead of the cops.

That was the real reason the party was called the Felons' Ball. Though Trey, Leo, and Ben Marsh were arrested on multiple occasions, the charges never stuck: evidence went missing, witnesses recanted. There were rumors of bodies in the lake, weighted down with concrete and steel blocks, although Natalie was never sure how much of that was family mythmaking. In the end, Uncle Leo was the only one of the three who did jail time, serving two years in a minimum-security prison near the North Carolina border for manufacturing illegal liquor in the George Washington and Jefferson National Forests. By the time Cassie and Kaitlyn were old enough for school, their mother had convinced their father to go clean, but Natalie was pretty sure that he still pined for the days when he'd been a dangerous man. A chance to relive those days was the best present that Kaitlyn could have given him, and Natalie was a little jealous that she hadn't thought of it herself.

"Where on earth did you get those pictures?" their mother asked, voice choked as if she too was struggling not to cry.

Kaitlyn beamed. "I found some old boxes up in the attic."

Her father paged past Ben again, caught in flight as he dove from the floating dock. Then Natalie caught a glimpse of a face she hadn't seen in years: Ben's teenage son, Lanny, standing on the deck of his father's houseboat, wearing swim trunks and a sailor's cap, his arms spread as if he was daring the world to come and get him. She felt her stomach give a funny kind of twist.

Just at that moment, Ben ambled across the deck to peer over her father's shoulder, and Natalie held her breath, wondering how he'd react to the sight of the son who, as far as she knew, he hadn't spoken to in years.

"What you got there, your baby pictures?" he asked Trey.

"Just about," her mother said. "Chronicles of our misspent youth."

Ben put his finger down to stop her father from flipping a page. He was in dark jeans and a blue T-shirt that most men his age would have bought in a bigger size, and she was pretty sure she could pick out a tiny red mark on his neck where she'd bitten him the night before. "That was when the tree blew down in that storm back in '94," he said, but then he seemed to lose interest, his eyes flicking briefly to Natalie's face before moving on.

She exhaled quietly. Ben had pictures of Lanny all over his boat, in frames and in the corner of the bathroom mirror and stuck to the mini fridge; surely it wouldn't disturb him to know that the Macreadys wanted to remember him too.

"I saw a couple bears on the bank out by my place," he said to no one in particular. "A mama and two cubs."

"Say you saw a bear?" Lester Singletary shouted from the other side of the porch, hiking up his waistband as if ready to pull out a six-shooter.

Kaitlyn's husband, Luke, came around the side of the house and walked toward them. Natalie was surprised to see that her brother-in-law was wearing his deputy uniform, the star pinned to his chest glinting in the pale sunlight. At the slate path that led to the porch, his path intersected with Cassie's and they walked up the steps together, Luke putting a hand on her back and leaning close to say something that made Cassie stifle a laugh. "Happy birthday, sir," Luke called to her father, who raised his hand without looking up from the photo album.

Luke made eye contact with Kaitlyn and Natalie and motioned them away from the crowd gathered around their parents. "Y'all need to come with me," he said under his breath. "I've got to show you something."

6.

He led them to Natalie's car, the silver convertible her father had bought her when she moved back to Ewald after college. Over the course of the day, it had been blocked in by Land Rovers and Audis with private-school decals affixed to the back windows.

From this angle, everything looked fine, and Natalie was about to tell Luke to get to the point when she circled the front and saw the damage. The windshield had been smashed, the crazed glass that remained forming a frame for the interior, glass scattered over the console and glittering across the leather seats.

Kaitlyn shrank back. "Oh my God, what happened?" she said, voice muffled by the hand over her mouth.

"Ben said there was a bear," Natalie began, and then stopped when she realized how stupid that sounded.

"I've seen a lot of things, but I've never seen a bear carrying a hammer," Luke said. Despite the grim tone of his voice, his smile had a certain smugness, and Natalie couldn't help wondering if he was enjoying himself just a little. Luke lived for the accidents and catastrophes that reinforced his belief that the world was one big dumpster fire; it was why he'd become a cop in the first place.

"But how did he get away?" Kaitlyn asked. "Wouldn't someone hear the noise?"

Luke shook his head. "It would make a crash, but it's loud up there at the house, and you can't see this spot from the back windows. All he had to do was give it a tap and get the hell out of Dodge."

Suddenly Natalie understood why they kept saying *he*. "You think Croaker did this?"

"You didn't hear him this morning," Luke said. "I don't know what he's on, but it's definitely not happy pills."

She shook her head stubbornly. "But how could he think he'd get away with this? There are a hundred people wandering around here."

Luke smirked. "Well, he did get away with it, didn't he?"

Natalie gave him a look, and he turned serious. "I'm going to call the sheriff and file a report, but I'd rather not tell your dad until the party's over," he said. "The last thing we want is a bunch of middle-aged guys dressed like Bugsy Siegel playing vigilante in the woods."

Kaitlyn circled the front of the car again, surveying the damage. "You should call your insurance," she said to Natalie. "Let's tape some plastic over it for now and talk to Daddy in the morning."

Natalie knew they were right. The men were liable to go off half-cocked, particularly when they'd been drinking, and who could tell what might happen if they ended up face-to-face with Croaker Farber? The back of her neck tingled, and she whipped her head around to scan the line of trees at the edge of the yard, the branches of the great oaks stirring slowly in the wind.

She spent the next hour on the phone with State Farm while Luke wrote his report and Kaitlyn taped the window, deftly tearing a garbage bag in half and ripping off strips of duct tape with her teeth. Natalie was still on her parents' insurance, so there was no chance of keeping the incident a secret even if she'd wanted to. Her father would see the claim when he checked his email tomorrow, and as she sat on hold, she tried to predict what he would do next. The old version of her dad would have engineered a quid pro quo, slashing Croaker's tires or jumping him on the way out of a bar, but these days, Trey Macready was more subtle. He'd find a way to get his revenge while also ensuring plausible deniability.

"Where the hell have y'all been?" he said when she, Kaitlyn, and

Luke returned to the party. They'd missed four rounds of the tournament, and the teams were taking a break, refilling their drinks before the semifinal round. "I was just about to send out a search party."

Natalie could tell from his tone that he was truly annoyed, not just pretending to be, and she leaned over his Adirondack chair to kiss him on the cheek. He'd thrown on a blue windbreaker that smelled like smoke over his gangster suit.

"Who's up next?" she asked, and her father nodded at the board they'd carried out to the court. Most of the names had been crossed out; eight remained, including Ben, her father, and Jay.

"So how does it feel to be fifty?" she asked, pulling up the chair closest to her father's. "Did you see your life flash before your eyes when we sang 'Happy Birthday'?"

She'd always been the best at charming him out of a bad mood. He smiled reluctantly, pulling a cigar from the inside pocket of his jacket. "Those pictures threw me for a loop," he said as he bit the end. "A blast from the past, that's for sure."

Natalie nodded, but she was only half paying attention, her eyes moving to the sliding glass doors that led to the living room. Ben had just stepped through them onto the deck, but he didn't return her gaze, making a wide circle around the cluster of partygoers until he ran straight into Luke's mother, Cindy, who batted her eyelashes at him and flicked the long red hair that was definitely either a weave or a wig over her shoulder. Cindy wore glittery gold sandals with a pink dress that was all wrong for both the party theme and the season, and she was drinking a cosmo that had already stained her upper lip bright pink.

Natalie wasn't sure why, but Cindy had never liked her. Maybe it had to do with Kaitlyn, who Luke's mother seemed to believe had tricked her son into marriage, though everyone else knew that it had been Luke going after Kaitlyn and not the other way around. Cindy ran a day care out of her ranch house near the hospital, though from what Natalie had seen, she didn't seem to like children very much.

Natalie moved closer, and Cindy paused her conversation with

Ben to give her a faux hug, placing her fingertips on Natalie's shoulder and leaning forward until their cheeks brushed. "Can you believe it?" Cindy said, widening her eyes. "I'm going to be a grandma! Or a *glam*-ma," she amended, with a wink toward Ben.

"Congratulations," Natalie said, offering a thin smile as she tried to catch Ben's eye. She'd hoped they could share a moment of silent commiseration on Cindy's awfulness, but he seemed to be avoiding her gaze. She felt hurt. He'd never ignored her like this.

"I heard your mother is planning another big party for Anjali's baptism," Cindy went on, her mouth tightening in a way that emphasized her wrinkles. "Do you know what she wants the babies to call her?"

Natalie blinked at her, confused. Anjali was only six months old; she didn't call anybody anything. "*You* know," Cindy said with a fake laugh. "Is she going to be Grandma or Granny or what? Honestly I can't stand any of them. Maybe I can be Gigi or Nana."

"There's always Big Mama," Natalie said, and Ben barked out a laugh that he tried to turn into a cough.

Cindy's plumped-up lips thinned slightly. "It must be so nice for you and your sisters and their families to be together again," she said. "I just hope it doesn't make you feel too left out."

For a moment, Natalie was too surprised to react. Though she knew she'd never been a favorite with Luke's mother, Cindy had never come for her like this, and Natalie knew instinctively that it had something to do with Ben's presence. Cindy either knew about the two of them or she had sensed something, and she wanted, for reasons of her own, to embarrass Natalie in front of him. Had there been something between the two of them back in high school, or maybe later, after Ben's wife died? Natalie had a vague memory of rumors to that effect, but she wouldn't have cared at the time; Ben was just a family friend back then, as devoid of erotic interest as her pastor or high school principal.

"No ma'am," Natalie said, pasting on a sugary grin. "I'm happy just the way I am." She took a step back from the group, annoyed with herself for getting pulled into Cindy's trashy bullshit in the first place.

On the other side of the porch, Trey Macready pushed himself up from his chair. Everyone knew how to read that signal: the semifinal round was starting. Cindy hurried back to her place at the edge of the court. Natalie turned around to say something else to Ben, but caught only a glimpse of his back as he headed for the bar, leaning close to the bartender and pointing to the hidden bottle that Natalie's father saved for his most favored guests.

7.

At first Natalie thought the bottle must be for someone else. Even after the bartender poured Ben a tall glass and he slugged it down as if it were water, she told herself she must be missing something; maybe it wasn't liquor after all, even though it looked just like the nameless, unlabeled brew that Trey kept secreted away to pass with a wink to investors and state legislators on nights just like these. She tried to make her way over to Ben, but someone shouted, "Play ball!" in an umpire's shrill voice, and her father strolled to the court through a wave of applause. Natalie was swept down the steps to the yard, where the guests were lining up on either side of the court.

She knew exactly how the rest of the evening would proceed. After the bocce tournament, some of the guests would take the chartered boats back to the Lake Monroe Resort on the far side of the lake, while others would stick around for barbecue and her father's secret stash. Her father and Ben and Uncle Leo would repeat the old stories of the sheriff chasing them through the backwoods, their voices rising in competition through the night. Anjali would get fussy, and Cassie would leave to put her down in the guest house; Kaitlyn would fall asleep on the couch. The guests would shed their jackets, and then ties and even shoes. If it had been a warm night, people might have gone skinny-dipping, but after seeing the weather forecast, her father had planned a series of bonfires instead. The high school boys he'd hired were already piling up branches and setting out fire starters along the quarter mile of private beach.

Natalie moved up front to sit on the grass beside Cassie, who gave her a quick smile that didn't reach her eyes. Anjali was in a portable playpen, bundled in a sweatsuit with ears on the hood that made her look like a tiny bear. Natalie wondered if this was the right time to tell Cassie about everything that had happened in the past twenty-four hours—Amanda's collapse, the threats from Croaker, the smashed car window—but she was afraid that Cassie might turn it around and blame her. The family consensus had always been that Natalie was immature for her age, and Cassie would probably find a way to suggest that if she'd been more responsible, none of this would have happened. "Are y'all having fun?" Natalie asked instead.

"Jay is loving the tournament," Cassie said. "You'd think yoga would have mellowed him out, but he's literally the most competitive person I've ever met."

Natalie could believe it. She'd looked up the videos of Jay from his days as a professional surfer on YouTube. Watching him now, she related in a deep, almost physical way to the concentration on his face, the coiled strength in his body as he squared up to the bumper at the head of the court. He released the pallino, and it rolled down the artificial turf to stop exactly where her father would have wanted it, just inside the four-foot line. Her father slapped Jay on the shoulder, leaning close to say something that made them both laugh.

Ben threw next, and his ball went wide, coming to a stop just past the center. Everyone knew then that the game wasn't going to be close, and the hum of conversation picked up on the sidelines, people already looking forward to the final match. When Ben moved away so the other team could take position, Cindy had to grab his arm to stop him from stumbling, the muscles in her forearm tightening. His face was pale, slick with sweat despite the stiff breeze.

"You're shivering," Cassie whispered, and Natalie realized that she was right. Her cardigan was thin for the cold night, and the skin of her forearms prickled like chicken flesh. Cassie took off her cashmere shawl and wrapped it around Natalie's shoulders. "Can you get us keys to the studio tomorrow?" Cassie asked, leaning in close. "We both have some ongoing Zoom appointments, and I don't want to bother you every time I need to get in. But don't worry, Jay and I understand that it's your space. We just want to know how we can best support you."

Natalie tried not to roll her eyes. Cassie talked this way as a matter of course, but no amount of wellness-industry jargon could disguise the fact that as guest teachers, Jay and Cassie were basically taking over the studio for the next three weeks. They would be teaching some of Natalie's classes and hanging out in her office, and she knew they would be secretly judging the way she ran her business, no matter what they said to the contrary. Jay's competitive approach to bocce was one more sign that they weren't really hippies, regardless of how many pairs of harem pants Cassie might own. They were secret hustlers, and Natalie respected the type-A ambition under all their talk about balance and contentment. It was a quality that both she and Cassie had inherited from their father.

"I haven't had a chance to tell you what happened in my class last night," Natalie whispered. "Do you remember Amanda Maxwell from high school? She's Amanda Vergotti now. She's been coming to the studio, and last night she kind of collapsed in one of my classes. She's fine, but I wanted to bring it up in case you hear about it from the students."

Cassie gave a Botox frown, the inside corners of her eyebrows wrinkling slightly. "That must have been *so* scary." Natalie knew her sister well enough to predict that the sympathetic response would be followed by questions about waivers and incident reports, but before Cassie could ask any questions, raised voices drew their attention back to the court.

Ben and Cindy were arguing. Natalie couldn't hear what they were saying, but Cindy was holding Ben's elbow, and his face was red with anger. Her father looked ready to step in, but then Ben pulled away and threw the ball—aiming, Natalie thought, for an elegant fuck-you, a way of indicating to everyone present that he didn't care about the loss of the game. But the effort to shake Cindy's grasp had thrown him off balance, and the ball went wide, landing in Anjali's playpen and rolling to a stop on the blue vinyl mat.

For a moment Natalie couldn't make sense of what she'd seen. There was what happened—her niece unhurt, the ball lying harmlessly on the bottom of the playpen—but then there was what could have happened, and the two narratives seemed to overlay themselves, no-harm-done reality competing with a vision of the baby knocked backward, the ball cratering a hole in her fragile skull. Anjali, like the rest of them, seemed to need a minute to process the fact that she wasn't dead, but then she started to cry, the one tooth in the lower half of her jaw standing up as her mouth gaped open in a wail.

Jay shoved Ben in the chest. There was something different about the way he was moving, Natalie thought—a clumsy tension in his muscles, the usual easy grace dissipated.

Cassie lunged toward Anjali and gathered her in her arms. "Jay," she said in a warning tone, but he didn't even look at her.

Ben took the hit, but kept his balance and then put his hands up in a placating gesture. "Man, I'm sorry," he said, and Natalie could tell that he meant it. He had scared himself. "Listen, I would punch myself in the face if I could. Is she all right?"

He tried to peer around Jay to get a glimpse of Anjali, but Jay grabbed him by the collar. It was the first time that Natalie had really understood the difference in strength between them. She'd thought of Ben as a strong man, but Jay seemed ready to lift him off the ground with one arm. "If you'd hurt my daughter, I would fucking kill you," he said, his voice low enough that Natalie had to concentrate to make out the words.

Her father shouldered between them and put a hand on each of their shoulders. "Gentlemen, why don't we take some time to cool off?" he said. "Jay, my friend, I don't think I've gotten a chance to show you my new boat. I've got a handmade Chris-Craft down there with a bottle of Buffalo Trace under the seat."

Natalie could tell that he was talking off the top of his head. He knew that Jay couldn't have cared less about the boat or the bourbon, but the chatter had the desired effect, breaking his focus on Ben and bringing him back to himself. Jay moved off with her dad, and Natalie took Ben's arm, for the first time not caring who might see them together or what they might think.

He was shivering, with an old man's wild, vacant look in his eye. "I almost killed Cassie's baby," he muttered. "I almost killed her."

"It's okay," Natalie said, though of course it wasn't, not at all. She took off the shawl and wrapped it around his shoulders.

They passed Cassie, encircled by a crowd of women as she jiggled Anjali in her arms. The yellow ball still lay in the playpen. Natalie was surprised the whole thing hadn't collapsed.

"I'll take you back to the boat," she said to Ben. "You just need to sleep it off." He was crying like a child now, with big racking sobs that shook his whole body. He'd be ashamed later, she thought, when he remembered all the people who had seen him like this.

Before they reached the dock, Luke stepped out of the crowd. "I'll take him," he said to Natalie. "You should stay with Cassie."

She watched them walk away, Luke with his hand on the older man's shoulder, grip firm as if he was about to push Ben into the back seat of a police car. Ben would be all right in the morning, she told herself, but she felt a pang of guilt that she would come back to later—as if it had been an omen, a warning she'd chosen to ignore.

8.

When Natalie let herself into the guest house, where Cassie and Jay were staying, the first thing she saw was Anjali, playing with foam blocks on a blanket on the floor. She flashed Natalie a grin and waved a red block, apparently unaffected by the somber mood of the room.

Natalie's mother was doing her best to salvage the evening. She sat on the couch beside her oldest daughter, making bright conversation about nothing in particular. After more than thirty years with Trey Macready, their mother excelled at soothing and redirection, but Natalie felt a surge of irritation when she thought of how often her mother was called upon to exercise those skills on behalf of men who couldn't control themselves. "Where's Jay?" Natalie asked as she sat in the armchair across from them.

"Went for a walk," Cassie said with a wan smile that seemed to contain a hint of apology. "He just needed to be by himself for a while."

Her mother glanced at her watch. "Goodness, it's past dinnertime," she said. "Natalie and I will get you a couple of plates from the kitchen so you don't have to brave the crowd."

Cassie nodded without looking up. "Don't forget that Jay is vegetarian."

"Just the side dishes, then," her mother said. When they'd closed the door behind them, she leaned over and whispered to Natalie, "We had a time calming Jay down, let me tell you. He looked about ready to hit somebody, not that I'd blame him."

But Natalie knew better than her mother how foreign physical violence must be to Jay's sense of himself. It was impossible to imagine him really hurting Ben, no matter what the other man had done. Ahimsa, or nonviolence, was the first of the ethical principles of yoga, and Jay talked about nonharming at least as much as he talked about stacking your ears over your shoulders and keeping a neutral spine. "How does Daddy feel about not finishing the tournament?" Natalie asked.

"He'll be fine," her mother said. "He wanted to follow Ben out to the boat and give him a piece of his mind, but I told him that would just have to wait."

As they stepped into the circle of light by the back steps, it struck Natalie that her mother looked harried and drawn. It was a sharp contrast to the photos of her on this same lawn twenty years ago, laughing with a hand up to shade her eyes. "Are you okay?" she asked.

Her mother tried to smile. "I'm fine, honey," she said. "Just worn out." She put an arm around Natalie and hugged her to her side.

For the rest of the night, Natalie played the good daughter, escorting groups of guests down to the docks, where the boats waited to ferry them back to the resort. Her father brought the diehards into the den and showed them his collection of NASCAR memorabilia, including a die-cast model of Dale Earnhardt's Chevy Monte Carlo, explaining to anyone who would listen that the original stock car racers had been moonshiners, trained to race on the mountain back-roads where they outran the revenuers, and that Virginia's own Curtis Turner had been a personal friend of his daddy's. Natalie poured drinks and handed around cigars until she was finally allowed to fall into bed around two. The moon shone through her bedroom window, but she didn't move, too tired and tipsy to get up and close the shades.

She wondered if she should have insisted on taking Ben back to his boat. They'd never found time for the conversation he'd mentioned that morning, not that it would have been possible after what happened at the tournament. She couldn't deny that the last twelve hours had changed the way she saw him. He was no longer the easy good-time guy who'd made every night they spent together feel like a party. He was her father's best friend, a middle-aged man in crisis whose very presence in her life raised complications, and if he'd decided that their relationship had run its course, maybe he was right.

For hours she lay in a half stupor, drifting in and out of dreams. She was in a hospital bed, watching a storm outside, rain so heavy that it seemed to want to drown the whole earth. Then she was in the water, her body sliding down under the waves even as she fought to pull herself to the surface.

Natalie sat up suddenly, heart hammering in her chest. Cassie's shawl, she thought—the one she'd tucked around Ben's shoulders before Luke led him away. Natalie had been able to tell just from the texture that it was high-quality cashmere, but neither Ben nor Luke would have cared, even if they'd been sober. Neither of them would have thought to prevent the shawl from falling off the bench or trailing in the dirty water at the bottom of the boat.

Cassie had been too distracted by what had almost happened to Anjali to remember the shawl last night, but surely the loss would occur to her in the morning. If it was gone, or ruined, she would never let Natalie forget it. The story would be raised at Thanksgivings and birthday parties for the rest of their lives, just another example of Natalie's habitual carelessness.

Natalie threw on leggings and a sweatshirt and tugged her hair into a ponytail. The moon was low in the sky, but still bright enough for her to pick her way down to the boathouse and pull a rowboat into the water. It was freezing on the lake, far colder than she'd expected, and her teeth were chattering so hard that her jaw was sore by the time she tied up at the cleats on Ben's houseboat.

Her eyes had grown accustomed to the dark, and she saw it before she realized what she was seeing—a figure sprawled just inside the door to the cabin. She sighed. It was lucky that he'd managed to make it inside before he passed out, where there was no chance of rolling into the water.

Natalie stood, steadying herself against the rocking of the deck.

"Ben," she said, but he didn't stir. She stepped inside, her right foot skidding across the wood before she grabbed the doorframe for balance. He must have dropped a bottle. She reached for the light switch, wondering why he'd fallen off the wagon after so many years of sobriety. If she'd driven him back to the boat, they could have talked about it, but now there would be no chance of rousing him until the morning.

Blood. It was everywhere, smeared across the planks, forming pools on the wood. Ben's bare feet were painted red on the bottoms. She bent down beside him and took him by the shoulders. His head rolled back, and she put her fingertips to the cut across his neck as if she could close it by applying pressure. Dark-red slashes marked the skin of his hands and arms.

Blood on her hands, blood on her knees, the blood that had spilled across the floor soaking into the fabric of her leggings. Handprints in blood covered the planks, as if he'd tried to get up again after falling to the deck. She was talking to him, or to herself: "Wake up," she said, "baby, wake up," but she couldn't even do that, she could do nothing, she could make nothing right.

9.

Their mother had given each of them a pill. Natalie had no idea
what it was, but she'd swallowed it eagerly, only too glad to bet
on whatever brand of oblivion Rosemary's medicine chest had to
offer. Now Kaitlyn was asleep at the foot of her bed and Natalie was
sitting with her back against the headboard, so numb all over that she
could have stuck a safety pin into the skin of her palm and not felt a
thing.

He was dead, she told herself, but her mind skittered away from
the finality of it. It was a bad movie she'd watched—the body a prop,
the blood only ketchup. Her own screams, still echoing in her mind,
had been merely acting. She felt as if she was floating above herself,
observing her body on the bed. When she looked down at her hands,
they looked strange and misshapen, like a stranger's gloves picked
out of a box at Goodwill. Ben had said he wanted to talk to her about
something, and then he'd been murdered. Maybe he'd known he was
in danger. Maybe he'd planned to tell her what was going on after the
tournament, but instead she'd turned away, determined to keep her
distance on the one night he really needed her.

Her eyes flicked to the door as it slid open. It was her mother,
wearing jeans and a light-blue sweater, her gray-blond shoulder-
length hair perfectly curled. "How's my baby girl?" she asked gently,
leaning against the doorframe.

"Still here," Natalie replied, and was relieved when her mother
seemed to take the words at face value.

"The sheriff wants to talk to you," her mother said in a stage whisper. "We've got him set up in the dining room. He said it wouldn't take long."

Natalie rubbed her eyes. "I just need to sleep," she said, a whine creeping into her voice. "I already gave a statement." Her memories of the deputy who'd arrived at her parents' home in the early morning hours and asked her to walk him through the discovery of Ben's body were spotty at best, but she knew she'd signed something.

On any other day, her mother would have said something sharp about Natalie's bad attitude, but today she simply nodded. "I'll say you're not up to it," she said, turning from the door. "I told your dad it was too much."

But the only thing worse than having to talk to the police was being treated like a child. "No." Natalie threw her legs over the side of the bed. "I'll get dressed. Do I have time to take a shower?" She'd washed off the blood when she first got back to the house, but she still didn't feel clean. Once again she could smell herself, a rancid fear sweat that turned her stomach.

At the foot of the bed, Kaitlyn stirred and then sat up, yawning into her fist. "Mama, do you need help?"

Their mother was a small woman, but when she drew herself up to her full height, she never failed to impress her daughters. "You girls don't need to do a thing," she said firmly. "I made a coffee cake with raspberry jam, and they can damn well wait until you're ready."

Everything Natalie knew about murder came from books and movies. She prided herself on always being able to guess who did it, but now her mind went back and forth like a pinball. Who would want to hurt Ben? Who would hate him enough to open up those bloody holes in his chest? That's the word that had come to her last night: *holes*, not *wounds*; skin gouged, the hidden inside uncovered. She stood in the shower until her fingertips puckered and the ridges in the tiles had made grooves in the skin of her feet. Suddenly her stomach wrenched and she threw up quietly into the drain, cupping her mouth so her mother wouldn't hear her retch.

Her father was the only one in sight when she came downstairs, slumped forward on the couch with his elbows on his knees. "Hey darlin'," he said, lifting his shaggy head from his hands, voice so slow and dragging that for a moment she wondered if he'd had a stroke and she was about to lose him too. She bent down and hugged him around the neck, and he patted her absently on the shoulder.

Natalie perched on the back of the couch. "Where is everybody?"

He took a moment to think about it. "Your mama is making some calls," he said finally. "Kaitlyn and Luke went over to the guest house to tell Cassie and Jay what's going on. The police are in the dining room."

"Did anyone else stay here last night?" she asked, looking around for shoes kicked off under a chair or ties draped over a lampshade. "Anybody crash in the guest room?"

Her father shook his head. "Lester and Cindy and Leo were the last of them, and they left right when you went to bed. I was dead to the world until you came in around five."

Natalie nodded. She wanted a cup of coffee, but she couldn't muster the strength to walk to the kitchen.

"The crazy thing is," her father said, "that Ben was about to sell that boat."

"What?" Natalie pushed her wet hair back from her face. "He was?"

The surprise and interest in her voice hadn't seemed to register. "He was looking to retire and move down to Florida full-time," her father said without raising his eyes. "I told him fifty was on the early side, but he had plenty of savings, and the truth is, we could have hired an engineer straight out of college and paid him about half as much. Then somebody comes along and stabs him in the middle of the night. It must have been a drifter or something, looking for valuables. I wonder how much cash Ben kept around."

The numbness had come over Natalie again, and she wondered if she might be having an unusually specific dream. "Mama says I'm supposed to talk to the police," she said.

"That new sheriff seems pretty bright," her father said. "He's from Tyndall. I know the family. I'm sure he'll get this all straightened out."

That was how she knew there was a part of him that was thinking about Macready Contracting and Excavation. Her father wanted to know who had killed his best friend and chief engineer, and he wanted to know right now, before bad press had time to affect his business. Seeing that sharp, familiar look on his face made her feel just a bit better. The world may have been turned upside down, but her father was still her father.

Natalie stood up. "Luke told me about your car," her father said. "You might as well talk to the sheriff about that while you're in there. He'll want to know that pissant Croaker Farber was hanging around last night."

She started to walk away, but he was still talking, staring into the empty mug in his hand. "Poor Ben," he said under his breath. "He never really got over it after Lanny left."

The new sheriff's name was Hardy Underwood. Her father had donated to Underwood's campaign, and Natalie had heard him say that the new sheriff had served in the marines after college and worked in Atlanta before moving to Ewald. She'd met him only once, when her father had taken her as his date to Underwood's election-night party. In his acceptance speech, the new sheriff had quoted from Robert Frost's "The Road Not Taken," and ever since, Natalie had thought of him as Two-Roads-Diverged-in-a-Hardy-Underwood.

From what Natalie had heard, even when old Sheriff Shifflett chased Trey and Leo around the county or arrested them for this or that liquor violation, he'd always been friendly toward the Macreadys, and there was no reason to expect that things would be any different under Sheriff Underwood. The good ol' boys were still in charge, and that was probably to the benefit of her family in the big picture, but Natalie wondered how Underwood's loyalty to the establishment would affect the investigation. It seemed unlikely that he'd be fired up to look into a murder at a party that included the bank president, the superintendent of schools, and two members of the Virginia General Assembly among its guests.

When she walked into the dining room, she acknowledged to herself that under different circumstances, she might have found Hardy Underwood attractive. Physically he was her type: big and broadshouldered, with a thick beard that made her wonder if he had to shave his back. He was wearing a uniform, the same brown one that Luke wore, with the stripe down the side of the pants. A radio squawked at the edge of the table, and he reached to turn down the volume as he motioned her to a chair. "First of all, I'm sorry that you have to go through this," he said. "I know you already talked to one of my deputies, but I have a few additional questions, if you think you're up for it."

"I thought detectives were in charge of investigations like this," she said. "I don't mean any disrespect, but that's always the way things happen on TV."

"They don't make crime shows about places like Ewald," he said. "Our office is too small to justify hiring a detective. I worked as a homicide investigator in my last job, so I'm it."

"In Atlanta?" As soon as the words had left her mouth, she felt that it was a ridiculous thing to ask at that moment. Surely a police interview did not demand polite small talk.

Sheriff Underwood paused to show that he was aware that she was asking him questions rather than the other way around, and that he'd decided to tolerate it. "That's right," he said. "So tell me about Ben Marsh." He leaned back in his chair. "I hear that he and your daddy had been friends a long time."

"Since they were kids," she said. "Ben was just always around. He had a son who was my sister Cassie's age, and they'd come over for barbecues or to go out on the boat." For the first time it occurred to her that Lanny Marsh probably hadn't heard that his father was dead, since as far as she knew, no one had any idea where he was. "You know about Lanny, right?" she asked. "Ben's son? He joined the merchant marines after high school, and I'm not sure my parents know how to get in touch with him, but he should be notified, right?"

The sheriff was nodding before she even finished talking. "Yes ma'am, we're looking into that. Now, can you tell me when you arrived at the party yesterday morning?"

Natalie had tried to prepare herself to conceal her relationship with Ben, but now the last night they'd spent together came back to her, unbidden: the way his face had relaxed in sleep; the way he'd held up the pile of clean clothes, so pleased by the surprise he'd prepared for her. "About ten," she lied. "Ben came a little later. Maybe around ten thirty."

"Did it look to you like he'd been drinking? I heard that he'd fallen off the wagon in the last couple of weeks."

Her eyes flew up to meet his, but his face didn't give anything away. "I didn't really talk to him," she said. "We were all on the deck, and then Luke came to tell me that somebody had broken my car window. Did you hear about that? We thought it might be this guy named Croaker Farber. I think his real name is Travis, but everyone calls him Croaker." She repeated the story about Croaker coming up to Luke at Tractor Supply, only vaguely aware that she was giving the details an entirely different significance than she had yesterday, when she'd wanted to believe that Croaker was no danger to anyone.

The sheriff nodded, but he looked skeptical. "I saw Luke's report on the smashed window, but I don't see the connection," he said. "Any thoughts on why Croaker would want to target Ben Marsh?"

Natalie chewed her lip, considering how much of the truth she wanted to tell him. "There was a boat crash," she said finally. "About twelve years ago, when I was in high school. We were coming back from a bonfire at the resort—me, my sisters, Luke, Croaker, and Ben's son, Lanny. Croaker turned the wrong way and hit one of the pylons on the Highway 82 bridge. My dad has a lot of friends, and Croaker thought that he and Ben leaned on the judge to get him a longer sentence. That's what I heard, anyway."

Sheriff Underwood didn't write anything down, and she had a

feeling that he'd heard this story before. "I'm sure we'll be in touch with Mr. Farber," he said. "Anyone else you think we might want to talk to?"

"I don't know," she said. "I think Ben was scared." She'd thought that when she paddled up to the dock on Friday night—the way he'd waved his gun around before she'd even had a chance to speak. "You could talk to Luke's mom, Cindy Caldwell," she offered. "She was Ben's partner in the bocce tournament, and they were arguing about something. I don't know what."

This time he did make a note, but he kept his eyes on her, his brows drawn together as if he were puzzled by something. "It sounds like you were paying a lot of attention," he said. "Why did you go out to Ben's boat last night? I know about your sister's shawl, but couldn't that have waited till the morning?"

Natalie's mouth was so dry that her lips felt like paper when she rubbed them together. Underwood was talking as if she might be a suspect, and for the first time it occurred to her that the police had only her word that Ben was dead when she arrived.

She turned to make sure the door was completely closed. "I did have another reason," she whispered. "But it has to stay between us. I don't want my family to know."

She expected him to tell her that he couldn't make any guarantees when it came to the investigation, but again he simply waited, his eyes trained on hers. "Ben and I were seeing each other," she said. "I did want to get Cassie's shawl, but I also wanted to check on him. I wanted to make sure he was okay."

Suddenly she wanted to cry so badly that her throat burned, but the tears didn't come. Underwood waited until she'd taken a deep breath. "How long had you and Ben been in a relationship?" he asked quietly.

There was a knock at the door, and Natalie's mother stuck her head in. "I wanted to see whether y'all might like some more coffee," she said. "I just put on a fresh pot."

Sheriff Underwood put his hand over his mug as if he were at

Shoney's. "I think I'm topped up for the moment, Rosemary," he said. "Would you mind closing that door behind you?"

When she'd gone, Natalie leaned forward, whispering, "That's why I can't talk here. I'll come down to the station tomorrow if you want, or meet you somewhere, but I can't do it here."

The look on his face unsettled her. It was too intense, too searching, and she wondered if she'd put herself in a bad position without realizing it. She knew from the legal dramas her mother loved that you weren't supposed to talk to the police without a lawyer present, but neither of her parents had suggested calling Mr. Singletary that morning. They wanted to find out who had killed Ben, and it seemed self-evident that the best way to do that was to share everything they knew with the police.

Then again, her parents weren't aware of all the factors that might make Natalie uniquely appealing as a suspect. Not only had she discovered Ben's body, but she'd been sleeping with him for most of a year.

She was afraid that Hardy Underwood would press her to talk now, but instead he simply sighed and dropped his eyes to the legal pad in front of him. "Can you walk me through what happened when you went out to the houseboat? Everything that you remember."

Natalie nodded and recited the story just as she had for the deputy that morning, but her mind wasn't there. She was drifting away, returning to their trip to the condo on Big Pine Key. On the second day she'd gotten food poisoning, and they'd had to cancel a charter boat trip. Ben had brought her toast and tea in bed, and then they'd made love, more gently and tenderly than they usually did. Here in her parents' dining room, she was describing the blood on the planks to Sheriff Underwood, but she was also seeing the slow wheel of the fan and hearing the palm fronds tap against the shutter. If Ben was beside her on that white bed, kissing her deep and slow, he couldn't also be dead, lying gray-skinned on that blood-slicked floor. She decided that she would stay there as long as she could. The sunlight rippling on the ceiling reminded her of water.

10.

When the sheriff dismissed her, Natalie retreated to the glassed-in porch they called her mother's study. The den was her father's territory, with the mini fridge and the NASCAR collectibles, but the study was Rosemary's, decorated in white and muted pastels, with framed photos of her daughters hanging on the walls. Because of the lack of insulation, no one used it after Labor Day, but it was a good place to keep out of the way and feel nothing. Natalie wrapped herself in layers of blankets and lay on a wicker chaise longue, looking out at the lawn.

It was like watching TV. Men in orange vests swarmed over the dead grass. The preponderance of law enforcement made it look like a standoff at an armed compound, and her father, standing in the middle of it, could have been the cult leader, his face red despite the cold, wild hair grizzled. He was talking to Luke, both men standing with their arms crossed over their chests. Dark clouds scudded across the sky, and she could tell just by looking that the wind was sharp, the temperature close to freezing.

She wondered if the sheriff had questioned Luke. He'd been the last person to see Ben alive, when he took him back to the boat. That fact alone would seem to make him an obvious suspect, but she could think of no earthly reason why he would have wanted to hurt Ben Marsh.

But he would have plenty to say about Croaker Farber. Luke would have repeated the same old story they'd all been telling for the past twelve years: how Croaker, drunk, had driven them into the bridge pylon, catapulting them into the water, knocking Cassie unconscious, and breaking Natalie's collarbone. It was the story that had led to Croaker's conviction—the story that might have spurred him on to smash her windshield, and maybe much worse.

But Natalie had never been sure it was the real story. Maybe, she thought now, she should have told the sheriff that she'd always believed it was Lanny Marsh who'd been driving the boat that night. Natalie was passed out when they smashed into the pylon, but her last memory was of Lanny walking toward the captain's chair, saying that he was going to take over from Croaker and drive them home. If her sisters and Luke had lied to protect Lanny, that wrong should be righted, whether or not Croaker had fucked up her car. Besides, the more she thought about it, the more it strained credibility to think that Croaker could be dumb enough to announce his desire for revenge to Luke outside Tractor Supply and yet smart enough to smash Natalie's windshield, lurk in the woods for a few hours, stab Ben to death, and then get away without being seen.

She turned off notifications on her phone. Clearly reports were trickling in that something had happened out at the lake, though no one seemed to know exactly what. She had eighteen texts—from high school friends, from students at the studio—and the thought of opening even one of them made her so tired that she put her head down on a throw pillow.

Then she was asleep. She couldn't help it. She was hungover, and she'd hardly been to bed the night before. She waded through uneasy dreams that disappeared as soon as she heard her mother come in, closing the door behind her and sitting quietly on the silk ottoman at Natalie's feet. "Feeling better?" she asked when Natalie opened her eyes.

Natalie shrugged. When she was little, her mother had put the back of her wrist to her forehead to see if she was sick, and she'd always been able to gauge her daughters' emotional states just as easily. At times, Natalie had resented her ability to take the temperature of her mood within seconds, but now she was grateful that her mother knew she didn't want to talk about her feelings. "I told him about what happened to my car," she said.

Her mother nodded. "Well, that's good. They asked Daddy for a list of everyone who came to the party. Lucky I'd printed out the spreadsheet I use for the invitations."

"Is the sheriff still here?"

"He says he's finishing up," she said. "I just made him another plate of ham biscuits. That man certainly has an appetite."

It didn't surprise Natalie to know that her mother already had the sheriff calling her by her first name and asking for seconds. Rosemary Macready always knew what to say, what to wear, and how to make any man she spoke to feel like the most fascinating person in the world. For Christmases and birthdays she gave the softest pajamas, the perfect books, candle sets that smelled of peonies and sunshine. When Natalie and her sisters were sick as children, she'd made homemade chicken soup and rubbed their feet with essential oils. Natalie had wondered sometimes whether all this caretaking was really a way of expressing love, or simply a collateral effect of her mother's insistence that every aspect of her life be perfect.

"If you're ready to get up, I could use some help figuring out how to feed everybody," her mother said. "We have leftovers, but I'm not really sure what to do with them."

Natalie glanced outside. The light was dimming, the sun hidden behind a layer of clouds. Her father and Luke had disappeared, and the guys in the orange vests seemed to be finishing up too. "I'll help," she said.

But of course her mother already had a plan. Last night the leftover brisket had been packed into Tupperware in the chest freezer; Natalie's job was to heat it up and somehow make it look appetizing on the long, delicate platters from her parents' wedding china. Her mother toasted the buns and heaped leftover coleslaw into serving bowls; Kaitlyn made a salad. The ritual of preparing food gave them something to do with their hands, and created the impression that the routine of life was proceeding as usual.

She was arranging the buns in stacks on a round plate when Sheriff Underwood stuck his head through the door. "Thanks for all your help today, Rosemary," he said. "We're going to get out of your hair now."

Natalie's mother wiped her hands on a dish towel. "Sheriff, if there's anything else we can do, you just let me know. Ben Marsh was a friend of ours for many years." Something seemed to catch in her throat then, and Kaitlyn put her arms around her while Natalie showed the sheriff to the door. On the porch, he turned to look at her. "I'd like you to come by my office tomorrow," he said in an undertone. "It's important that I hear about Mr. Marsh from the people who were closest to him."

She nodded to show she understood and shut the door behind him. When she got back to the kitchen, Kaitlyn was patting their mother on the back. "Mama, why don't you lie down for a while?" she said. "It'll take another ten minutes to heat up the mac and cheese."

Their mother looked tempted. "Someone should run over and tell Jay and Cassie when we're eating."

"I'll do it," Kaitlyn volunteered, but as soon as their mother had left the room, she turned to Natalie and said, "Want to go for a walk?"

They climbed the cliffside steps down to the dock. It looked now like a storm was blowing in, one that would bring the cold needling rain of late fall. Dried leaves tossed in the roiling water. Natalie kept looking toward the mouth of the cove, though she knew she couldn't see Ben's houseboat from this angle. She wondered if they'd removed his body yet, and if so, where they'd taken it. "Does Uncle Leo know what happened?" she asked as she took out her Marlboro Lights.

"Daddy called him," Kaitlyn said.

That was probably how the gossip had spread, Natalie thought. Once her uncle knew, everyone in town would know too. "Do you think it'll be on the news?"

"Luke said a van from Channel 10 tried to drive down Southridge

Road," Kaitlyn said. "The sheriff had it blocked off, and he told them to turn around, but I'm sure they'll be back."

Natalie put the cigarette to her mouth but didn't light it. Channel 10 was out of Roanoke, nearly a two-hour drive from Ewald County. Would Ben's murder be a national story? The presence of two Instagram yoga influencers would surely increase the interest, and she wondered if she should warn Cassie to delete her posts from the past two days before it was too late. "It sucks about what happened to your windshield," Kaitlyn said. "I don't know where I'm going to find another car I can afford."

Natalie fumbled for her lighter, embarrassed to admit that she'd completely forgotten about her promise to sell her old convertible to Kaitlyn when she bought a new car in the spring. "I can't think about that now."

"I know." Kaitlyn sat down, her legs hanging over the edge of the dock. "You were sleeping with him, weren't you?" she asked, not looking at Natalie.

"What?" Natalie's hand was trembling, and she stuffed the lighter back in her pocket. "How did you know?"

"I mean, I remember how you were about Lanny back in high school. It makes sense—they look so much alike. Then the night before last at the studio, I got a look at your phone screen and I saw that Ben was calling."

Natalie looked away. Leave it to one of her sisters to point out that twelve years before she'd fallen for Ben Marsh, she'd been head over heels for his son.

"Do Mama and Daddy know?" Kaitlyn asked.

"God, I hope not," Natalie said. "It's not like we were going to get married. It wasn't a serious thing."

"You mean *you* didn't take it seriously," Kaitlyn said.

Natalie felt a chill that might or might not have been from the knife-sharp breeze that cut straight through her fleece jacket.

"Natalie," Kaitlyn said, shaking her head, "did it really never occur to you that this might have something to do with you?"

11.

They decided to eat at the big table on the upper level of the boat-house. "A change of scene" was how Natalie's mother sold it to the rest of them, as if a different backdrop would somehow make them feel better.

The table was still laid with a white cloth from the party the night before. From here they could look down on the beach, where Natalie's father, who'd refused to sit down for dinner, was arranging the materials for another bonfire. His gray hair blew wildly around his head as he stacked the branches in a rough pyramid. The whole thing looked pagan, as if they were preparing to enact some gruesome propitiation of the gods.

Predictably, no one had an appetite. Picking at her barbecue, Natalie was still thinking about what Kaitlyn had said down on the dock. When Natalie asked her how she could possibly be responsible for Ben's murder, Kaitlyn had waved it away, mumbling that she shouldn't have said anything. Natalie had pushed, but getting her sister to talk when she didn't want to was next to impossible, and finally she'd dropped it.

But Natalie could imagine only one explanation that made sense. Kaitlyn had been implying that their father had found out about Natalie and Ben and been so overcome with rage that he'd picked up a knife and stabbed his best friend again and again. Natalie couldn't believe it. Trey Macready certainly wouldn't have been happy to find out that his daughter was sleeping with a man twice her age, but it wouldn't have sent him into a homicidal fury. Even if he'd been in-

THE FELONS' BALL 57

volved in shady business decades ago, surely Kaitlyn didn't believe that he was still capable of the kind of violence that had been alleged against the Macreadys in the past.

On the other hand, her father had more than one reason to be angry with Ben. It wasn't just that he was sleeping with Natalie; there was also the fact that only hours before his death, he had nearly brained Trey Macready's only grandchild. Natalie thought about what her mother had said on their walk back from Cassie and Jay's cabin, about how Trey had wanted to go out to Ben's boat and give him a piece of his mind. She felt nauseated and pushed her plate away, hoping no one would notice.

"I can't believe you pierced her ears," Rosemary said to Cassie as she batted her eyelashes at the baby across the table. "It must have hurt so much, and at that age they can't understand it."

Cassie's face went still in that way that meant she was making an effort not to roll her eyes. "It's traditional in Indian families."

"People circumcise babies every day," Kaitlyn offered. "Imagine how much that hurts."

Natalie took her plate into the kitchenette and scraped it into the trash. She wanted a drink, she thought—or no, that wasn't it. She wanted to be drunk already, so heedlessly, stupidly drunk that she would blurt out the whole story of her affair with Ben without even realizing she was doing it.

The door swung open behind her. "Here," Jay said in a conspiratorial hush, opening his hand and showing her a white pill nestled in his palm. He was looking over her head, as if they were doing a drug deal in the hallway of a club.

"What is it?"

"Just a Xanax. I hate to fly."

She swallowed it dry, glancing over his shoulder to make sure that no one had followed him in. "Did the police talk to you today?"

He leaned back against the counter. "They wanted to hear the story about the ball landing in Anjali's playpen. I guess someone told them I said 'I'm going to fucking kill you.'"

Indignation filled her. "But you didn't threaten him. You were just upset."

"Don't worry about it," Jay said. "The sheriff seemed to get it."

She wondered how he could be sure. Jay had been one of only a handful of people of color at the party, and if she were him, she would have wondered whether the rumors going around had more than a little to do with that fact. But she had no idea how to raise such a sensitive subject with him now, when they'd never talked about anything more personal than how to engage your glutes in a forearm plank. "I'm so sorry about this," she said. "It's awful that you're in the middle of it."

"Hey, what are you apologizing for?" he said, pulling her into a hug. The embrace felt awkward; they'd hugged before, but only briefly, one of those quick side things where you separate almost before you lean in. This was a real hug, their bodies pressed fully together, his chin resting on the top of her head. She wanted it to go on longer. She wanted to put her head down on his shoulder and cry until his T-shirt was soaked through.

Cassie walked in, and Natalie pulled back abruptly. "Dad says the bonfire's almost ready," Cassie said, slipping her arm around Jay's waist and leaning against him.

Natalie felt herself flush. Being caught embracing her hot brother-in-law felt wrong somehow, but if Cassie was unbothered, maybe Natalie shouldn't worry about it either. Touching people was literally Jay's job, after all. "Anybody up for raiding the liquor cabinet before the bonfire?" Cassie asked. "You know Dad's going to give a half-hour eulogy."

The door swung open again and Luke came in, forcing the three of them even closer. "Y'all better get out there," he said to Cassie and Natalie. "Your mom dropped one of her earrings in the sand, and she and Kaitlyn have about gone blind looking for it."

"Luke, what happened when you took Ben back to the boat?" Jay asked. "Did he say anything to you?"

"Not really," Luke said, as if the question bored him; surely his colleagues at the sheriff's department had gone over this a half-dozen times already. "He was in bed when I left. I asked him if he needed anything, and he said he was just going to sleep it off."

Cassie, who had turned to root around in the cabinets, emerged triumphant with a bottle of Hendrick's Gin. "This ought to get us through the night," she said. "Can somebody grab those plastic martini glasses from the cabinet? I think there's a jar of olives in the fridge."

They found their father standing by the blaze, flames reflected in the glasses he'd been too vain to wear the night before. "Y'all took your sweet time," he said, but it was a routine kind of grumbling, thunder in the distance.

"Should we say a prayer?" her mother asked. "I think it would be nice."

They screwed their martinis into the sand at their feet and joined hands, Natalie between her sisters, with Cassie's wedding ring digging uncomfortably into the underside of her middle finger. "Lord, I'd like to thank you for the life of Benjamin Alan Marsh, who blessed this family with his love and friendship for more than forty years," her father began.

Forty years, Natalie thought with a surge of heartache. She remembered that Ben and her father had met as children, but she'd never done the math. Someone you'd known for forty years was as much a part of you as any family member. As her father went on about Ben's career, his love of practical jokes, and the impact he'd had on Ewald County, detailing each element of the dead man's personality as if he was introducing Ben to Jesus at a Rotary dinner, Natalie's gaze settled on Luke, on the other side of the circle. Instead of his deputy uniform, he wore jeans and work boots with a dark cable-knit sweater that had probably been a gift from her mother. Luke wasn't as handsome as Jay, but there was an authority about him that reminded her of her father. He was looking at Cassie, but when he felt Natalie's eyes on him, he glanced back toward the fire.

Luke had said that Ben was in bed when he left last night. She could picture it so clearly: Luke pulling up to the side of Ben's house-boat, helping him out and checking to make sure that Ben was settled before he left; Ben lying down with his eyes on the ceiling, telling Luke he just needed to sleep it off and would see him in the morning.

When Luke left, Ben might have listened to the party noise for a while, but it would have died down around midnight. After that, there would have been nothing but the shushing sound of waves on the bottom of the boat, the gentle movement that had rocked her to sleep so many times. It was hard to imagine that someone could have sneaked up on him, even when he'd been drinking. He would have heard a kayak scraping against the wood, the thump of hands and knees as the killer transferred their weight to the dock.

From Ben's bed, it would have been an easy reach to the 9mm in his built-in bedside table, but the gun wasn't beside him on the dock. It was true that she hadn't been looking for it, but she was sure she would have noticed a gun if it had been anywhere in the vicinity of where Ben was found. If he'd heard someone pull up to the dock after Luke left, Ben would have grabbed it automatically. She knew that better than anyone after what happened on Friday, when he'd nearly shot her by accident.

If Ben hadn't reached for the gun, that could mean only one thing. It meant that whoever had pulled up to the dock that night, it was someone he'd expected to see.

12.

The house was quiet when Natalie got up the next morning. She padded downstairs in a bathrobe and bare feet and popped a pod in the Keurig, staring out the window at the back lawn and the pale rim of sky above the line of woods. She'd had a dream about Jay, and it bothered her that she couldn't remember the details. It hadn't been sexual, not exactly, but she recalled clearly the weight of his body on hers. Maybe he'd been adjusting her, lengthening her spine in a forward bend, the way he would in class.

She'd never told anyone, but it was Jay, not Cassie, who had first sold her on yoga. Not long after they started dating, Natalie flew out to LA to meet her sister's new boyfriend, and Cassie took her to the studio in Malibu where he was teaching at the time. The studio was famous for its celebrity instructor divas, Cassie explained as they drove up the coast. There was one who was famous for demanding absolute silence as soon as she walked into the room, and another who Cassie had seen tear up the class roster and throw it in the face of the front-desk attendant who'd accidentally left off one student's name. Natalie had fiddled nervously with the hem of her sweatshirt. Her knowledge of yoga extended no further than a few online tutorials, and Cassie had promised that she would take her to a beginner class, but this didn't sound like the kind of place that catered to newbies. What if Jay criticized her form in front of everyone, or called her out for her twenty-dollar mat and Target athleisure?

But Jay wasn't like that. She already knew from Instagram that he was handsome—tall, with lean muscles, high cheekbones, and a slightly asymmetrical nose that kept his face from being intimidatingly perfect—but she was surprised to find that he was also nice. He gave her an enthusiastic bear hug when Cassie introduced them, and during class, which wasn't too hard after all, he seemed to pay her special attention. When he put a hand to her spine or adjusted her arm by a few degrees, something clicked in her body and everything made sense. By the time they got to the resting pose at the end, Natalie had tears in her eyes.

When Cassie had talked about the mind-body connection, Natalie thought it sounded like hippie nonsense, but after her first class with Jay, she knew that Cassie was onto something after all. It was as if the weight of all the hurt she'd carried since the boat crash and Lanny's disappearance had suddenly lifted. Jay seemed to her less like a teacher than a magician, vanishing her pain with a touch of his hand.

The Keurig sputtered to a stop, and Natalie reached for the mug. "Will you make me one of those?" said a voice behind her.

She jumped, coffee scalding her wrist. Kaitlyn was curled up on the couch with an afghan over her legs. "Take mine," Natalie said, moving into the living room. "God, you scared me."

Kaitlyn reached to switch on the lamp. "I lay down to rest for a few minutes after dinner, and I guess no one wanted to wake me. I haven't been sleeping very well."

She scooted over to make room for Natalie on the couch. The light made the outside seem darker, the two of them enclosed in a private space. Cassie and Kaitlyn were only a year and a half apart, but it was Kaitlyn and Natalie, with three years between them, who had been paired when they were children. "The younger girls," her mother had called them to distinguish them from Cassie, who was always simply herself.

Now that the light was on, Natalie was sure she could detect the evidence of insomnia on Kaitlyn's face—the drawn cheeks, the hollows beneath her eyes. "It's not about Luke, is it? Did y'all have a fight or something?"

She didn't know why she'd asked. She'd noticed no evidence of tension between Kaitlyn and Luke. Maybe it was the way he'd reacted when she caught him staring at Cassie across the fire the night before—his eyes flicking away as if he'd been doing something wrong.

"No, we didn't have a fight," Kaitlyn said, picking at a loose thread in the afghan. "I told you, I'm just tired. Why are you up so early?"

"Habit, I guess," Natalie said. Six to seven was normally her practice time, but she felt too antsy to roll out her mat right now, her mind on the appointment with the sheriff later this morning.

Kaitlyn blew on her coffee and set it on a coaster. "I talked to Amanda yesterday," she said. "She's back home. I could tell she wanted to ask about Ben, but I didn't want to get into all that. I think Daddy's right, and it must have been some stranger. I've heard about people squatting on empty boats before. Maybe somebody thought Ben's was abandoned, and then they freaked out when they realized he was there."

"I like that theory better than your other one," Natalie said. "You really messed me up down on the dock when you said it might have something to do with me."

Kaitlyn's face went still. "I don't really believe that," she said. "I think I was in shock yesterday. I can't imagine how awful it was for you, finding his body like that. And then I made it worse by giving you more to worry about."

Natalie felt a sudden urge to lay her head in Kaitlyn's lap and tell her everything, about Ben's last words to her on the morning of his death and her fears that she might have been able to help him if only she'd insisted on being the one to take him back to the boat. But before she could move, they heard the creak of the stairs. It was their father; they could hear him sighing, then whistling the first bars of "Morning Has Broken." Kaitlyn grabbed Natalie's hand and squeezed, and Natalie squeezed back, feeling a rush of gratitude for her middle sister, who knew her better than anyone in the world and somehow, inexplicably, loved her in spite of it.

Though no one had actually told her not to leave the property the day after Ben's murder, Natalie hadn't even considered going to work. She'd canceled all the classes, and Luke had driven into town to stick a sign on the door. It had seemed essential that the family stick together, but when she told her parents that she had to go into town on Monday morning to answer a few more questions for Sheriff Underwood, they agreed without hesitation. The Macreadys might not have been ready to go back to business as usual, but clearly their daughters were no longer expected to hang around the house.

Cassie volunteered to go with her and take Anjali for a walk in her stroller while Natalie talked to the sheriff. "I'm surprised that Daddy hasn't called a lawyer," Cassie said as they pulled out of the driveway. "I expected him to have Lester Singletary over there the second the police set foot on the property."

Natalie downshifted, frowning. Her father had insisted that she drive his Chevette until her windshield was replaced, but she hated driving stick, and the flash car embarrassed her. "Maybe that's a good thing," she said. "Maybe he's heard that the police don't consider us suspects, so he doesn't feel like he needs a lawyer."

"Are you kidding? Mom and Dad were Ben's closest neighbors," Cassie said, ticking off on her fingers, "Luke was the last one to see him alive, and you found the body. I'm sure we're at the top of the list."

Natalie felt her breath tighten in her chest. Surely, as Kaitlyn had said, there was someone else—some violent drifter, some disgruntled employee or former friend who might have had it in for Ben. Maybe she'd been wrong about the reason Ben hadn't grabbed his gun. Maybe he hadn't expected anyone, and had simply been too drunk or too sleepy to clock the noises from outside. "Daddy probably wants to show the police he's on their side," she said. "If he called his lawyer right away, it might seem like we're hiding something."

But Cassie, leaning her head against the window, no longer seemed to be listening. "This whole thing is so surreal," she said. "We live in LA, which is an actual dangerous place, and I've never even had my car broken into. Then we come back to this little town in Virginia, and there's a murder."

"It's not like that's a regular thing, though," Natalie said, keeping her voice light. "I mean, I'm pretty sure that boredom is a bigger problem in Ewald than murder. People always say that it's a great place to raise kids."

Cassie snorted. "Depends what kind of kids, I guess." She and Natalie exchanged a look, and Cassie clicked her tongue against her teeth, as if faintly irritated by her sister's incomprehension. "This whole baptism thing," she said. "Why is Mama making such a big deal about it?"

Natalie realized she was squinting and flipped down the visor. "What do you mean?"

"Jay was raised Hindu," Cassie said. "He's not practicing, but I'm not exactly a practicing Christian either. I don't understand why she has such a bug up her ass about Anjali being baptized."

"I thought it was all settled," Natalie said, aware that it was a lame response but unable to come up with anything better. It had never occurred to her that her niece would not be baptized at First Presbyterian, in the same long lace-trimmed white dress that Natalie and her sisters had worn. "I mean, if you don't want to do it, just tell her, I guess," she added quickly.

Cassie sighed. "It's just so tone-deaf. She wants to dictate every part of my life, just like she does with you and Kaitlyn."

For a moment, Natalie was too stunned to speak. "Is that what you think?"

"I'm not trying to hurt your feelings," Cassie said. "But you're still living at home, Natalie. Daddy bought your car; he put together the funding when you were building your studio. It's a good gig, don't get me wrong, but at some point you're going to want out from under their thumb."

Natalie stiffened but said nothing. Women without sisters were always telling her how lucky she was. "I always wanted a sister," they'd say, as if they were talking about an American Girl doll or jelly shoes. She knew exactly what they were picturing: spontaneous slumber parties where they whispered secrets and braided each other's hair, or long text threads where the person who knew you best in the world offered unconditional love and encouragement, regardless of how misguided or just plain dumb your decisions happened to be. That was part of it, sometimes, but it certainly wasn't the full truth of their relationship. For every time she felt a surge of the fierce affection and bone-deep loyalty that was the Hollywood version of sisterhood, she felt twice as much frustration, especially when it came to Cassie. Her oldest sister always seemed to keep her at a distance, as if Natalie never quite measured up to her expectations.

They'd turned onto the Square, and Natalie was surprised to find that it looked even more downtrodden than usual, as if she was seeing it through Cassie's eyes rather than her own. Unlike Marlborough Springs, on the southern side of the lake, Ewald attracted few tourists, and the beauty of the mountains that encircled the town seemed beside the point when contrasted with the low, shabby buildings. The sheriff's department was located in the old courthouse, a two-story redbrick building with peeling columns and ornate masonry. As soon as Natalie shifted into park, Cassie popped out and unfolded her stroller from the back.

"Text me when you're done," she said. "I just hope Anj doesn't have a blowout. I bet not one of these places has a changing table."

Natalie watched her sister and niece disappear around the corner of the Square, as out of place in downtown Ewald as if they'd stepped from the pages of a magazine. She felt a surge of resentment. As much as she loved her sister, admired her, and wanted to be like her, she couldn't deny there were times when she would have liked to see Cassie knocked down a notch.

She was reaching over to grab her purse when someone knocked on the passenger-side window. She started, and her forehead hit the horn as a face appeared in the glass: Sheriff Underwood. "Sorry," he mouthed, miming cranking down the window. It struck her as an old-fashioned gesture, and she wondered if he was even older than she'd thought.

"I saw you from my office," he said when she'd turned the key and hit the button for the power window. "I wasn't sure if you knew your way around the building, so I thought I'd come out and meet you."

When she asked Luke about his new boss the night before, he'd said that Underwood was weird. "Weird how?" Natalie had persisted, but Luke only shrugged, unable or unwilling to put his dissatisfaction into words. She knew he'd been just as impatient with the old sheriff, who owned a dairy farm and, especially as he neared retirement, cared far more about his Holsteins than he did about the future of a county rife with prescription drug abuse and the property crime that came with it. As a child, Natalie had always hated it when they ran into Sheriff Shifflett in town because he and her father chatted for so long that she and her sisters ran out of games to play. Those long, aimless conversations about cattle and water levels in Lake Monroe had reinforced her sense that she lived in a town where nothing ever happened. Though she knew in some vague way that Sheriff Shifflett's father had arrested her father when he was young, and even sent Uncle Leo to prison, the rapport between the two men had made it seem that those long-ago stories were just a myth, unreal as an episode of *The Dukes of Hazzard.* The way her father talked about those times, it was as if moonshining and being busted was all part of a game he was playing, one where even adversaries knew the rules and could walk away as friends.

When Shifflett finally retired, Luke hadn't wanted the job himself—too much politics, he'd told them, and too much responsibility—but he'd hoped they'd put up someone who knew the county and its people. Hardy Underwood had come off well enough during the campaign, but Luke had detected a big-city slipperiness in his tone and manner. As Natalie turned off the Chevette and got out, she wondered why Underwood had really come out to meet her—if he was just polite, or if he hoped to wrong-foot her in some way by catching her off guard. God knew she could have made her way around the undersize courthouse without his help.

Inside he led her through the metal detector and then down a long hallway that reminded her of an old hotel, with beige carpet and whitewashed radiators lining the walls. People were walking back and forth between the offices, and Natalie knew most of them well enough to say hello to, though she noticed that she seemed to be getting some strange looks. She avoided their eyes, fighting the urge to cross her arms over her chest.

At the end of the hall the sheriff directed her through a kind of waiting room, where a young receptionist with a bad bleach job was buffing her nails, and into his inner office, closing the door behind them. It was smaller than she'd expected, and painted a queasy shade of green that she couldn't imagine he'd chosen. The desk was cluttered with papers; pictures lined the walls, including a photo of Underwood in his marine uniform and a series of school pictures of two pretty brown-haired girls.

"I have news, but I'm not sure if it's good or bad," he said as he took a seat behind his desk. "Croaker Farber seems to have an airtight alibi for Saturday afternoon. Apparently he went on a bender in Tyndall County and ended up getting in a fight with a couple bikers. One of them cut him with a bottle, and he didn't get released from the hospital until eight p.m."

Natalie sensed that Underwood wanted to test her reaction to this story. She had no idea what he was expecting or hoping for, but she didn't like feeling manipulated. She swallowed down the rising panic in her chest. "Okay," she said. "What am I supposed to do with that information?"

The sheriff was still watching her with curiosity. "My point is, even if Croaker didn't smash your window, somebody did, and I'd certainly advise protecting yourself."

Natalie bit her lip, wondering if Luke had told Underwood about the Glock 19 with the pink skin that her father had given her for her birthday one year. She'd kept up her certification at her father's insistence, but she'd never liked the idea of carrying a gun. "Protecting myself in what way?"

Underwood smiled, as if this was just the question he was hoping she'd ask. "I guess first of all by being safety-conscious," he said. "Park in well-lit areas. Don't go out alone at night. You're a smart woman, so I'm sure you've heard all this before. By the way, you didn't see a knife on Ben's boat on Saturday night, did you?"

A shiver started in the soles of her feet and traveled up through her body. "No," she said. "I mean, I don't know if there was one there or not—I wasn't looking. Are you saying that you didn't find a weapon?"

This time, she wasn't surprised when he didn't answer her question. "I bet half the men at that party were carrying, and probably some of the women too," he said. "So I can't get my head around why Ben would be stabbed, when there are cleaner and more efficient ways to kill somebody right there at hand."

She felt flattered that he'd jumped right into the difficulties of the investigation, as if she had something to offer in that regard. "Maybe it was a crime of passion," she said. "Isn't that what people say about stabbing? People get angry, and then they turn around and there's a knife in the block by the cutting board."

As soon as the words were out of her mouth, she wished she could take them back. If Ben's murder originated in passion, it must have been committed by someone who knew him well, and who knew him better than her family? Who knew him better than her, the woman he'd been sleeping with for most of the past year? "But don't listen to me," she added hastily. "I guess your mind just wants to come up with a story to explain a situation like this."

The sheriff said nothing. He didn't even nod. He was one of those men who knew how to use silence to make people nervous, and it was clearly working, Natalie chattering on without even thinking about what was about to come out of her mouth. "I really don't know how much more I can tell you about Ben," she said. "It wasn't like other relationships, where you sit down and tell each other all about your families and your hobbies. We kind of skipped over that stage."

"That makes sense," Underwood said. "I assume you'd known him your whole life, right? How did you get together?"

Natalie hesitated. "I wasn't a teenager or anything, if that's what you're insinuating."

He lifted an eyebrow. "I didn't say you were."

"That's one reason we kept it a secret," she said. "Older men and younger women get together all the time. There's nothing unusual about it. But if it turns out that they've known each other for a long time, people think it's grooming or something."

"Like Elvis and Priscilla," Hardy offered.

She paused. It was a reference her father would have made. "Ben loaned me some money," she said. "When I was first starting out. I could have gone to my dad, but he'd already financed the construction, and if he'd given me a loan, it would have come with all kinds of conditions. Ben didn't even want me to sign anything."

"Did you pay him back?"

"Not yet," Natalie said. "I was going to, but he never acted like there was any hurry."

The sheriff nodded. Everything about his body language indicated that he was open, receptive, not judging or criticizing her, and Natalie wasn't sure why she couldn't quite bring herself to believe it. "You asked me about Lanny Marsh yesterday," he said. "We're still trying to track him down. Did you know him well?"

"Of course I knew Lanny," she said. "We were friends."

He was watching her closely. "Friends?" he repeated. "Or more than friends?"

Natalie crossed her legs and then uncrossed them, pressing her hands to her thighs. "We never dated or anything like that," she said. "I was only fourteen, and he was eighteen. He talked a lot about wanting to get out of Ewald, and I used to fantasize that maybe he'd take me with him. But then he ran away."

Hardy pushed himself back from the desk and threaded his hands behind his head. "I heard something about that," he said. "I'm not sure if I've got all the details, though."

Again, she considered how much she really wanted to tell him. Her family never talked about Lanny Marsh—not where he had gone when he left Ewald County, and certainly not what he'd done right before he left. If she was going to tell Sheriff Underwood the truth about the boat crash, it might as well be now. She took a deep breath and jumped.

"You know how I said that Croaker blamed us when he went to prison? It wasn't just that my dad and Ben had an in with the judge. I always thought that maybe Lanny, not Croaker, was the one driving."

"But you were on the boat, weren't you?" Underwood asked. "How could you not know who was driving?"

"I was passed out," she admitted. "I was only fourteen, and I'd gotten into my dad's liquor that night. In the hospital, everybody told me that Croaker had been driving, so of course I believed it. But later, when I thought about it, I was sure that Lanny had been at the wheel when I blacked out."

His face was expressionless now, and she had no idea whether or not he believed what she was saying. "So you're assuming that your dad and Ben lied."

Natalie grimaced. "I think Daddy was just trying to help," she said. "Lanny didn't have a great childhood. His mother died of cancer when he was only three or four, and Ben was a heavy drinker back then. Daddy said that Lanny was like a son to him. We always went to his football games, and I think Mama might have gone to his parent-teacher conferences when Ben couldn't make it. That was what made it so awful, when Lanny—"

She stopped, hoping that the sheriff would assume that she was referring to the boat crash. But she could tell from the slight lift of his eyebrow that he'd caught her hesitation. "Lanny left home not long after that, didn't he? Did he talk to you about it before he left?"

Natalie shook her head. "I was still in the hospital then. Lanny had been talking about joining the merchant marines for years, so no one was really surprised. He always said he was going to drive out to LA and jump on a ship as soon as he got a chance, and when Ben went to rehab, I guess that seemed like the perfect time. But he took some things of Daddy's when he left—this Brooks & Dunn NASCAR die-cast, and a Curtis Turner that was Daddy's favorite. That was what really broke Daddy's heart."

The sheriff nodded, as if this was more or less what he'd expected. "I saw your dad's collection, but I don't know a thing about NASCAR," the sheriff said. "What's a die-cast, and what kind of money are we talking about?"

"A die-cast is like a model car," Natalie explained. "Like a Matchbox car, but bigger. I think it's made in a mold or something. The Brooks & Dunn was really rare, so it was worth a few thousand dollars, but the Curtis Turner wasn't worth anything. He grew up not far from here, and he was Daddy's favorite driver. He thought Lanny took it just to be spiteful."

"Did your father report them missing?"

"I'm not sure," Natalie said. "I know they spent a lot of time trying to get the police to look for Lanny, but he was eighteen, and they said they couldn't do anything. Obviously that was more important than the collectibles, but I did catch Daddy searching for the Curtis Turner die-cast on his phone one time. I think he was hoping that Lanny might have posted it for sale."

Underwood unlaced his hands, his eyes trained on the empty wall behind Natalie's head. "And nobody ever talked to Lanny again? Not even his dad?"

"Ben got postcards from him," she said. "He used to flip through them once in a while, but I never read them or anything. I really hope y'all can find him. I can't imagine finding out that my dad had died and nobody had even told me about it."

The sheriff paused, laying his hands flat on the desk. "Let's go back a little bit," he said. "Now you know I'm not telling tales out of school when I say that your family used to be involved with some nefarious activities. That's just a statement of fact; you know it, I know it, everybody knows it." He spread his palms as if to indicate that awareness of the Macreadys' criminality extended to the edges of the known universe. "What I can't figure out is when they quit. I've read all the interviews and the transcripts from your uncle's trial, but there's nothing in the reports that indicates that those stills up in the national forest were ever destroyed."

"You should ask my dad," she said, feeling even more nervous now. "I don't know anything about that stuff. I was just a kid back then."

"And you and Ben never talked about it?" he pressed. "He never told you stories about their glory days?"

"No," she said. "I swear."

Underwood held her gaze for a long moment, but something in his expression had changed, as if he'd believed her denials and concluded that she had nothing useful to offer him. She couldn't tell yet if she felt offended or relieved.

"When I first came in, you said I should protect myself," she said. "What did you mean exactly? If you don't believe Croaker had anything to do with what happened to Ben, what do I need to protect myself from?"

He scratched at his sideburn, pursing his lips as if he wasn't sure how to answer. It was so quiet, she could hear the fan blades spin and the plastic blinds tick against the glass. "You'd probably know more about that than I would," he said. "Do you have any enemies? Anybody who might mean you harm? When you're close to somebody who's murdered, you have to ask yourself if there might be a message in there for you."

She felt a buzzing in her ears, like the beginning of a headache. "If we're done, I should get back and meet my sister."

But now that their interview was officially over, he didn't seem in any hurry to see her leave. "Do you know I've never taken a yoga class?" He kicked back in his chair. "I've been thinking I should try it out. I have some sports injuries from way back, and I think it might help to stretch everything out."

"You should come by the studio." She reached into her purse for one of the free-class cards she kept in the inside pocket. "Increased flexibility can help with long-term discomfort like you're describing, but it also has a lot of other benefits. You'd be surprised at how much better you'd feel."

Halfway through her spiel, she began to worry that he might see this as another kind of invitation, but he simply tapped the card against his palm and slipped it into his pocket.

Though she would have preferred to make her own way, he walked her down the hall again, past the window of an office that seemed to be for paying bills or submitting forms. Beverly Peck was standing in line and called out, "Morning, Sheriff," her beady eyes sweeping over Natalie, who cringed inwardly. Beverly worked at the bait and tackle store out by the marina, and by noon every fisherman between here and Marlborough Springs would know that Natalie Macready had been seen at the courthouse that morning.

At least the sheriff didn't walk her all the way out to the parking lot, instead opening the door for her and looking out, shading his eyes with his hands. "That's a nice little Chevette you're driving," he said. "That's not what the insurance gave you, is it?"

"It's my dad's car," Natalie said. "I'd rather just get a rental, but he says it's safer to drive a car that everyone can recognize as mine."

"Well, it's sure as hell conspicuous," Underwood said as he turned back toward his office. "Everybody's going to see you coming."

13.

It wasn't that she'd lied to Hardy Underwood, or not exactly. It was true that she knew virtually nothing about her family's moonshining business, which had ceased to be a viable commercial enterprise around the time she was born. From what she'd heard, production in Ewald had all but stopped after the big federal raids in the late nineties. Her grandfather Macready's farm supply store, which had once sold seven million pounds of sugar and half a million one-gallon containers in a single year, had been forced to close its doors, and he'd died soon after. Her father had left behind the lucrative days of delivering the county product to the back doors of bars in the cities of the Southeast and concentrated on their legitimate business, and after Uncle Leo served his time, he'd joined his brother at Macready Contracting. That was the official story—the one that her father himself had surely shared with the sheriff before he'd written a sizable check to his campaign.

But it wasn't the whole truth. Natalie could remember the mini fridge in the den that throughout her childhood had been stocked with mason jars, some clear as sunshine, others tinged deep blue, yellow, or purple with muddled fruit. She'd assumed these were gifts from friends, as Hardy had suggested, but she didn't know that for sure. When they were very little, their mother had told the girls that it was medicine that was dangerous to children, and none of them had gone further than opening the door and running their fingertips along the long line of colored glass. Until they were teenagers, of course. Until the night of the boat crash.

No one ever asked Natalie what she remembered from that night. She'd answered the police's questions at the hospital, but once they found out that she'd passed out after the boat left the dock and didn't wake up until Luke pulled her onto the bank, they'd seemed to lose interest, and that was fine with her. They had so many other accounts to chase, ones that must have seemed more interesting and more relevant. In the years since, Natalie had heard her sisters' stories of that night so many times that they'd become as real to her as her own memories. She could see the tall, shirtless boy palming the wheel—could see, as if in a movie, the boat turning at a too-sharp angle as it approached the bridge that ran over the top of the TVA dam. She could see the pictures that had been printed in the newspaper the next day: the police headlights illuminating the lakeshore; Croaker with his head in his hands.

She'd had a new outfit for the Felons' Ball that year, a skintight red minidress that she'd bought with her allowance and sneaked past her mom. Cassie said it looked slutty, but once Natalie put it on, she knew that the real reason Cassie didn't want her to wear the dress was because she'd known Natalie would look prettier than her. The dress clung to Natalie in all the right places, showing off her new cleavage and the roundness of her ass. In a concession to the weather, she paired it with shearling boots and a long white cable-knit cardigan. Kaitlyn did her makeup, giving her a smoky eye and lipstick that matched the dress exactly. "Just keep your face out of the light when you see Mama," Kaitlyn warned. "She'll say you look like a streetwalker."

Natalie had rolled her eyes. The last thing she wanted to do that night was be around their parents. Lanny had been flirting with her for months now, putting a hand on her waist or lower back anytime he passed her in the hallway, leaning too close to whisper funny or outrageous comments in her ear. This was her chance to show him that she was ready to learn whatever it was he had to teach her.

Lanny was like the other guys she knew, but also different, and that was what she liked about him. He'd refused to apply to college in the fall, saying that he could make a good salary by hitchhiking out west and jumping on the first boat he saw, and he'd get to see the world at the same time. He was the one who'd explained to her that the merchant marines weren't like the regular marines; the correct term was actually merchant mariner, which referred to any worker on a cargo ship with a US flag. "I don't know where the fuck he even got this idea," she'd heard Ben say to her mother in their kitchen late one night. "It's like he wants to get as far away as possible." Ben Marsh never would have asked her opinion, but Natalie could have told him that that was exactly the point.

But finding time with Lanny at the Felons' Ball was harder than she'd expected. He was with Croaker and Luke, the three of them making the rounds of the adults, saying yes ma'am and no sir, answering questions about the football season and accepting hearty pats on the back. Luke was the one who usually bought the beer for the group, since he was over six feet and could grow a real mustache, as opposed to Croaker's scraggly peach fuzz. He lifted weights even in the off-season, and sometimes Natalie saw him running along the side of the highway in basketball shorts and a sweatshirt with the sleeves cut off. Luke had been after Cassie since middle school, and though Cassie acted like she was too good for him, Natalie had always expected her to give in eventually. As far as Ewald County boys went, she could do a lot worse than Luke Caldwell.

Natalie liked both Croaker and Luke well enough, but she found it hard to pay attention to them when Lanny was around. It wasn't just his looks that attracted her. He was passably cute, with a tall, rangy body and the kind of pointed, mobile face that made him look interesting rather than handsome, but there was more to him than that. She loved the way his eyes moved over her, with a gaze that warmed her body from the top of her head to her curling toes. Most of the boys she knew were bashful about sex, stealing glances at Natalie and her friends and then turning away, as if embarrassed by their own lust, but Lanny was the opposite. He made Natalie aware of her own desire—made her feel the force that was inside her, like a seam of lava running to her core.

While Lanny and his friends made the rounds, Kaitlyn stayed behind the buffet table serving puff pastry appetizers, and Natalie lounged in a beach chair behind her, fending off the cold with an insulated cup of white lightning and orange juice. She was on strict orders from Cassie to limit herself to one drink—"I'm not sneaking you in the house if you get sloppy," her sister had insisted—but Natalie found the limit insulting. She wasn't a child, for God's sake. She'd been sneaking the occasional beer at parties for the last year at least, and she could handle far more than one sip of her father's moonshine. It was in her blood, after all.

The bocce tournament had ended, her father and Ben Marsh crowned champions again, when Lanny appeared at the arm of her chair. Natalie hadn't seen him coming, and she sat up suddenly, wishing she could check her makeup. "It's on," Lanny whispered, his eyes scanning the crowd rather than her face. "I got the keys to your dad's boat."

Natalie gave him her widest smile. "I'll go anywhere with you," she said, and now Lanny did stop and look at her, his eyes traveling down from her face to her body. She shifted slightly to let her cardigan fall open, and his grin widened. "Well, damn, girl," he said, his accent getting stronger, the way it always did when he was drinking. "Let's get the hell out of here then."

They left the party and made it across the lake without incident, but the bonfire was disappointing—mostly college students from out of state who had no interest in sharing their weed with a bunch of locals—and it wasn't long before Luke decided they should relocate to the party boat. "Come on," she heard him whisper to Lanny, who was standing by the fire. "The plan was to get some alone time." Luke looked meaningfully at Cassie, and Lanny grinned.

Screams of laughter came from down the beach, and Natalie turned to see that Kaitlyn and Amanda Maxwell had fallen on the sand, Kaitlyn's body draped over Amanda's. Instead of struggling to their feet, they flipped over so Amanda was on top of Kaitlyn and they were both covered in sand from head to foot. "Shit," Cassie said, sitting on the picnic bench beside Natalie and setting her red Solo cup down with so much force it dented the plastic. "We'll have to hose her off before we get home. Or throw her in the lake."

Natalie took a defiant sip of her screwdriver. "You should throw Luke a pity fuck tonight," she said. "It's the least you could do. He's been mooning after you since fifth grade."

"Are you okay?" Cassie asked, her eyes narrowing critically. "Mama and Daddy are going to flip if you come home hammered."

But Natalie didn't care. The night had already soured for her. On the way to the resort, she'd sat on Lanny's lap, his hands on her hips, and she'd been sure that this was it: she'd turn her head at the right moment, and he'd kiss her at last. Several times she'd tilted her chin his way, but he'd always been distracted, taking a sip from his beer or yelling something to Croaker at the wheel. Maybe he was just a flirt, Natalie thought. Maybe he agreed with Cassie that he was too old for her, and all the attention he'd paid her had been a kind of joke. Now he had his arm around one of the college girls, a cute blonde wearing a shirt that was even more low-cut than Natalie's dress. Natalie finished her drink in one swallow, barely flinching when the harsh burn scalded the back of her throat.

That must have been what put her over the edge. She tried to hide it as long as she could, but by the time they headed back to the boat, she could barely stand and had to put an arm around Croaker's shoulder for support. "I knew it," Cassie said bitterly. "I knew she'd get fucked up, and now they're going to blame me."

"You shouldn't have let her have Dad's liquor," Kaitlyn murmured. "That shit is like one hundred and sixty proof."

"Nah, she's fine," Luke replied. "We'll make her some coffee and she'll be sober as Sunday morning."

They laid her across two seats with her head on Lanny's lap, Natalie concentrating all her energies on not throwing up on him or on her new dress.

"Hey," he whispered. "You all right?"

"Mmph," Natalie replied. She felt miserable, and not just because her stomach was twisting like a rubber band. She raised herself on her elbows and tried to plant a kiss on Lanny's lips. He tolerated it for a moment, but then turned away. "Easy there, jailbait," he said, patting her on the shoulder. "Your daddy would kill me. Hey," he called to Croaker, who turned to look back at them. "I should be the one driving. I'm more sober than y'all motherfuckers combined."

Lanny slid Natalie's head onto the seat cushion he'd vacated and stood up. Just before she lost consciousness, she realized with a sense of despair that she'd had her first kiss after all, and on the very worst night of her life.

What came next: cold. Waking up on her side with lake water spew-ing out of her mouth, as if she'd already begun retching while still unconscious. Men in uniform lifting her onto a gurney, and then her mother running along beside it down the long hall of the hospital, tears streaming down her face. When she woke up the next time, clean and dry and lying in a white bed in a white room, Natalie kept expecting someone to get mad at her for drinking, but no one ever did, and in the weeks and months that followed, she began to get the feeling that her parents were so happy that she was alive that she could get away with just about anything.

At times, Natalie thought she could recall what had come before: the impact, the flight through the air, the feeling of drowning, and then Luke's arm around her waist, towing her to shore. The dread and panic of sinking through the murky water, and then being lifted, saved. Sometimes she was sure that the memories were still in there, buried in the network of fascia and in the folds of her brain. But what she'd learned was that it was better not to remember. She didn't have to relive the trauma of that night, didn't have to process and integrate her almost-death under the surface of the lake. No matter what Cassie said on her podcast, no one gave you a prize for forcing yourself to go over the most painful parts of your past. Sometimes, Natalie thought, it was better to just forget.

Back at the lake, Natalie pulled in behind her mother, who was unloading groceries from the trunk of her BMW. From the side of the bags, Natalie could tell that she'd driven all the way down to the Harris Teeter in Tyndall County, nearly an hour away. It was where she always went when she was stressed or upset, coming back loaded with fancy ice cream and overpriced almonds. Natalie and Kaitlyn joked that their mother never needed to come to a yoga class, since she could go to Harris Teeter instead.

"I got lots of vegetarian things," their mother said as she unloaded the bags. "Do you know what to do with tofu, Cassie? I've never really understood what it was for."

"You can do a lot with tofu, Mom," Cassie said, unbuckling Anjali from her car seat. "I'm going to check on Jay."

Natalie followed her mother up the wooden steps into the kitchen, where she set a bag overflowing with kale and broccolini on the counter. Before she had children, her mother had worked as an interior designer, and while most of the other houses on the lake were decorated in rustic chic, all honeyed wood and signs declaring that LIFE IS BETTER ON THE LAKE, the Macready family had patterned wallpaper, white molding, and countertops of Carrara marble. "Where's Daddy?" she asked.

"He texted when I was on my way back and said he was going for a walk. He was going to try to make it over to the resort and have a scotch at the bar, but he'll probably call in half an hour and want us to pick him up from the side of the road." On her way to the refrigerator,

Rosemary stopped and looked at Natalie with concern, putting the back of her wrist to her daughter's forehead. "Why don't you lie down for a bit?"

Natalie pulled away. "Do you know where that photo album is? The one Kaitlyn gave him for his birthday?"

Too late she remembered that the album was supposed to be from both of them, but her mother didn't seem to notice. "What do you want that for?" she asked as she slotted a jar of kimchi into the shelf on the door.

"I didn't really get to look at it the other night. I wanted to see the pictures of you and Ben and Daddy when you were young."

"It's in my room," her mother said, still peering into the refrigerator. "On the bookshelf by my desk. Just make sure to put it back when you're done."

By "my room," Natalie knew her mother meant not her bedroom but the glassed-in study where she read and paid bills, and where Natalie had sprawled to watch Sheriff Underwood's henchmen scour their property for clues. Today the bright sun made the room warmer and more cheerful, glittering off the waves of the lake. Natalie pulled the red leather album from the lowest shelf and settled on the chaise longue, pulling a blanket from the wicker basket up over her legs.

The pictures must have started in the early nineties, Natalie guessed from the color of their jeans and from Uncle Leo's haircut, which was perilously close to a mullet. Natalie paged past photos of picnics and Thanksgivings, with a few Polaroids of herself and her sisters as babies that Kaitlyn had stuck in seemingly to fill the pages. Ben was in nearly every photo, a fixture of their family. Here he was as she'd never known him—Ben propped on the dock with a beer in his hand, holding up his middle finger to the camera.

Her father, drowning his sorrows in the bar at the Lake Monroe Resort, was permitted to mourn his friend in theatrical ways. He could wear his pain openly, secure in his right to the exaggerated pageantry of grief, but Natalie didn't have the same privilege. For the time being, the shock of finding Ben's body could explain away her low mood, but that wouldn't last forever. She flipped numbly through pictures of her dad and Ben fishing on the lake and clinking bottles at her parents' wedding, wearing ruffled baby-blue shirts under their tuxedos that she hoped had been intended as a joke.

The front door opened, and Jay came in, dressed in track pants and hiking boots. His hoodie was pulled up over his face, but he pushed it back as he looked in on Natalie. "Hey," she said without moving. "Cassie was looking for you."

Her mother came out of the kitchen, wiping her hands on an apron. She was quicker on the uptake than Natalie had been and rushed to Jay's side, placing a hand on his arm. "What is it?" she asked, looking up into his face. "Is Anjali all right?"

"I found something," he said, his voice hoarse. "In the woods."

It was a kitchen knife, a generic one that looked like it could have come from any black-handled set sold at Walmart or Target. The knife lay on a patch of dead leaves about two feet off the path, as if it had been tossed there in a hurry. Natalie put her hands up instinctively and stepped back, almost tripping over a root.

"Did you touch it?" her mother asked Jay in a hushed voice.

"No," he said. "I almost stepped on it, and then I ran over to the house to get somebody." He was sweating, Natalie noticed, despite the cool air. He made an odd snorting sound, as if he were sucking phlegm back up into his sinuses, and when he wiped the sweat off his forehead, she saw that his hand was shaking.

"Maybe it's not what we think it is," Natalie said, her eyes drawn back to the rust-colored stain on the blade. "Maybe somebody used it to skin a rabbit or something."

Even as she spoke, she realized how implausible that sounded. Luke and her father were both hunters, and she'd gone with them often enough to know that no respectable outdoorsman would use a kitchen knife to skin an animal, nor would they just toss it into the woods when they were done.

"Are we missing a knife?" she asked.

Her mother ignored her. "Does anyone have their phone? We need to report this."

Footsteps crunched over the leaves, and they all jumped. "What's this, a party?" her father said, his face flushed from the scotch and the long walk from the other side of the lake. "Why didn't anybody invite me?"

Natalie gestured to the knife without saying a word. Her father stepped closer than she'd dared to, bending down with his hands on his knees to peer at the blade. "Who found it?"

Jay cleared his throat. "I did. I was coming back from a walk and decided to take a shortcut from the lake path." He pointed, and Natalie followed the direction of his eyes to the lake, just visible through the bare branches.

Her father put his arm around Jay and drew him aside as he pushed a button on his phone. "Luke?" he said. "Y'all need to get your crime scene guys out here again. I think we found the murder weapon."

Natalie and her mother stood to the side, waiting. There was no further need for their presence, and it was exasperating but also a relief. Everyone had concluded, through some strange code she'd never learned to read, that this was Men's Business, and that her feelings and observations were superfluous for the present time.

But if they had asked her opinion, she could have told them something that they didn't seem to have realized yet. If the Macreadys hadn't been suspects up to this point, they surely would be now.

14.

Jay spent the rest of the day at the station, but when Natalie saw him at dinner that night, he was his usual easy self, asking her mother about interior decorating and her father about his new boat in a way that seemed to denote genuine interest.

That was what Natalie had first noticed about him, when Cassie had taken her to his class in Malibu: Jay had a knack for making every student in the room feel as if they had his individual attention, as if he was conscious at the same time of Natalie's burning hatred of back-bends, and someone else's bad knee, and someone else's tight lower back, and holding each of them in the light of his calm confidence in their potential. She wondered if Sheriff Underwood had treated Jay like a suspect that afternoon, and wished she could explain to him just how impossible it was that the Jay Desai she knew could be a murderer. It wasn't just the fact that violence was antithetical to yoga. It was that Jay's entire personality was predicated on the seren-ity radiating from him. If that was fake, then everything about him was fake.

Her mother had served baked tofu and roasted potatoes, and Na-talie was watching her father push the little white cubes around on his plate when Kaitlyn said to Cassie, "Have y'all thought about going home?"

Cassie, who had been trying to coax the baby to eat the tofu she'd mashed into an unappetizing paste, paused with her fork in the air. "What?" she said blankly.

Kaitlyn glanced around the table. "Well, it's such a sad situation, and you don't really need to be here, so . . ."

Cassie carefully wiped her mouth, though Natalie hadn't seen her take a bite. "Actually, I've been thinking about enrolling Anjali in day care. If there's a trial, Jay might need to testify."

"Someone needs to be arrested before there can be a trial," their father said, just as Rosemary piped up, "But I could watch her!"

Cassie shook her head firmly as she reached for the steamed broccolini. "It's too much. Anyway, kids this age are better off with other kids, where they can be socialized. I talked to your mom," she said to Luke. "She thinks she has a place for Anj at You Are My Sunshine starting next week."

Luke nodded, but in a way that made Natalie wonder if he'd been paying attention. He tended to tune out when the women in the family were talking. "When's the funeral for Ben?" he asked her mother.

She filled her wineglass again before she answered. "We're having a memorial service," she said. "He wanted to be cremated. Since his family is gone, I suppose we're the ones who need to plan something, but I haven't given it much thought yet." She had an air of being put upon, as if they'd demanded that she decide on a venue and choose the hymns right that minute, and Natalie wondered if she was annoyed with Cassie for taking the socialization of her only grandchild out of her hands.

"Would it be okay if I said a few words?" Jay asked. "Not at the service—I was thinking after dinner tonight. I thought it might be helpful to see what another tradition would have to offer in a moment like this. But only if you're comfortable with it."

He was looking at Natalie's parents, and after a fraction of a pause, her mother said, "Thank you, Jay. That would be lovely." Trey said nothing. He had made his face entirely blank, as if he'd decided to pretend he was somewhere else.

Natalie was surprised that her mother had agreed to Jay's offer. She didn't want to think of her parents as the kind of people who were uncomfortable with different belief systems, but the more she thought about what Cassie had told her on the way to the sheriff's department that morning, the more she had to admit that their mother had been pushy about the baptism. Did she really think that the fate of Anjali's eternal soul depended on whether or not she was raised in the faith of her Macready forebears? Natalie had never heard her say anything negative about Jay or his family, but then again, they'd never met the Desais, who had moved back to India after Jay's father retired. Her mother had said once that all those spices in the food must give people indigestion, and another time that she didn't know how Indian women could walk in those bulky wrap dresses, and while both comments had made Natalie cringe for her, she'd never called her mother out on it. She had never challenged her parents about anything meaning-ful. She'd disobeyed them and sneaked around behind their backs, but she'd never confronted them when she thought they were wrong, not once in her whole life. Even the thought of it made her palms sweat.

No one objected when Luke and Trey disappeared after dinner, presumably to smoke cigars at the boathouse. Jay helped the women clear the table and put away the leftovers, and then the five of them sat down on the Persian rug, Cassie at the edge of the circle with An-jali on her lap. The sisters were comfortable sitting cross-legged, but Kaitlyn fetched a throw pillow for their mother, who winced a little as she lowered herself onto the soft cushion.

"I'd like to lead you in a chant," Jay said when they were all seated, pressing his hands to his heart. "Please repeat after me: 'Om namo Narayanaya.' "

"Om namo Narayanaya," they said obediently, though Natalie saw Rosemary raise her eyebrows. No one had told her there would be chanting.

After they'd repeated the chant three times, Jay touched his fin-gertips to his forehead. "Look," he said, spreading his hands with a deprecating half smile, "I'm not a particularly deep guy. From ages fourteen to twenty-one, I spent most of my waking hours on a surf-board, and if there's one thing that people know about surfers, it's that we're not too bright." Natalie and Kaitlyn giggled obligingly, and even their mother smiled.

"I don't want to sit here and tell you I've got it all figured out," Jay continued. "I didn't know Ben Marsh very well, but he was close to some of you, and that means he's important to me too. In a situation like this, it's tempting to sit here and pontificate about life and death and what it all means, but I'm no guru, that's for sure. Honestly, all I know is that a tragedy like this prompts me to return to the present moment. It reminds me that that moment is all I have, whether I'm a newborn baby"—he smiled at his wife with Anjali on her lap—"or an old dude tottering around on my last legs." He made his voice wobbly, leaning forward as if supporting himself on a cane.

Jay put his hand flat on his heart, and after he glanced around the circle with an encouraging smile, the others did the same. He closed his eyes, and they did too. "I'd like to invite you to observe the sensation of your heartbeat," he said. "It's an autonomic function, so it's not something we think about a lot. If you take the time to sit with it, though, you'll realize that it's a little metronome reminding you to be here now. Be here now," he said again, and after a moment of hesitation, the women said it with him, their palms pressing into their sternums. "Be here now. Be here now."

It was perfect, Natalie thought. She had no idea if this was Jay's take on a verse from the Yoga Sutras, or if he'd cribbed it from a self-help book, or if he'd made it all up on the spot, and it didn't matter. The important part was that he spoke with total conviction and sincerity, as if, despite his denials, he really did have some uncommon access to spiritual wisdom. This was why *Hashtag Yoga* had cracked ten thousand listeners per episode, and why Jay and Cassie had half a million followers when other yoga influencers had trouble breaking a hundred thousand. Her arms felt tingly, and she realized she'd broken out in goose bumps. Cradling Anjali with the other arm, Cassie had discreetly raised her phone to chest level while her husband was talking, and Natalie realized that she'd filmed the whole thing.

15.

Kaitlyn and Luke were staying over. After they cleaned up, Luke put on a movie, but Natalie didn't bother following the plot, which had something to do with four college buddies taking a road trip to Vegas with a pet monkey. She picked at her cuticles and thought about Ben being cremated, his poor torn body fed into the yawning flames. No one would ever acknowledge that she had a right to be there. She was the closest thing he'd had to a girlfriend at the time he died, but no one would ever know it, and it was her own damn fault for insisting they keep the relationship a secret. If she'd put everything out in the open, maybe Ben would have trusted her with his own secrets. Maybe, she thought, he might even still be alive.

She didn't realize she'd fallen asleep until she felt her mother standing over her. "Jay left his wallet," her mother said, waving it in her hand. "I was going to ask Luke to take it over to the guest house, but I don't want to wake him. Your father's already in bed. Do you think I should call Jay to come get it, or just wait for the morning?"

Natalie looked at Luke stretched out on the other side of the sectional, mouth open, snoring lightly. "I'll do it," she said.

Her mother shook her head. "Absolutely not. You're not going out in the dark alone."

Natalie sighed. "Mom, why did you wake me up if you didn't want me to take it to him? You can watch me from the kitchen window."

Her mother glanced at Luke and Kaitlyn's sleeping forms, and Natalie was surprised when she said, "All right." Perhaps she'd weighed the unpleasantness of an argument with her youngest daughter against the negligible risk of Natalie being attacked by a kitchen-knife-wielding madman and concluded that it was better to let her have her way. "Flick the porch lights on and off so I'll know you've made it."

Natalie expected the outside light to come on when she stepped off the porch, but nothing happened. She stood there for a moment in the dark, scuffling the dead leaves at her feet. It wasn't like she really needed the light, she told herself; she'd walked this path a thousand times, maybe more. The guest cabin had started its life as a playhouse for her and her sisters, which Trey Macready had added on to over the years until he'd concluded that he might as well make it a permanent structure. The walk was less than a quarter mile across the backyard and through a short stretch of woods, and Natalie could see the cabin's porch light through the waving limbs of the bare oaks.

She shivered and zipped her coat up to her chin. *Be here now*, she told herself and took off across the yard at a fast clip, wanting to break into a run but fearing the branches that could have blown down in yesterday's winds. The air smelled of dead leaves and woodsmoke, and through her fear, she felt a rush of adrenaline that was almost a kind of pleasure.

Cassie answered the door and put a finger to her lips. "We just put the baby down," she said, taking the wallet from her hand. "Are you coming in?"

"For a minute," Natalie said, looking past her to Jay, who was on his mat in the middle of the living room, stretching into a downward dog. The soft burr of a white noise machine came from the loft, where Anjali slept in the five-hundred-dollar Scandinavian crib their mother had ordered for Cassie's infrequent visits. Natalie flicked the lights by the front door and turned back to wave at Rosemary, watching from the kitchen window.

"Sorry," Jay said, smiling at her between his arms. "I haven't been able to do my usual practice for the past couple of days. I can't do anything in here without bumping into a wall."

Natalie watched as he kicked up into a forearm stand, his body straight and strong as the trunk of a tree. If she thought about it too hard, she began to wonder if there was something wrong with admiring her brother-in-law's alignment when he was wearing those Manduka shorts, which were basically a Speedo with a couple inches of thigh coverage, but how could she help it? "You know, I go into the studio before class," she said as he flipped his arm position to turn the forearm stand into a tripod headstand. "I usually leave around five thirty, and no one else comes in until after seven. You could come with me if you want."

Jay thumped down to sit on his heels. "Really?" he said, looking at his wife. "Cassie will be your biggest fan. I know I'm driving her crazy falling out of scorpion pose ten times when Anjali is trying to sleep."

"Oh my God, yes," Cassie said, rolling her eyes. "Please, get him out of here."

Her tone was light, but Natalie couldn't help doing a double take. The response had been too quick, and something about Cassie's tone made it sound as if she really meant it. But as far as Natalie had been able to tell from social media, Cassie and Jay were happy together—certainly happier than Kaitlyn and Luke, who sometimes argued about money and Kaitlyn spending time at the studio when Luke thought she should be at home. Natalie wished she and Cassie were close enough for her to ask her sister what was going on, but she knew that Cassie wouldn't have welcomed that conversation. She'd made it clear by now that she didn't want to open up to Natalie or vice versa. "Happy to help," Natalie said.

The studio was her favorite place in the world. She loved the feeling of the bamboo floor against her feet and the slight smell of sweat that never quite went away, even after they'd burned about a hundred candles. She loved the arty black-and-white photos of her and her sisters lining the wall behind the desk: Kaitlyn in a simple balance pose with the sole of one foot pressed against the opposite leg, Natalie in an extended side plank, and Cassie in a backbend that made her look like a contortionist. Even on the worst of days, Natalie felt her pulse rate lower the second she walked through the door.

Some mornings, when it was still dark when they arrived, she forgot about Jay altogether. Sometimes, after she'd started her practice, she disappeared into the routine, the way she would have in an empty room: the slow joy of her body opening up, her muscles loosening. She lost track of time and thought of nothing but the sound of her own breath, her heartbeat like the roar inside a seashell.

But as soon as the sun came up, angling straight in the eastern-facing windows, everything changed. Now she could see him, and he was doing poses she'd never even attempted, the kinds of poses that people were thinking of when they said that yoga meant tying your body into a pretzel. Jay could flip from a handstand into a backbend and back again. He could put one foot behind his neck and rise to a standing position, hands at his heart. Sometimes Natalie sat back on her heels and simply watched, the way she might at Cirque de Soleil.

"Could you give me a hand with dropbacks?" he asked one morning, catching his breath after a series of arm balances she'd never even seen on the internet. "I don't need you to help me up, but if you could just stand there, it would be a big help. I'm feeling a little creaky in my lower back today."

She was pretty sure she knew what to do. Though she'd never attempted one, she knew that a dropback is when you stand at the front of your mat and bend back, bringing your hands down to the mat before standing up again. The teacher was always stationed in front of the student, sometimes holding their waist, but often simply standing there for moral support. Natalie readied herself, lunging forward on her right leg and tensing her arms, just in case Jay had overestimated himself and needed her help after all.

Since they'd begun practicing together, she'd been careful not to look at Jay in a way that might denote sexual interest, but now she had no choice. He dropped easily back to the mat and popped up again, as if a coiled spring in his spine had tensed and released. Her eyes fell to his bare chest, the sweat shining on his collarbone, his pecs and abdomen, and then to his crotch. It wasn't her fault, she told herself. What was she supposed to do, close her eyes?

"What is the sequence you're doing?" she asked when he finally stopped and lowered himself to a seated forward bend.

"I've been working on the third series of ashtanga," he said, his voice muffled as his face pressed into his shins. "It's taking me a while to get through it, and it only gets worse from here. Fourth series is super gnarly."

Gnarly, she repeated to herself. He had that California way of talking that she'd only heard on TV before they met. What, she wanted to ask, could be more gnarly than standing up with your foot behind your head? What was next, levitation? "You know, you could add in some advanced poses too," he said, making a gesture that took in her whole body. "You have the strength and flexibility. You could do more, go deeper. I could teach you."

"Oh." She dabbed at her face with a towel, hoping she could blame it on the heat. "I don't know if I can drop back and grab my ankles today. Maybe we can work up to it."

He smiled in a way that made her breath catch in her throat. "We can go as slow as you want," he said.

16.

She thought maybe she should feel guilty, but it wasn't like they were doing anything wrong. Like everyone else, she'd heard the stories about the yoga gurus who harassed or even assaulted their students, and she'd listened to the episodes of the podcast where Jay and Cassie discussed how teachers could respect students' personal boundaries by creating a safe space and always asking before making a hands-on adjustment, but to Natalie, these so-called ethical guidelines had always sounded like bullshit, rules made for a theoretical world rather than this real one. Jay never touched what her mother used to call her "bathing suit area," but often she could feel his hand moving just outside or above, the sweep of it sparking a slow electricity beneath her skin.

She found him attractive, that was undeniable, but she wasn't sure she really liked him all that much. Jay usually had a private online class right after their joint practice, and after the fourth or fifth time Natalie heard him start asking the student to ground herself in the breath and repeat "Be here now," she started closing the office door as soon as she heard the ping of the Zoom notification. He always sounded sincere, but maybe, she thought now, that wasn't the same as actually *being* sincere. Maybe, as her father had once told her, the greatest con men were the ones who didn't even know they were running a con.

Still, she didn't really consider quitting until they got to deep backbends. In the studio lit only by the flicker of the electric candles,

Jay directed her through a sequence: this many sun salutations, then poses to elongate and strengthen. He stood over her, one foot braced on either side of her body, and used his hands to encourage her rib cage to spread and open as she lowered her head to the floor and reached for her feet. She felt as if something was cracking in her chest. She was slick all over, every inch of her, and then she was suddenly lightheaded, weak as water. She turned on her side and she was crying, racking sobs that poured out of her as she listened in a kind of horror. She wondered if this was how Amanda had felt spewing blood over the laminate, amazed by all the ugliness that turned out to be inside her.

"Hey," Jay said. "This is totally normal." He sat cross-legged beside her and handed her a towel that she used to dab at her eyes, thanking him in a whisper. "Believe it or not, I see this a lot. There's emotional stuff in there that you're stirring up."

The tears continued, even when she told herself sternly to stop crying. "I thought I was just being a baby about it," she said. "That's what Cassie said, when I told her how much I hated backbends."

Jay put a hand on her knee. "You don't have to be a psychiatrist to know that there's a connection between physical and emotional trauma. Everybody has it, but as a yogi, you're actually working your way through it, which means that you're miles ahead of most people."

Natalie nodded, tossing the towel toward the laundry basket in the corner. She had no idea what Cassie had told Jay about the boat crash, but surely he knew that Natalie had been injured and spent time in the hospital. She wondered if he would ask her about it, and if he did, how much she wanted to tell him.

"Take me, for example," he said before she could speak, drawing his knees to his chest and lacing his arms loosely around them. "I don't know if Cassie's told you, but I was into some bad stuff when I was a teenager. My dad was really strict, and I wanted to be as unlike him as possible. I would try anything once, but then somebody took me surfing, and it changed my whole life. Suddenly I was on my board just about every minute that I wasn't eating or sleeping. I was never going to be the best, but I had some sponsorships, and I got invited to some of the big tournaments. Then one weekend I went up to northern California with some buddies and I wiped out. The board broke, and my leash got tangled in the rocks. Finally I got my ankle strap off and came up, but that was the longest ten seconds of my life."

When he paused, Natalie recognized the look on his face. It was what she'd felt when he'd put her in that backbend—something resurfacing in the body that you never even knew was there. "Anyway," he said, rubbing a hand across his face, "I came out of it with a broken arm and a broken ankle, but it could have been much worse. I probably could have gone back to surfing after six months or so, but I just couldn't bring myself to get back on the board. Instead I just sat in my apartment, and for a while my insomnia got so bad I was actually hallucinating. Then a friend suggested I try a yoga class."

Natalie waited, but he was smiling now, as if the message of the story was self-evident. She felt a vague sense of disappointment. "And that's it?" she said, more sharply than she'd intended. "You went to a yoga class and you were cured?"

"It wasn't that easy," he said. "But things got better. Trust me, it'll be the same for you."

But that was the problem: she didn't trust him, and she couldn't shake a feeling of dissatisfaction. If Jay really understood her—had seen into her, as he sometimes seemed to—he would be able to admit that yoga wasn't going to magically solve all her problems. It wasn't going to change the fact that she'd found Ben Marsh's body, or that she'd no idea what she was doing with her life. *Being here now* wasn't going to help with any of that.

"I'm not a guru," Jay said from time to time, but in that self-deprecating way that seemed to imply that he really was a guru, simply a modest one. A man like that could be all things to all people, she thought, and maybe never even realize that he was lying the whole time.

17.

By the time Luke came by, Jay was in the shower and Natalie was dust-mopping the studio. "Easy," Luke said from the doorway. "What did that floor ever do to you?"

Natalie flushed and dropped the mop, which clattered to the floor. "Sorry," Luke said, holding up a paper bag marked with the logo of Ewald Coffee. "I just got off the overnight shift, and I stopped by to bring y'all breakfast."

"Kaitlyn hasn't come in yet," Natalie said as she peeked into the bag, which held two scones, one blueberry and the other cranberry-orange. "But as long as you're here, could you take a look at the sink in the women's locker room? It's been leaking for weeks."

Luke rolled his eyes but said he might as well. "You want to show me which one?"

She led him through the door and pointed to the folded towel under the U-bend. Luke got on his knees and peered at the pipe. "This is probably loose," he said, shaking it a little. "Y'all still got that toolbox in the office?"

Natalie went to get it. Kaitlyn was always teasing her about calling Luke or their father to take care of jobs that she could have handled perfectly well on her own, but fixing the sink seemed like the least Luke could do after he'd given Kaitlyn such a hard time about taking the job as studio manager. Though they never seemed to have enough money, Luke disliked the idea of Kaitlyn working outside the home, and had made her promise to give up teaching yoga after the baby was born.

The problem with Luke, she thought, was that he had her father's overbearing personality without her father's sense of humor. Instead of looking at life as a comedy, he thought of it as an action movie where he would at some point be required to prove his toughness on a grand scale. In restaurants he sat with his back to the wall so no one could sneak up on him. In crowds, he found the nearest exit and sized up the people who stood between him and the door. It had always seemed a little over-the-top to her, but it was probably one of the qualities that made him a good investigator. "Hey, did you ever figure out anything about that knife?" Natalie asked as she slid the toolbox across the floor.

"Nothing to figure out," Luke said. "It's just a regular old kitchen knife, no blood, no fingerprints. Hardy's thinking about calling in the state police so we can get some kind of expert testing, but with the capabilities we have, there's no way to know if it's even the knife that killed Ben. Can you hand me that clamp?"

Natalie held it out on her open hand. This was a possibility she hadn't considered. What if the stain on the knife wasn't blood after all? Then the damning proximity to her family became nothing more than an unlucky coincidence.

"How is Kaitlyn feeling this week?" he asked as he slid under the sink.

Natalie grabbed the laundry basket of fresh towels and began folding. "What do you mean, how is she?" she said. "You live with her."

"I wanted a second opinion. I feel like she's been having a hard time—with the pregnancy, and what happened to Ben on top of it."

Natalie draped a towel over her arm. "Like she's depressed or something?"

"Didn't say that, but I'm not sure I like her spending so much time with Amanda Vergotti. She's been over there three times this week. I guess they're playing tennis again."

This was news to Natalie. "She's probably feeling bad about what happened in my class," she said. "She's just checking on Amanda to make sure she's okay."

Luke wiggled his boots in a way that seemed to indicate doubt. "You might not remember, but Amanda was *wiiiild* back in high school." He drew out the word, his tone savoring and contemptuous at the same time. "I always wondered if there might have been something going on between her and Kaitlyn. They were too close, if you know what I mean."

"You mean 'going on,' like in a sexual way?" Natalie scoffed, but then she thought of the night of the boat crash, Kaitlyn and Amanda rolling over and over in the sand at the bonfire.

"I'm not judging her or anything," Luke said. "What Amanda does is her business. I'm just not sure I want her spending time with my wife."

"You're out of your damn mind," she said, holding a stack of towels against her chest and kicking the sole of his boot lightly. "Why don't you just ask Kaitlyn about it?"

"I was thinking maybe we should see a counselor," he said. "Cassie and Jay did, back in LA. He was telling me about it the other night after dinner. He wants more kids, but Cassie's not sure."

"Really? Did he say why?"

"Nope." Luke rattled the U-bend. "He said she just wasn't sure she wanted them."

Natalie picked up another towel. Cassie would not want to slow down, she thought. She would not want to risk her figure. No one wanted to say out loud that you had to be pretty and thin to succeed as a yoga teacher—the talk was always about health and self-care—but that didn't change the fact that the most famous teachers were all supple, gorgeous supermodel types. If you were pregnant, people would say you couldn't do this pose or that pose, and then after you had the baby, you'd have to worry about getting your body back. Cassie had already done it once; having another child would set her back at least a year.

On the other hand, a pregnancy would be great social media content, and Natalie felt a surge of complicated jealousy when she thought of it. Of course she'd be happy if her sister had another baby, but the thought of Cassie and Jay popping up in her Instagram stories, glowing parents of another adorable newborn, made her hate her life a little bit. Maybe that was one of the reasons she'd gotten so much gratification out of Kaitlyn taking the job as the studio manager: for once, one of her sisters was following her instead of the other way around.

"Maybe the whole family needs to see a counselor," Natalie suggested. "Maybe we can get a group rate."

Luke smiled sardonically as he lifted the lid of the toolbox and fit the wrench into its slot. "Not a bad idea," he said.

If it hadn't been for that conversation with Luke, Natalie wouldn't have offered to teach Kaitlyn's beginner class that morning, and she wouldn't have been at the front of the room when Hardy Underwood tiptoed in, five minutes late, and laid down a loaner mat with exaggerated courtesy. Natalie missed the next cue, and one of the regular students had to remind her, in an exasperated voice, that they hadn't done the left side in crescent twist.

Natalie expected him to be terrible. Large men were usually lacking in flexibility, and he'd told her he didn't know anything about yoga. He should have been stumbling and falling out of poses, beet-red and frustrated, but instead he followed along just fine, responding to her cues and sometimes even anticipating them. He'd taken his shirt off, and though he didn't have Jay's twelve-pack abs, he was more the kind of guy she usually went for, the kind with hands that could lap themselves around her wrists. She kept glancing over even when she didn't mean to. "Spread your legs," she said as the students lay back into savasana, and then quickly corrected herself: she'd meant *relax* your legs, not *spread* them. She could see Hardy's shoulders shaking quietly, a grin spreading over his face.

In the hallway after class, she confronted him. "You're not a beginner."

"I am, but thank you for the compliment," he said as he toweled off the back of his neck. "I've done a few YouTube videos. An old girl-friend told me it was good for cross-training."

"Do you want to sign up for a pass?" If he was going to hang around anyway, she might as well make some money off him.

Hardy made a noncommittal noise, pulling a blue T-shirt over his head and tossing his towel into the hamper in the corner. "Is there somewhere we can talk?" he asked. "I won't take up too much of your time."

She felt a prickle on the back of her neck. This must be related to the investigation, if he'd bothered to seek her out at work. "Come with me," she said, and grabbed her jacket from the hook before leading him out to the picnic table.

It was cold out, but not the usual dingy gray cold that you ex-pected in early December. This was a bright, clean cold, the dew on the grass sparkling like tinsel. Only one car was parked in the lot, a tiny red boxy thing with Georgia plates. To her surprise, Hardy pulled a key fob from his pocket and pushed it twice, the car beeping agreeably.

"Is that yours?" Natalie could hardly believe it. The last thing she would have expected him to drive was a Mini Cooper.

Underwood shrugged. "It was my ex-wife's," he said. "When we divided up our assets, it made sense for me to take the car, and since I drive my sheriff's vehicle most of the time, I haven't gotten around to selling it yet."

"You were *married*?" she asked, unable to keep the note of accusa-tion out of her voice.

"For seventeen years."

"Jesus Christ," she snapped. "How old are you?"

He smiled, but the pause before he spoke told her that he'd noted her response. "I'm thirty-nine. Is that a problem?"

She thought of the two girls she'd seen in the pictures in his office. Seeing that he wasn't wearing a ring, she'd assumed they were nieces, but maybe not. "Do you have kids?"

He leaned back, resting his elbows on the table as if he planned to stay a while. "Twin girls. They're teenagers now. I don't really mind the car, though it's not a Chevette, that's for sure. I guess you know how to drive a manual?"

Natalie pulled her cigarettes from her pocket. "Daddy always used to say that everybody around here, boy or girl, should know how to drive stick, shoot whiskey, and gut a deer."

The sheriff watched her with a faint smile. "And you smoke too?"

"Yeah, so?"

He shook his head. "You're just full of contradictions, that's all."

The flirtatious tone had crept back into his voice, unsettling her. Her mother would be so happy to see her with a man like Sheriff Hardy Underwood—a man who could be depended on, a man who would keep her safe. Luke, the cop, had always been her favorite of her sons-in-law.

Hardy made a motion to the table as if inviting her to sit, but instead she leaned against the wall and crossed her arms over her chest. "Did I say something wrong?" he asked, still with a trace of a smile on his face.

The words might have mollified her, but she didn't like that he sounded amused, as if they'd both agreed that she was being unreasonable. "Why would you get divorced after seventeen years?" she said. "I'm really asking. After you've been together that long, what could you find out about each other that you didn't already know?"

Again he made her wait, and she remembered that he'd said that he wanted to ask her some questions, not the other way around. At any moment, he might tell her that she'd gone too far, crossed some line that she damn sure should have seen coming. Every time he answered, and chose to show her more of himself, they were taking their interaction further from the professional into the realm of the personal, and he wanted her to know that he was letting it happen.

"There was some trouble in my department," he said. "There was an officer-involved shooting that got a lot of attention, and then an investigation by internal affairs that dragged on for months. I wasn't implicated, but friends of mine were, and when I tried to defend them,

I got suspended too. After that I was drinking too much for a while, and my wife got sick of it. I guess she was sick of me in general." He pointed at the pack in her hand. "Can I bum one of those?"

Natalie tossed it on the table, and he nodded thanks. She took the lighter from her jacket pocket and placed it beside the cigarettes. "I'm sorry that happened," she said. "The job, and your wife. Everything."

"I'm not," Hardy said around the filter. "I don't like being away from the girls, but they're going away to college in a year anyway, and I never liked Atlanta. Spent more time sitting in traffic than I did with my own family." He stretched his arms above his head and gave a big, exaggerated yawn. "You know, I think I will sign up for one of those passes you told me about. I sure could use some time to lie on the floor in the dark."

He wanted to make her laugh, Natalie realized. He wanted her to play along—to chide him for pretending not to understand what yoga was—but she had spent her whole life hitting her mark, and she was tired of it. "You should buy a mat too," she said, stubbing her own cigarette into the mortar between the bricks. "I wouldn't rely on the loaners. We clean them, but just imagine how many strangers' feet have been on those things. You can pick up a mat for twenty bucks at Walmart, or I can order you a good one with my discount. Which is the way to go, if you're really ready to commit to something new."

"Oh, I'm not one of those guys that has trouble with commitment," he said with an easy smile. "I'll see you soon, Natalie." When he turned to wave from halfway across the lot, she realized that she still had no idea why he had come.

18.

If Underwood's goal was to unsettle her, he'd succeeded. It was still entirely unclear whether he was flirting or investigating, or somehow trying to do both at the same time, and that uncertainty made it impossible for her to know how to act. There were a hundred different reasons why she shouldn't even consider getting involved with Hardy Underwood, but she couldn't deny that he was on her mind. That was probably the intention, she decided—not to attract her but to unnerve her, in the hope that her vulnerability would work to his advantage.

When she got home, she found her mother down at the boathouse, packing plates and glassware into a cardboard box. She smiled at Natalie without pausing what she was doing. "So many things migrate down here over the summer," she said. "And then I can never find anything I want."

"Can I help?" Natalie asked. It was after five; at this time of day, her mother and father should have been in the living room in front of the fire, observing their ritualistic cocktail hour—a glass of wine for her, a tumbler of scotch for him—but since Ben's death, all their routines had gone awry.

"You could put the casserole in the oven," she said. "That would be wonderful. I put it on preheat, but then I got distracted down here."

Natalie nodded, but then she lingered, running her hand along the edge of the white dining table that was only marginally less expensive than the one in the house. "I drove by the bank on the way home," she said, "and I saw something kind of weird. Luke's truck was parked under one of the parking lot lights, and Cassie was in the passenger seat."

Her mother placed another wineglass in the box. "Are you sure it wasn't Kaitlyn?"

Natalie gave her a look that her mother chose to ignore. It was true that the sisters looked alike—all brown-haired and pretty, with the same hazel eyes and the same thin build—but they didn't look *that* much alike. "Even if it was Cassie, I'm not sure why that's worth mentioning," her mother went on. "They were probably talking about Kaitlyn. I know Luke is worried about whether she's losing too much weight. I wish she'd go back to the doctor."

That was plausible, Natalie conceded. They could have been talking about Kaitlyn's health, or even Luke's bizarre theory about Kaitlyn and Amanda. Maybe it was only Natalie's own not entirely sublimated desire to cross a line with Jay that had made the scene in the parking lot look suspicious. She picked up a coffee cup with a cartoon of Snoopy typing on top of his doghouse. "Does this stay or go?"

Her mother made a face. "I don't want that in my house," she said. "Before you go, we set a date for Ben's memorial service. It'll be the Wednesday before Christmas. It's the one day that week when the church doesn't have any services or pageant rehearsals."

Natalie passed the mug back and forth between her hands. She'd come to terms with the fact that no one was going to acknowledge her closeness to Ben or her right to grieve him—how could they, when so few people knew they had been together?—but it still made her sad to think of his service at First Presbyterian, the pews that were usually reserved for family empty as Jesus's tomb. "I've been thinking about Lanny," she said.

"What about him?" her mother asked, with the steeliness in her voice that always made Natalie brace herself.

"Shouldn't we try to find him?"

"I don't know what you mean. He's dead, Natalie."

The words weren't entirely a surprise. Of course she'd wondered before if Lanny might be dead. Guilt for the theft and for letting

Croaker take the fall might have kept him away for a while, but not forever. "But how do you know for sure?"

"Because we've looked. Five years ago, Daddy hired a private detective. He went everywhere that we thought Lanny had a reason to be, and he couldn't find hide nor hair of him. The detective told us that he'd probably died without identification, and no one ever claimed his body." Her mother spoke the words matter-of-factly, but with a brittle edge to her voice that suggested that she'd prefer to avoid the whole subject.

Natalie sat heavily in one of the wicker chairs. "Did the shipping companies have any record of him?"

"The detective couldn't find one." Her mother lifted a plate from the cabinet and reached for the newspaper. "Though it's possible that he changed his name and got new identification. The detective says that happens sometimes."

Natalie could tell from her mother's tone that she was supposed to leave it alone, but she couldn't help herself. "Don't you even care?" she said, her voice coming out shriller than she'd expected.

Her mother turned to look at her, setting her hands on top of the box as if this conversation required great patience. "You're not the only one who has feelings, Natalie."

For a moment, Natalie felt ashamed. She did know that her mother had cared for Lanny. After the death of his own mother, he'd been in and out of the house nearly every day, playing checkers with their dad or making himself a peanut butter sandwich in the kitchen. As the girls had gotten older, he hadn't been around as much, but that didn't mean her mother had lost her affection for him. "I don't know what you want me to do," Rosemary said. "Of course we feel terrible that Ben won't have any family at the service, but we can't just conjure Lanny out of thin air."

"I'm sorry," Natalie said. She wanted to ask if maybe they should try again, maybe hire another detective, but she knew that even the suggestion would set her mother off. She never wanted to talk about anything she believed to be in bad taste, which included anything having to do with sex, death, or scandal. From the evidence of the old photo album, Natalie was pretty sure that Rosemary Macready had once been looser, more easygoing, but she had no memories of that woman. If Natalie was going to get more information about Lanny Marsh, there was no point in trying to get it here. She'd have to go talk to her dad.

19.

In Natalie's opinion, the best thing about Macready Contracting and Excavation was that it couldn't be seen from the studio. Natalie knew why her father and uncle had insisted that Ewald Yoga had to be located on this particular corner; they already owned the land, and it would have been ridiculous to buy new property when they had plenty of space right here. Still, she was grateful that they'd at least kept in place the line of trees that screened the chain-link fence at the back of the equipment lot. Even in winter, when the leaves were down, you had to squint to make out the shapes of bulldozers and concrete mixers clanking along the gravel.

She'd tried to convince Kaitlyn to go with her to see their father. When Natalie let herself into the office that morning, she'd found her sister curled on the corduroy couch in the corner under a layer of the woven blankets they used as props in the restorative class. "Holy shit," Natalie said. "What happened? Did you and Luke have a fight?"

"What are you talking about?" Kaitlyn yawned. "I came in early to meditate, and I couldn't keep my eyes open, so I curled up in here."

Natalie sat on the other end of the couch, fiddling with the zipper on her sweatshirt. At first she'd wondered if it was simply the fluorescent light that hollowed her sister's cheeks and painted shadows under her eyes, but now she knew better. Without the long shapeless sweaters she wore over her yoga clothes, Kaitlyn looked painfully thin, her wrists like sticks. "How much weight have you lost?"

"I'm *fine*," Kaitlyn repeated with an edge to her voice. "I just haven't been sleeping."

She leaned back, the blankets slipping to show her belly. Natalie hadn't still fully gotten used to the idea that Kaitlyn was pregnant, but it seemed even stranger when she compared the firm roundness of her middle with the rest of her sister's body. "When is your next doctor's appointment?" she asked. "Because I want to go with you."

Kaitlyn shook her head, still yawning. "This is the first appointment Luke could get off work for. I think he wants it to be just the two of us."

That was good news, Natalie thought. She'd worried that Luke might be the problem, but if he was taking off work to escort his wife to the obstetrician, things couldn't be that bad between the two of them. She drummed her fingers on the arm of the couch as she studied the side of her sister's face. "Have you been hanging out with Amanda lately?"

"What?" Kaitlyn yawned again, but Natalie had seen the look of fear that flashed over her face before she replaced it with fatigue and confusion. "Sometimes. There's a tennis court in her subdivision, and we've been playing a couple of times a week. Why do you ask?"

"Does your doctor know you're getting that much exercise? Are you sure that's safe?"

"What the hell, Natalie?" Kaitlyn made a face, looking genuinely annoyed now. "Are you asking if it's going to make me bleed from my vagina?"

"If there's something going on, you can tell me," Natalie said. "I understand if you need time away."

"For God's sake, this has nothing to do with Luke," Kaitlyn snapped. "I'm still taking the medication. I'll gain it all back and then some once I stop throwing up."

"Okay, don't have a hissy fit about it." Natalie glanced at her watch. She was late, and it was clear that Kaitlyn wasn't interested in a heart-to-heart right now. "Will you walk over to Macready's with me?" she asked. "The insurance company is on my ass to send them the deed to the convertible. I was supposed to do it two weeks ago. If you're there, maybe Daddy won't lecture me about how irresponsible I am."

Kaitlyn shook her head. "I need coffee," she said, patting Natalie's shoulder, and Natalie knew she couldn't push any harder without causing a fight. Strangers always thought that Kaitlyn was the sweetest of the sisters, but you couldn't make her do anything she didn't want to. As their father always said, she was contrary as a two-headed goat.

Behind the studio, she took the path that kids and dogs had made through a gully choked with trash and empty bottles, the corrugated roof of Macready's just visible now, like an airplane hangar with faded white vinyl siding. A wind had kicked up, skittering dead leaves against the curb. Two expensive-looking dump trucks were parked next to a small hill of gravel in the corner of the lot, with a brand-new earthmover beside them. The sign over the door was freshly painted, even down to the two little pine trees on either side of MACREADY CONTRACTING. On her way up the metal steps to the front office, Natalie stopped to knock the dirt off her tennis shoes.

"Honey, you come right over here and hug my neck," Renée Howard said as soon as Natalie walked through the door. Renée had been secretary to her father and Uncle Leo since they'd first started the company in 1998. *Secretary* was the term she used; it was even printed on her business cards, and once, when Natalie had brought her a card that read "Happy Administrative Professionals' Day," Renée had rolled her eyes and said she didn't know why they were always inventing new words for things.

Today her gray pantsuit looked businesslike from the waist up, but when she moved out from behind the desk, Natalie could see that she'd kicked her shoes off and left them under the desk, revealing a pair of pink polka-dot socks. "I tell you, I just can't believe it about Ben," she continued in a whisper, keeping her arm looped around Natalie's shoulder. "Of all the people for something like this to happen to. I told your daddy, I think it must have been somebody on drugs. Nobody in their right mind would ever hurt that man."

It wasn't far from her father's theory that a drifter had somehow drifted all the way out to Ben's houseboat. Natalie hoped she was right, but she wasn't sure she could make it through yet another conversation about Ben's murder. "Is my dad here?" she asked, and Renée nodded.

"He's in his office. Did he tell you that we got those new maps with your ad on them?" She handed Natalie a small stack of maps showing a hand-drawn outline of Lake Monroe. "Take as many as you want."

Natalie flipped the map over and inspected the ad for Ewald Yoga, right under the giant logo for Macready Contracting and Excavation. "Thanks," she said as she slipped the stack into her purse.

"You know what I heard the other day?" Renée whispered. "You know that old abandoned boat out by Ben's place? Apparently somebody reported seeing a light on in there on the night of the Felons' Ball."

Natalie knew the boat she meant. The old party boat she'd always avoided on the way to Ben's. "What do you mean, there was a light on?" she said. "That place hasn't had electricity for years."

"Well, sweetheart, they could have had flashlights," Renee said. "It gives me the chills just thinking of it. That's probably where the killer was hiding while the party was going on, and then when he knew Ben was back home, he snuck over there and stabbed him to death. It's enough to make your blood run cold."

Natalie was surprised and annoyed to find her eyes filling with tears. She'd been the same way in the weeks and months after the crash, breaking into sobs or trembling in panic at the oddest times, sometimes prompted by nothing more traumatic than the sound of a slamming door in the distance. For a moment Renée looked confused, but then she gasped and pulled Natalie into her arms again. "Oh Lord, I forgot that you're the one who found him. Will you ever forgive a stupid old woman for putting her foot in her mouth?"

Natalie wiped her eyes with the side of her hand. "It's fine," she said. "But I should go in and see my dad." She smiled at Renée and turned toward the door to her father's executive office suite, trying not to think of Ben lying on the deck, Ben's eyes blank as glass as she'd leaned over his body.

Her father was behind his big desk with his feet up on a chair, doing nothing in particular as far as Natalie could tell. He pulled out a folded piece of paper and slapped it into her palm. "Come out to the lot with me," he said. "I got to check a truck battery."

She followed him out of the office. As he pushed open the door to the back lot, he said over his shoulder, "I'm glad you stopped by. The sheriff was here this morning."

Natalie felt a flutter in her chest. "Did he say something about me?"

Her father lifted his eyebrows. "No, nothing about you. He wanted to know if I'd seen Ben drinking at the party. I told him not that I recalled, but I thought it was a strange question. What would that have to do with his murder?"

"He was definitely drinking." She recounted the moment when she'd seen Ben point at a bottle behind the bar, hoping her father wouldn't ask why she'd been so interested.

His father nodded as he walked around to the back end of a detached semi, dusting his hands on his legs. "Hardy was asking me what made him fall off the wagon. I told him I wished I knew."

Natalie wished she did too. "I was just talking to Mama about Lanny," she said. "She told me that you hired a private detective to look for him. Do you think I could talk to him?"

"Why would you want to do that?"

Natalie perched on the bumper of a dump truck parked a few feet away. "Maybe there's something else we could do to find him," she said. "Don't you think Ben would want that?"

"Baby girl, let's leave the investigation to the police," he said with a sigh as he bent over the battery, lifting off the plastic top. "Hardy Underwood knows about Lanny. If he thinks looking for a needle in a haystack is a productive use of his time, he can do that. Based on what that detective found, he's either living under a different name or he's deceased, and either way there's not much more we can do."

"What about the memorial service?" she asked. "Couldn't we post an announcement in a newspaper or something, in case Lanny is still alive?"

"Well, I'm sure the obituary will be in the *News-Gazette*," her father said. "But I'm leaving all the planning to your mother. I always do."

He smiled as if this were a charming eccentricity on his part. "Why?" Natalie asked. "Why does Mama have to do everything? Why does she have to plan the service, when Ben was your friend in the first place?"

He picked up something that looked like a giant cheese grater with a temperature gauge on it and used pliers to attach it to one of the truck wires. "You sound like Cassie," he said. "Your mother and I have our own way of doing things. She takes care of everything at home, and I take care of everything outside of the home. Maybe that seems old-fashioned to you girls, but it's worked for us for thirty years. As far as Lanny goes, Ben could have hired his own detective if he wanted to look for him. He never did, and it's probably because he knew there was nothing to find."

Natalie swallowed a lump in her throat. She'd always believed that Ben never talked to her about Lanny because he was ashamed of what his son had done on the night of the boat crash, but what if it was more than that? What if he hadn't mentioned his son because he would have had to tell her that Lanny was dead, and he didn't want to say the words out loud? "I guess he kept a lot of secrets," she said. "Maybe most people are like that."

She'd meant it as a general statement on human nature, but her father seemed to take it personally, and also to take offense. "Not me," he said brusquely. "I'm an open book. I'm like one of those water-logged Tom Clancys at a beach house, the ones you can't get to stay shut no matter how hard you try."

20.

But what her father said wasn't true. There were a thousand things his daughters didn't know about him—things they'd never cared enough to ask, like what he actually did all day when he wasn't checking truck batteries, and things they'd never been brave enough to ask, like whether he'd ever hurt anyone back in the day when moonshining was still a thriving business in Ewald County. Natalie might have been his favorite, but she was no more able than Cassie or Kaitlyn to face the freezing stare he would turn on her if she interrogated him about his past. He had transformed that past into the Disneyland spectacle of the Felons' Ball, and Natalie knew that was the only version he'd ever allow his daughters to see.

It wasn't enough. When Natalie got back to the studio, Kaitlyn was teaching her ten a.m. class, and Jay and Cassie were nowhere to be found. Natalie shut herself in the office and took out one of the maps of Lake Monroe that Renée had given her. Her father planned to leave them at businesses that tourists frequented—hotel lobbies, bait shops, convenience stores. It might convince a few of them to spend a rainy vacation day sweating through a yoga class, and a select few might want to give Macready Contracting a call about putting up a second home on one of the last lots for sale in Maplewood Estates. She put her finger on the spot in the blue water where Ben's boat would have been, and then moved it a little down and to the left to mark the location of the abandoned party boat. She grabbed a pen and made a tiny X on the expanse of blue water. That was where they'd been headed the night when everything had started to go wrong.

      Natalie couldn't remember much about the days after the boat crash, but she did remember the rain. It started the next day and kept on for nearly two weeks straight, through Thanksgiving and into the first week of December. She lay in her bed at the hospital eating the pumpkin pie that her mother had brought in a Tupperware container and watching rain pound the metal roof outside her window. She was upset that Lanny hadn't visited. Like Cassie and Kaitlyn, he'd been released from the hospital on the night of the accident, but unlike her sisters, he'd never stopped by to bring her flowers or a teddy bear or even a card. She kept asking, and finally her mother told her the truth. "He's gone," she said. "He can go wherever he wants, of course, but I wish he'd waited until his father was back from rehab and tried to have a conversation with him about this merchant marines business. Surely there must be a better solution than taking off in the middle of the night."

Over the weeks after she left the hospital, Natalie managed to piece together the full story. On Thanksgiving night her mother had woken around midnight because she'd thought she'd heard someone pulling down the driveway, but she'd been too tired to get up to look. The next morning Lanny's car was gone, along with the two die-casts—the Brooks & Dunn and the Curtis Turner—that Trey kept in glass cases on the mantel in the den. Cassie and Kaitlyn claimed that Lanny hadn't said a word to them about leaving town. He was simply gone, and when they finally called Ben in rehab to see what he wanted to do, he said not to worry about it, that Lanny would come home when he was ready.

But that had never happened—not when his father graduated from the six-week program and came back to Ewald; not when Lanny's class graduated from high school; not when his father was stabbed to death on the deck of his houseboat. Even through the years of his son's continued absence, Ben had stayed sober, but then, for some reason that she still didn't understand, he'd started drinking again in the weeks before the Felons' Ball.

Someone must have noticed. Even if Ben had managed to keep his fall from the wagon from Natalie and her parents, he must have let the secret slip somewhere. If she could find out where he'd been drinking, and with whom, maybe she could discover what had been bothering him. Maybe if she could answer just this one question about Ben's death, she wouldn't feel so bad about everything she'd failed to see.

You only had to spend an hour or two on Lake Monroe to realize that it wasn't round at all. They made it look round on the map, but that was only by cutting off the inlets, the byways and oxbows, that made up more than half of its two-hundred-and-forty-mile perimeter. If the mapmakers had drawn the lake accurately, it would have looked more like a spider, legs stretching out into remote hollows and mountain passes, taking over any space low enough to be filled.

That was because it wasn't a real lake. A hundred years ago the valley had been mostly wilderness, the riverbank supporting a patchwork of subsistence farms on the outskirts of Hazel Creek, the only town worth the name. Because of its remote location, the area had been largely untouched by the Civil War, with few local men fighting on either side of the conflict, but eleven men and boys from the valley had died in World War I. In the decades that followed, Hazel Creek had produced a lieutenant governor, a coach for the Baltimore Orioles, a federal judge, and a marginally successful lady poet whose verses were later included in the 1965 Westinghouse time capsule.

When the Tennessee Valley Authority decided to dam Hazel Creek, they had a long list of reasons. Men in gray suits traveled to the valley with bags full of plans and flyers, and presented them to the farmers in town halls and local churches. The dam would supply power not just to the valley and nearby Ewald but to cities on the other side of the state. The lake would also be a tourist attraction, benefiting the economy of the isolated mountain county. The TVA decided to christen the new lake after a wealthy local farmer who was one of the first to agree to sell his land. The administrators hoped that his example would encourage other citizens to give in and cede their property to the government, and it may have had the desired effect, but there were still holdouts. According to legend, a woman who had lived every one of her eighty-plus years in the same house shot herself in her kitchen with a rifle her father had brought home from the Civil War. A man climbed to the church roof and refused to come down for three days. The biggest stalemate had to do with the graveyard, which would be out of reach of the floodwaters, but no longer reachable by road.

"How do you know all this?" Jay asked, crooking his elbow on the window ledge. Anjali had fallen asleep before they left downtown, her head fallen to the side and a delicate baby snore issuing from her mouth.

"My great-granddaddy was the pastor at Hazel Creek Baptist," Natalie said. "My mom's grandfather. He wrote all these letters to the state legislature claiming that the graveyard was sacred ground and that everyone buried there was going to heaven. He'd had some kind of vision of the Rapture and bodies floating up out of the ground, and somehow he got the Park Service to sign an agreement with the families of the residents that they'd run ferries across the lake once a year on Decoration Day so people could keep up the graves. Meanwhile, like I told you, my Macready great-grandfather was drawing up an agreement that moved the line of the national forest farther back so he could keep his property. That's what we come from—politicians on the one side, holy rollers on the other."

Jay peered out the window at the blue sheet of water unrolling beyond the guardrail. "Is the town still down there?"

"Well, they didn't bulldoze it," Natalie said. "People say the lake is haunted, of course. They say there have been way more deaths here than you'd expect from a lake of this size, though I don't know if there have been studies or anything."

Before she spoke, she hadn't been thinking of Ben. She was thinking only of the drownings—people who had fallen from boats, struck their heads while diving, or driven into the water where Southridge Road made a ninety-degree turn by the old post office. She knew that plenty of locals believed in the curse, and even after his murderer was arrested, it was likely that Ben would still number in the unofficial list of the victims of Lake Monroe.

"I saw the ghosts," she said. "Or at least I thought I did, after the boat crash. Everyone said I was only in the water for a few minutes, but I have these memories of sinking down under the waves and being really scared at first, but then the fear went away and I saw all these people, just walking around on the lake bottom like it was a normal thing to do. Kaitlyn was the only person I told about it, and she asked if it was like *The Little Mermaid*, but it wasn't. It was like they'd all gone on with their everyday lives. One woman held out a pie like she wanted me to smell it."

"It's probably good that you didn't tell people about that," Jay said, smiling at her.

"I know it didn't happen," Natalie said. "I'm sure I was just remembering the stories my grandmother used to tell me. She used to go on about how beautiful it was before the waters came. I don't think she was one of the people who chained themselves to their houses, but she definitely wished she had. She always said the government would cheat you if you didn't watch out. If she was alive, she'd be one of those people searching the sky for the black helicopters from the UN."

She was afraid she'd told Jay too much. Would he think that her grandmother's fear of the federal government carried the usual implications—that their family was a bunch of small-minded bigots, intolerant of change even when it was for the better? She didn't want him to think of her that way.

"I didn't believe it at first when Cassie told me that your dad and your uncle had been moonshiners," Jay said, turning in his seat. "It sounded like something out of a movie, and then all of you were so adorable and southern. I'd never met adults who called their father 'Daddy' before."

Natalie tried to detect if there was a note of mockery in his voice, but she couldn't find one.

"But Cassie and I are different," she said. "I mean from the rest of the family. I love them, but I don't want to be stuck in the past the way they are. That's why I started Ewald Yoga to begin with. I want to help this place grow with the times."

"That's an admirable goal," Jay said, and now Natalie was pretty sure that he was laughing at her, just a little, just like the rest of the men she knew.

Without it ever being discussed, Natalie had become the one who drove Jay home in the afternoons as well as driving him into town in the mornings. Cassie always had a reason for staying late: she had a call about a merchandising opportunity, or paperwork to do, or a private Zoom session with a client in Boston or Seattle. Natalie and Jay picked up Anjali at Cindy Caldwell's day care, and sometimes the three of them stopped on the way home at Ewald Coffee, sitting out at the picnic tables in the lukewarm sun and sharing a muffin broken into thirds. Today was cold and gray, though, and Natalie had asked Jay if anyone had given him a tour of the lake. She had a destination in mind, but he didn't have to know that yet.

As she turned onto Highway 82 and pointed out the concrete shell of the dam rising on their right, she wondered if he was interested in the history or just being polite. She cared about the valley because it was her history, because the people who had willingly given up their land and the ones who had hidden with their shotguns in barns and corncribs were her people, linked to her by blood if separated by time. Maybe, she thought, Jay's curiosity about Lake Monroe had to do with Anjali. The people of the Hazel Valley were her people too, and Natalie wondered if Jay knew how much Anjali resembled the Macready sisters in their baby pictures, with the same wide eyes, the same unruly cowlick.

Jay drummed his fingers on the window ledge. "Sometimes I

think Cassie is a little embarrassed by this place, and I don't get it. It's a cute little town."

The words stung, but they weren't really a surprise. "Well, Cassie wanted to get out of here as soon as she could," Natalie said. "She didn't tell us that she was applying to colleges out of state, I guess because she knew Mama and Daddy wouldn't like it, but once she started getting financial aid offers, they realized they couldn't stop her."

"Yeah, I get that," Jay said with a soundless laugh. "She's a power-house all right."

It could have been a compliment, but there was an edge to his words that made them sound bitter rather than affectionate. Natalie couldn't help putting it together with the other warning signs she'd noticed in the past few weeks, particularly Cassie's eagerness to have Jay out of the house in the mornings. "Is there something going on with the two of you?" she asked Jay without looking at him. "Is that why Cassie wanted to come home all of a sudden?"

He was silent for so long that she was sure she'd offended him, but then he sighed and turned his body toward her, leaning the back of his head against the window. "I guess you could say that," he said. "It's nothing to do with her, though. It's a problem with me."

Again Natalie felt as if the words were simply an echo, confirming something she'd already known. She thought of the times she'd walked in on Jay on his laptop in an empty studio, in an intense conversation with a single student in Minneapolis or Dallas or New York City. He charged a hundred and fifty dollars an hour for those private classes, and the students were always female, always acolytes chasing the magic of his Instagram posts through contact with the real-life Jay Desai. He did in-person workshops too, and it was easy to imagine what might have happened after hours in a faraway city after dinner with a worshipful student. Clearly he hadn't followed his own ethical guidelines, but what could be less surprising than that a powerful man should come to count on the adulation of strangers?

But it wasn't that at all. "I hurt people," he said. "Physically, I mean. It happened once in a workshop in Portland, and once in a private class in Miami. I tore a woman's rotator cuff. I was trying to help her into a bind, and I pushed too hard. Our insurance paid her off and she signed an NDA, but the story's gotten some traction on the yoga blogs, and it's probably just a matter of time before one of the big yoga magazines picks it up and all hell breaks loose. That's why we came to Ewald. I think Cassie is trying to figure out what's going to happen with her career once I become a liability."

"Why didn't anybody tell me about this?" Natalie asked, her voice rising. "I mean, I'm not saying I don't believe you—of course I do—but when you're going to be on my payroll for the next month, a heads-up would have been nice."

"It's not going to affect you." Jay shifted his posture, angling his knees toward the window. He'd dropped his smooth-toned yoga-teacher voice and sounded almost sulky. "It's not like this is LA or New York, where people actually know who I am."

Was he right? It was true that her clients, with the exception of Amanda Vergotti, had probably never picked up a copy of *Yoga Journal* or *Yoga International*. If they followed Jay on social media, it was because he was Natalie's brother-in-law, not for his advice on macrobiotic diets or the best way to get into a headstand without straining the neck. But Natalie might not have ever taken a yoga class if it hadn't been for Cassie and Jay. When she told people like Hardy Underwood how much better it would make them feel, how much happier, how much more confident, she was speaking about herself, who would probably be working in sales at Macready Contracting and Excavation if Cassie had never invited her out to California and told her that vinyasa was what all the celebrities did to stay in shape.

"I'm sorry, that was selfish of me," she said. "Can I do anything to help? I know what a good teacher you are."

He shrugged. "Cassie says that if we give it some time, the whole thing will die down. Usually when yoga teachers get called out, it's for something sexual, so maybe it'll work in my favor that I just injured women instead of sleeping with them."

His tone was sour, and Natalie reached over to take his hand. She wasn't thinking about the doubts she still had about how Jay had happened to stumble on the knife after Ben's murder. She wasn't even thinking about what he'd just told her. She was thinking that men were easily redirected, and that a blow to their egos could always be assuaged by the right application of attention and flattery. Jay's other hand moved to the base of her neck, rubbing at the tight muscles of her levator scapulae, the ones that Cassie said Natalie never activated properly in downward dog. "Damn, you're tight," he said, with a teasing, brotherly lightness in his voice that belied the motion of his hands. "You need to relax, girl."

"We should come back another day without Anjali and I'll take you up in the mountains," she said dreamily. "I can show you where the old stills used to be." Jay smiled at her and went on with his massage, and Natalie could feel her muscles turning to water, as if she'd slipped beneath the surface of the lake and been absorbed into it, that lost home she'd never seen.

21.

The idea to visit the resort had come to Natalie while she studied the hand-drawn map of Lake Monroe on the brochures. Tracing the lake's outline, she noticed that the businesses along Southridge Road and clustered at the marina were all marked on the map, each with a corresponding drawing. Natalie counted three bars and five restaurant/bars, including the Lake Monroe Resort, where her father had drunk away the afternoon after Ben's death.

If Ben had started secretly drinking again in the days or weeks before the Felons' Ball, chances were good that he'd gone to one of these businesses around the lake. Technically speaking, boating under the influence was just as illegal as driving above the limit, but the Virginia Marine Police were unlikely to enforce the law unless it happened to be Memorial Day weekend or the Fourth of July, when tourists descended on the lake in drunken hordes. Though Ben usually kayaked over when he visited the Macreadys, he also had a motorboat, a used Sea Ray he'd restored himself. If he wanted to knock back a few without worrying about getting pulled over at the end of the night, his best bet would be either to bring a bottle back to the boat or to motor over to one of the lakeside bars served by a public dock.

Natalie wanted to avoid trying the ABC store as long as possible. Since Virginia didn't allow supermarkets or convenience stores to sell hard liquor, the state-owned alcoholic beverage control store was the only place in town to buy anything from Popov to Macallan scotch, and it certainly wasn't out of the question that Ben had stopped by there if he planned to drink alone. The problem was that Natalie didn't know the managers, and she doubted her ability to sweet-talk a total stranger to giving up information about his customers. She would start with the lake bars, where her family were familiar figures and no one would require her to explain her interest in Ben Marsh.

Jay hadn't asked why exactly she wanted to know where Ben was drinking before his death, and she was relieved, since she wasn't sure she'd be able to explain it. What Kaitlyn had said on the dock on the night after Ben's death still bothered her. Maybe the sheriff too would jump to the conclusion that Ben's death was connected to his affair with the Macreadys' youngest daughter, and if he did, that assumption would lead him straight to her parents. She'd tried to direct him away from that possibility, but it would be even better if she could prove that Ben had been worried about something that had nothing to do with her family.

It had all made sense to her an hour before, but now she felt distracted and off her game. She could still feel Jay's hand on the back of her neck, and there had been a moment, when she leaned to pick up her purse, when she'd thought he might be about to kiss her. Their faces had come within inches of each other, and the way he looked at her had made her breath quicken and shivers run the length of her body, but at the last moment she'd turned away, opening the door and moving to the back to unbuckle Anjali from her car seat. "Don't tell anybody at home that I ordered a drink before five p.m.," she said, praying her voice didn't sound as wobbly as she felt.

She'd hoped that someone she knew would be tending bar at the resort. She'd imagined herself making small talk for a while, asking about holiday plans and mutual friends, finally easing into the subject of the murder and then backtracking to whether they'd seen Ben in the weeks before his death. That wouldn't be possible now, because the man behind the bar was unfamiliar to her, a suave-looking fellow with a blond mustache whose name tag read *Gus*. Surely that was a name he'd come up with for the job, Natalie thought. Only dogs were named Gus.

She ordered a Jack and Diet Coke, and Jay asked for a sweet tea. Gus gave him a once-over and looked hesitant, as if he could tell just from looking at Jay that he was not from the South. "Our iced tea is very heavily sweetened," he said, and Jay told him that sounded terrific.

The bar was quiet at this time in the afternoon, the low mahogany chairs empty of customers and angled to face the floor-to-ceiling windows. The room smelled of air freshener and lemon peel, and tinkly piano jazz played at a low volume in the background. It was a bar for people her father's age, and not the kind of place where Natalie would have hung out voluntarily. "I'm Natalie Macready, and this is Jay Desai," she began, Gus nodding in a bored sort of way before the words were even out of her mouth.

"I know who you are," he said. "Your dad was in here the other day."

"Oh. Great." Natalie tapped her fingers on the bar, wondering if Trey had shown him the high school cheerleading photo of her that he still kept in his wallet. She'd begged him to update the pictures of his daughters—or, better yet, to keep his photos on his phone like a normal person—but of course he never listened to her. "Well, you probably know Ben Marsh then."

Know Ben Marsh, she'd said, as if there were still someone to know. In books and movies, the murderer often gives himself away by talking about the victim in the past tense before anyone else knows they are dead, but now Natalie found herself doing the opposite.

"I *knew* Ben, yeah," Gus said, emphasizing the word a little as if to offer a correction.

It was the opening she'd been waiting for. "Did he ever drink here?"

Anjali stirred and began to cry, and Jay got up to walk her over to the windows. Natalie wished Gus would do something with his hands—polish the bar or inspect the glassware for water spots—but instead he just stared at her, a faint wrinkle appearing between his eyebrows. "With your dad, you mean?"

That wasn't what she'd meant at all, but the question made her wonder. "With or without him," she said. "I was just curious about whether Ben stopped in."

Gus didn't answer right away. He was looking over her shoulder, and she turned to see a party of middle-aged women in pastel sweaters who were seating themselves at a large table. She didn't have to look closely to know that they were out-of-towners, probably celebrating someone's divorce or cancer remission. The pitch of their voices made it clear that they'd been day drinking for a while. "God, I *love* spicy nuts," one moaned, before another popped in with a "That's what she said."

Natalie glanced at Gus. She probably only had a few seconds before the tipsy tourists bellied up to the bar to order their prosecco and skinny margs. "Ben and I were close," she said desperately. "Very close, actually. I don't know if you know this, but he was in recovery for twelve years, and then he suddenly started drinking again. I just want to know why."

"No," Gus said. Natalie looked back at the women again, hoping that the no was somehow intended for them and not for her. "Ben never came in here," he continued. "I knew him from mountain biking. He gave me a ride down from the parkway once when my bike had a flat tire, but I never saw him in here. Never saw him with a drink, for that matter."

Natalie set her empty glass down on the bar. The thunk of glass against wood was louder than she expected, and Gus focused in on her face for the first time. "You're the one who's married to a cop, right?" he said.

"What? No," Natalie said. "That's my sister, Kaitlyn."

"Oh," he said, already looking away toward the table of laughing women. "You're the youngest, then. The one who Trey said was still trying to get her life together."

22.

"Y ou know what would make you feel better?" Jay said on the way home. "Backbends."

Natalie gave a short laugh. "Guess again."

"I'm not talking about tonight," he said. "Tomorrow. You don't even realize how flexible you are."

She felt a pulse of anxiety that she tried to disguise with a studied yawn. "There's no rush," she said. "How about next week?"

She could feel his eyes on the side of her face. He hadn't touched her since they'd left the resort, but the temperature of the air between them had changed, and they could both feel it. She had tried so hard not to think of him that way, had tried to turn her head when he thrust up into poses that outlined every inch of his pelvis, but after their moment in the car earlier, she could feel herself weakening. Cassie had been pushing Natalie and Jay together ever since they'd arrived, and he'd just admitted they were having problems. If something happened between them, was it even Natalie's fault?

"You're ready," Jay said, his deep brown eyes locked on Natalie's until she forced herself to look back at the road. "You just don't know it yet."

She worried all night. What if she started bawling again? What if her back simply didn't bend that way, and when Jay tried to force her into the right position, something cracked or slipped? What if he put his hand somewhere they both knew it wasn't supposed be, and she had to decide once and for all whether she was really the kind of person who would fuck her sister's husband?

Around three thirty she checked her phone and was relieved to see a text from Jay: *Can't sleep. I'm going to try a little longer and then maybe go for a drive. OK if we take a raincheck?*

Natalie let out a long breath. *Of course*, she wrote back. *Get some sleep.*

But there would be no sleep for her. A little after five, she got up, put on the clothes she'd left out on the chair, and started coffee. She was delirious and achy with fatigue, but she felt an unexpected sense of purpose. She would throw her Marlboro Lights in the trash. She would get into the studio and force herself through fifty sun salutations, seventy-five, a hundred, until her arms felt like noodles and her breath came in staccato bursts. She would punish herself so thoroughly that she'd never have another sexual thought about Jay, not ever again. On the podcast, they always said to listen to your body, but that was what had gotten her into trouble in the first place.

It was late afternoon before it occurred to her that something might be wrong. Natalie had taught three classes that day and then spent an hour and a half trying to figure out the new scheduling app. Jay and Cassie had never come in, but they weren't on the schedule and she didn't think much about it until Kaitlyn called to ask her if she'd heard from Jay. "Cassie hasn't seen him all day," she said. "He took the car, and she had to call Mama to take Anjali to day care."

Natalie checked the clock: four thirty. She felt a twinge of alarm that she tried not to let show in her voice. "He texted me early and said he was going for a drive," she said. "Maybe his phone went dead, or he's out of service."

If Kaitlyn thought it was strange that Jay had told Natalie, rather than his own wife, where he was going that morning, she didn't say so. "Well, if you hear from him, let her know," she said. "She sounded kind of frantic."

But that night, Luke said that there was no reason to be concerned. "Maybe he's just blowing off steam," he said. "Or maybe he and Cassie got in a fight, and he decided to head back to LA. I wouldn't blame him if he needed to get away for a while."

Natalie didn't think that made any sense at all. Things might have been strained between Jay and Cassie, but he would not just head back to California without his wife and daughter, without saying a word to anyone. "Can't you search the guest house?" she said. "Or you could track his phone, right? To see if it's still around?"

Uncle Leo snorted. He'd come over to drop off some paperwork for Natalie's father and stayed for dinner. "Cassie would have to file a missing persons report before the police could get involved," he said, reaching for another piece of her mother's fried chicken. "And there's no reason to think this is a criminal matter. Unless Jay confided in you that the Russian mafia was after him?"

Natalie bit her lip and, to keep herself from snapping back, grabbed his mostly empty beer bottle and whisked it away to the recycling. It was just a joke, she told herself. Even if her uncle did have a preternatural ability to sniff out secrets that other people wanted to stay hidden, he'd have no way of knowing that she'd been flirting with Jay. Rather than trying to make her uncomfortable, he was simply trying to imply that Jay might have very good reasons for wanting to leave Ewald County.

And maybe he was right. Her father would have told her to take her own feelings out of the equation and look at the situation logically: Jay had a public altercation with Ben Marsh; Ben was murdered, and then, barely three weeks later, Jay disappeared. Natalie had to consider at least the possibility that she'd been wrong about him, that the open kindness that had beguiled her since that first class in Malibu had been just a huckster's trick, a strategy for getting vulnerable women to put their bodies in his keeping. If that turned out to be the case, she could live with it, satisfied with the fact that things had never gone further than a hand on the curve of her rib cage, fingers moving the skin on her thigh to simulate the outer rotation of the hip.

But what would it mean for Cassie and Anjali? Her mother and Luke were still talking in the dining room, their voices lowered, and Natalie was pretty sure she could guess what they were saying. The Macreadys needed to close ranks, as they'd done so often in the past. The most important thing, now and always, was to take care of their own.

The mood at the lake that night was like a repeat of the day after Ben's death, except now it was Cassie lying upstairs while everyone else bustled around the kitchen and living room, speaking in hushed tones and trying to find ways to keep occupied. "Quite a coincidence," Natalie's father said when she found him alone at the dock, smoking one of the cigars her mother wouldn't allow in the house. "First Ben, now this."

She climbed up on the railing and looked down at the lake, where waves tossed up plumes of white spray as they collided. "It's bad luck," she said, hoping that saying the words out loud would make them sound more convincing. "There's no reason to think that one has anything to do with the other."

Her father puffed on his cigar, saying nothing, though his expression suggested he was formulating a disagreement. "What I can't figure out is why they can't find the car. It's one thing for a person to disappear, but a car is a whole different deal. Unless he just ran away back to India and left it at an airport somewhere."

"Daddy, Jay never lived in India," Natalie said impatiently. "His parents moved back when they retired, but he was born in LA."

"Well, maybe he went to visit his parents then. What difference does it make?"

Natalie picked at a hole in the knee of her jeans. A cold wind was blowing, and she threaded her hands inside the sleeves of her coat.

"This is going to be hard on Cassie," her father said, hunching forward with his elbows on his knees. "It's a special kind of pain, to realize that someone you loved isn't the person you thought they were."

23.

All evening they talked only in groups of two or three, keeping their voices low, as if Cassie, lying in the guest room upstairs, might hear them in her dreams. Natalie stacked blocks with Anjali until she got fussy, and then Rosemary took the baby from her. "Sweetheart, will you check on your sister, please?" she whispered to Natalie over her shoulder. "Just see if she wants us to bring her any dinner. I saved her a plate."

Natalie took her time getting upstairs. Now that it was full dark, she could no longer hold on to the possibility that Jay had gone for a hike or a drive up on the Blue Ridge Parkway and lost track of time. Something had happened: either he'd skipped town, as her father had suggested, or he'd been hurt or injured. Maybe, she thought, he'd driven back up in the national forest, looking for one of the stills she'd told him about the other day. But Jay had never struck her as outdoorsy, at least not in the way of the boys she'd grown up with. He was a surfer, but he had no experience with the mountains, and he wouldn't be foolish enough to set off into the wilderness without telling anyone where he was going. On the landing at the top of the stairs, she pulled her phone from her pocket and texted Hardy Underwood: *I need to talk to you.*

Cassie wasn't in the guest room. Natalie checked the bathroom, and then her own room, but both were empty, the fringe of the curtains swinging in the breeze made by the open door. Her heart beat faster. Cassie could not be gone. Still, she raced down the back stairs, readying herself to run across the yard to the guest house and check every nook and cranny for some sign of her sister's presence.

But Cassie was standing by the back door, wearing the down coat she kept in the closet of the guest house for winter trips home from California. Natalie put a hand to her chest, hoping that her sister wouldn't pick up on how terrified she'd been. "Where are you going?"

"I'm tired of lying in bed," Cassie said without looking at her. "I have to get out of this house, or I'll lose my damn mind."

"Can I come with you?" Natalie asked quickly, grabbing her mother's black puffer jacket from the hook on the wall. Cassie shrugged, but didn't protest as Natalie followed her outside.

The forecast called for snow, and in the last moments of sunset the overcast sky had taken on a gloomy purple tinge. Cassie headed for the lake trail, switching on the flashlight on her phone. "Have you seen what's happening on social media?"

"What are you talking about?" Surely people couldn't know already that Jay had left, when it had happened only hours ago.

"It started on some news site," Cassie said as she scrolled through her phone. "There was an article about Ben's murder, and I guess somebody figured out that Jay and I were at the party that night. Look at the top comment."

Natalie scanned the article over Cassie's shoulder. The tone felt judgmental, with a veiled implication that the party had been some kind of redneck bacchanal, with guests including notable state politicians and "yoga influencers Jay Desai and wife Cassie." "Well?" Cassie demanded, and Natalie's eyes dropped obediently to the first comment.

She read it out loud: " 'When people learn the truth about Jay and Cassie Desai, there's going to be a shitstorm.' " She clicked on the little gray head beside the comment, which took her to an account with the user name *tami_figg*. "What truth?" Natalie asked, looking up at her sister. "Who is Tami Figg?"

"It's this woman named Tami Figueroa," Cassie said. "We did a weekend workshop once at her studio in San Diego. She claims that

Jay injured one of her clients. Apparently she fractured a vertebra, and Tami says that Jay talked her out of taking legal action. There have been others too. I thought maybe if we stepped out of the spotlight for a while, the whole thing would blow over, but being connected to a murder investigation isn't going to help."

Natalie thought of what Jay had said on the day they toured the lake: *I hurt people.* "I don't understand what the big deal is," she said, more forcefully than she'd meant to. "That's why people sign waivers, right? Besides, don't you have insurance?"

"I told Jay I'm getting out." Cassie stuffed her phone into her coat pocket. "I hate traveling. I hate marketing our lives as if yoga makes us shiny and happy all the time, when the truth is that we're just as messed up as everybody else. When we traveled, the students would absolutely fawn over him. Some of the women would compete for the towels he used to wipe his face. That was why he started putting so much pressure on himself, and on me too. Did you know I strained my hamstring so badly last year that I couldn't practice for a month? He wanted me to demo a split for a class of intermediate students when I wasn't warmed up. He always wanted us to do something new, something amazing, but what the fuck is the point of pushing yourself until you break your own body or somebody else's?"

Natalie almost tripped on a root, throwing out her hands just in time to catch herself on a spindly poplar. "So you told him you're quitting?"

"That's how I know that he left us," Cassie said. "I tried to talk to him about it a couple of days ago, and he was so mad that he almost punched a hole in the wall of the cabin. I think Daddy could hear us—he kept looking out the den window, and once he came all the way out on the porch, but Jay had calmed down by then."

Two days ago, Natalie thought. The day before she'd taken Jay out to the resort and he'd almost kissed her in the car. On the drive he'd been his usual relaxed, charming self, but she'd sensed that there was something wrong, something he wasn't telling her. "Are you going to report him missing?"

"Because more attention from the police would make our lives better somehow?" Cassie snapped. "Did you know that Jay was charged with assault back in high school? He slammed a guy's head into a wall so hard that his attorney claimed he had brain damage. Jay was acquitted, but you better believe that Hardy Underwood dug that one up pretty quick."

Natalie took a deep breath. "Are you saying that he's a suspect in Ben's murder?"

Cassie stopped where the trail turned, looking over the dark water to the twinkling lights of the marina. "I don't know," she said. "If you're asking if he's the type of guy who could be violent, then yes, I think he is. Jay talks a good game about the ethics of the practice, but I'm not sure he ever really believed in it."

Natalie had to admit that it all made sense. She'd had the same instinct that Jay had begun to believe his own hype, and that behind the shiny surface of his charisma, there were no particular spiritual gifts, no extraordinary empathy, but simply a man with an insatiable appetite for the admiration he'd learned to inspire. Still, it seemed to her that Cassie was overlooking an obvious possibility. Jay could have left town because he wanted to leave his family, or because he was running from the investigation into Ben's death, but it was also conceivable that he'd somehow gotten on the bad side of the same person who'd murdered Ben. Why did no one seem to be considering the possibility that instead of being the perpetrator, he might be another victim?

Her phone buzzed in her pocket, and she saw that Hardy had finally responded to her text: *Let me buy you dinner.*

Cassie was watching her. "Just tell me the truth," she said. "Did you sleep with him? I guess it doesn't matter in a way. Maybe it's even kind of my fault, since I kept trying to get him out of the house. Still, if you did, that was a really shitty thing to do."

Natalie felt her breath catch in her throat. "I *didn't*," she insisted, hoping the darkness hid the rush of shame and anger that scalded her cheeks. "He never touched me. I swear to you, Cassie."

She waited to see if Cassie believed her, but she wouldn't meet her eyes. The wind sifted snow from the branch above them, and Cassie held out her hand to catch it. "He was always complaining about being cold here," she said. "Californians are such wimps about cold weather. He said, 'I knew your hometown was a redneck shithole, but I didn't know it was a redneck shithole that was freezing all the time too.' "

They walked back to the house in silence. Cassie headed for the kitchen, but Natalie decided against following her. She didn't want to watch their mother fuss over Cassie, asking if she was feeling all right, if she wanted to stay the night, and what in the world she'd been doing outside all this time. Natalie didn't want to have to stand there with an empathetic look on her face when really she was furious— with Cassie, for accusing her of trying to sleep with her husband, and with herself, for putting them in a situation where the accusation conceivably might be justified.

In her room, Natalie sat down on the edge of her bed, thinking of the day after Ben's murder, when she'd lain in a stupor until she had to go talk to Hardy. It occurred to her that she'd never replied to his text, and she pulled out her phone to write: *I already ate.*

He responded immediately. *Let me buy you a drink then.*

Where?

You know that Texaco down the road from your studio? Best dumplings I've ever had, and they have some good beers on draft.

Natalie was hunting for a pair of jeans when her mother's voice floated up the stairs. "Sweetheart?" she called. "Do you have my jacket? I don't know what happened to it."

Natalie sighed. There was zero chance that Rosemary actually needed her puffer jacket tonight, but once she'd noticed its absence, she wouldn't be able to relax until it was back in its proper place. "Yeah, I have it," she called back. "I'll bring it down as soon as I get changed." Hurriedly she thrust her hand into the front pockets, feeling for the cigarettes she'd bought to replace the pack she'd thrown away that morning. Jay's disappearance had seemed like a more-than-adequate reason to give up on her resolution to quit.

They weren't in the first pocket she tried, so she went on to the second. Still no Marlboro Lights, but her fingers brushed something else—bits of paper, she thought, maybe crumpled grocery lists, until she drew them out and saw that they were photographs. Every one of them featured Lanny Marsh, alone on the beach or with his arms around Trey and Ben on the floating dock, or with Rosemary, who reached out playfully to swat him on the arm. The last had clearly been taken on Thanksgiving, and it featured Trey holding his carving knife over a steaming turkey, Lanny grinning to his right.

Natalie wasn't in that picture. She had still been in the hospital then, floating in and out of dreams of the village under the lake. She stared at the photo for a long time. Behind her father, the curtains were open, and through the glass she could glimpse the blurry slant of rain.

24.

She couldn't figure out if the late-night meetup that Hardy had suggested was supposed to be a date. In high school, her mother had told her that you could never accept a date with less than twenty-four hours' notice, because jumping right on a last-minute invitation would make you seem desperate. In addition, you could never say yes to a date that involved a fast-food restaurant, because a boy who respected you would be willing to save up for a nice meal. Natalie had thumbed her nose at her mother's advice back then, but like Rosemary's pronouncements about not wearing white after Labor Day and how a strand of pearls goes with everything, it had stuck in her head despite her best efforts. By her mother's formula, Hardy Underwood could not respect her, or he would have invited her for a candlelit dinner at Chez Josephine rather than dumplings at the Texaco.

She'd never eaten at the Chinese takeout at the Goshen Street Texaco, but she knew the family; Christy Wong had been in Cassie's class in high school, and her little brother Hunter was a championship swimmer who went on to college in Oregon on a full scholarship. Their mother was a short, pretty woman wearing sensible shoes and bright pink lipstick. "Hey there, Miss Valerie," Hardy greeted her as they approached the counter. "Two orders of dumplings and two number fives, please. Do you want a beer?" he asked, turning to Natalie.

Miss Valerie gave Natalie an assessing glance, as if trying to determine whether she was a love interest or a suspect. "Y'all can sit out on the screen porch," she said as she uncapped their beers. "We've got a space heater out there." Natalie thanked her and followed Hardy out the back door.

The screen porch was carpeted in green baize and clearly intended for summer use, the lone heater in the corner giving off a meager stream of warmth. The matching green picnic tables, flecks of paint peeling off their tops, had been leveled with matchbooks under the legs. Hardy reached out to clink his bottle against hers and settled back in his seat, smiling at her in a way that made her want to fiddle with her hair. "It's good to see you."

She didn't return the compliment. "I texted you because my brother-in-law is missing. Cassie's husband, Jay. No one's seen him since yesterday morning."

Hardy sipped his beer while she told the story: the text in the middle of the night, Jay's last words to Cassie, the Honda gone from its usual spot in front of the guest house. "You said 'missing,'" he said when she'd finished. "Are you suggesting that something's happened to him?"

Natalie unrolled her silverware, wrapped in a real cloth napkin that matched the table. "My dad thinks he ran away," she said. "So does Cassie. I think they're afraid he might have something to do with Ben's death. But what if he's not the one who hurt Ben? I know he threatened him that night at the party, but he didn't mean it. Jay's not a violent guy."

"You know him pretty well," Hardy said. Though his tone was neutral, without judgment, she couldn't help wondering if he'd made the same assumption as Cassie. Why did everyone seem to believe that she was the kind of girl who would fuck her brother-in-law only weeks after she discovered her murdered boyfriend's body?

The answer was uncomfortably obvious. Because she almost had been that kind of girl.

Miss Valerie came out with a tray loaded with dumplings and two plates of the number five, which turned out to be a stir-fried chicken and vegetables with a chili sauce. "I already knew about Jay," Hardy said as he speared a dumpling with his fork and dragged it through the dipping sauce. "Luke called me earlier today, but he says that Cassie hasn't been down to the department. Until she reports Jay missing, there's really not much we can do."

It was exactly what Uncle Leo had told her. "But what if the same person who killed Ben killed Jay too?"

Hardy didn't seem surprised by the suggestion. He took another bite and wiped his mouth carefully. "Like who?"

Natalie picked at the peeling paint with her thumbnail. "What about Croaker?" she asked. "Or what if there's some sociopath running around—some drifter out there who went to Ben's boat hoping to rob him, and then went after Jay because he thought he knew something?"

"There aren't as many sociopaths as people think," Hardy said. "I think it's between one and five percent, and studies suggest that murderers are actually less likely to be psychopathic or sociopathic than other violent offenders. If you want to get into the criminological side of things."

She was pretty sure that he was teasing her, the same way her family did. She didn't know him well enough to tease him back, but she was pretty sure she knew how to set him on the back foot. She drained the rest of her beer, feeling reckless. "Let me ask you a question for a change," she said. "Were you in love with your wife?"

He gave a soundless laugh and reached for his fork. "Pretty sure most people are in love with the people they marry."

"I don't think I was in love with Ben," she said. "I feel like if I'd really loved him, his death would have destroyed me. I still think about it a lot, and . . ." Her throat tightened, and she stopped, swallowed, took a drink. "It was an awful thing to see. I keep thinking that there was something I could have done if I'd gotten there sooner. But I'm sad because of the experience, not because of the loss. Does that make sense?"

For a moment he didn't move or speak, his eyes on her and his fork suspended above his plate. "What do you think love is, Natalie?"

Finally, she thought, a question she could answer without second-guessing or hesitation. "Feeling like you're two halves of the same whole," she said. "Like you're not sure where they end and you begin. That's how my parents are. I cared about Ben, but I don't think I ever could have felt that way about him."

Hardy took a bite before he responded, his chewing slow and methodical. "Do you think y'all were on the same page about that?"

"I think so," Natalie said, but then she wondered if she was telling the truth. She thought of the way Ben had looked at her on the morning of his death as he handed her the stack of clothes. He'd taken them to the laundromat, washed and dried and folded them, just because they were hers. She looked down at her hands. "I guess I don't want you to think I'm a bad person because I'm not more upset. You were probably expecting me to act like a grieving widow or something."

"I wasn't expecting anything," Hardy said. "I never do. People can react to a crime in all kinds of ways, and an investigator could get in trouble trying to interpret those reactions. You mind if we talk a little bit about Lanny Marsh now?"

"Lanny?" Once again he'd changed the subject quickly enough to make her head spin, and she wondered if this was one of the techniques they learned in investigator school. "Why, did you find him?"

He shook his head. "Found the postcards, though," he said. "From Manila, Singapore, places like that, but it's hard to track down a man in that line of work. Your daddy kept saying that Lanny had joined the merchant marines, but if that was the case, there would be some kind of record. Seems more likely to me that he just hitchhiked out west and hopped on whatever ship would have him. You do it that way, you don't leave much of a paper trail."

Natalie felt a surge of disappointment. She'd been holding on to the hope that there was some kind of central agency they could appeal to, but if Hardy was right, Lanny had purposefully avoided any such thing. "I did find something interesting, though," Hardy went on. "I was looking through Sheriff Shifflett's old notes, and apparently your dad invited the sheriff to search the house after Lanny left. Shifflett didn't find any sign of him, but he did find a refrigerator full of unlabeled mason jars. He didn't specify what he thought was in them, but I think I have a pretty good guess, don't you?"

Her mouth went dry, and she reached for her beer, forgetting she'd already finished it. "Come on, Natalie," Hardy said, his voice gentle now. "I know it must have occurred to you that your father and your uncle never stopped making liquor. Why should they, when Shifflett was willing to look the other way?"

"There's nothing illegal about keeping jars in a fridge," she said. "If there had been questions back then about where it came from, Sheriff Shifflett would have looked into it. I don't see what any of this has to do with Ben's murder, let alone Jay going missing."

Hardy nodded, looking away from her, as if to indicate that this was an interesting point of view that he couldn't be bothered to consider. "Or maybe your daddy doesn't actually do the brewing," he said. "Maybe he has friends who do, and they pass him the occasional jar now and again for personal use. You ever see anything like that around when you were growing up?"

Natalie tried not to think of the jars she'd seen in her father's mini fridge, purple and yellow and the eerie pale red of a blood moon. "No," she said. "Of course not."

He knew she was lying. He paused just long enough to make sure that she knew he knew, and then reached over to her plate and impaled her last dumpling. She wondered if she should tell him that you were allowed to eat them with your hands.

25.

The conversation with Hardy had left her flustered, as he'd surely intended. Clearly he was leaning toward the theory that Ben's murder and Jay's disappearance were somehow related to her family's past. She would have liked to dismiss the suggestion out of hand, but she wondered now if that was even possible. If her father and uncle had never stopped making liquor—if her father's identity as a legitimate businessman was just a cover story—then she had no idea what to think or whom to trust.

Her father and mother had made it clear that they weren't going to tell her anything. That left only Uncle Leo, but Natalie hated the thought of approaching him. He was so hard to read—jokey when she needed him to be serious, and acerbic, even harsh, when she just wanted a straight answer. Still, she had no choice. She had to talk to someone about Hardy's insinuations, and Uncle Leo was the only one left.

When she got to Macready's the next morning, Uncle Leo's big white truck was parked at an angle to the front door, as if he'd been in a hurry to get inside. When Natalie walked in, he was standing by the watercooler with his arms folded, talking to Renée. Capone ran up and sniffed Natalie's legs, and she scratched behind his ears.

Renée pasted a smile on her lips that didn't reach her eyes. "Hey baby," she said. "Are you looking for your daddy? He's got meetings out of the office today."

Natalie waved cheerfully, as if she hadn't picked up on the tension in the air. "Actually I'm here to see you," she said to Uncle Leo. "Do you have a few minutes?"

"For my favorite niece? Absolutely," he said, ushering her into his office with his arm extended in a courtly way.

Natalie took the seat across from him. It was an expensive chair, an Eames or some other executive-grade office furniture, but the seat was so low-slung that she felt as if her butt was sliding out from under her. "Have you talked much to the new sheriff?" she asked, crossing one leg over the other in an attempt to stay upright.

Leo continued shuffling the papers on his desk without looking up. "Hardy?" he said, as if there might be more than one new sheriff in town. "Yeah, we grab a beer over at the Silver Moon every now and then. He's single, if that's what you're asking."

Natalie refused to take the bait. "I went to talk to him," she said. "I wanted to tell him about Jay going missing, and I knew he had some questions for me about Ben. But then he started asking me about you and Daddy. About whether you're still making liquor."

Leo gave her a blank, flat glance that put her in mind of a Gila monster before opening the top drawer of his desk to bring out a cigar. She could tell from the label that it was a Cohiba, the same brand her father smoked. "That's interesting," he said, using his penknife to slice off the end of the cigar over the trash can. "He had questions for you about Ben, you said? About finding the body? Or about your relationship?"

She'd always known that the only way to keep up with her uncle was to try to stay two steps ahead of him, and yet somehow she'd failed to foresee this entirely obvious question. "I'm not spreading it around, don't worry," Uncle Leo said. "I understand why folks would want to keep something like that private."

Natalie didn't try to deny it. She thought of the day of the Felons' Ball, when she and Uncle Leo stood looking out at the lake, and he asked her if she knew where Ben was. Her instinct had been right: he'd been telling her he knew about them, though whether it was to needle her or to assure her that he'd keep their secret, she still couldn't tell.

"And don't you fret about the sheriff and his investigation," he said, looking down at his cigar. "We've got all that under control."

He hadn't said not to worry her pretty little head, but it was close. "But I don't understand why he's asking these questions," Natalie said.

Uncle Leo waved a hand dismissively. "There were some financial irregularities that came up when the sheriff went through our business accounts, and he decided that we must have gotten the still fired up again. He's barking up the wrong tree, though. The truth is that old Ben was making some deals under the table without our knowledge. He was writing off some of our equipment and then selling it to secondhand dealers and pocketing the profits. There are taxes owed, of course, but I believe that will all come out of the estate."

The relief she felt was so complete that all the tension went out of her shoulders, as if she'd just had a massage. "Do you think that had something to do with Ben's murder? Do you think it could have been one of those dealers who came after him?"

"Your guess is as good as mine." Uncle Leo crossed his legs at the knee. "Could have been a female too, some gal from his past come back for revenge. You know what Shakespeare said about a woman scorned."

Natalie didn't know if he'd meant the words to be painful, but they hit her like a jab to the throat. Uncle Leo had known Ben far better and longer than she, and if he thought Ben was the kind of guy who vengeful ex-girlfriends might come after with a knife, he would probably know. "But what woman?" she persisted. "Who could do something like that?"

"Honey, I can't tell you. It wasn't like he told me all about his conquests. I only knew about the two of y'all because he charged some dinners on the company credit card, and I had to ask him about it."

Natalie felt her face turn bright red. How could Ben have been so careless? "He wasn't doing so well at the end there," Leo continued. "You know he was drinking again before he died. At the Silver Moon, lots of nights I had to ferry him back to his boat after last call."

He sounded amused, but Natalie didn't think it was funny. "Mama said that none of you know how to get in touch with Lanny. I wish somebody would at least try. What if one of us ran away from home, and Daddy never even heard from us again?"

"If you did that, I'd say that you deserved what you got," Uncle Leo said as he reached for the Zippo on the blotter.

26.

ater Natalie would look back and think that she should have stopped there. She'd been given reasonable answers to all her questions. Jay had abandoned his wife and daughter. Ben had been killed by some outsider, a business owner or a jealous ex. Her high school crush had decided to spend his life wandering around the Pacific and would not be coming back. The stories she'd been given were plausible enough, and she should have found a way to be satisfied with them, as women claimed to be satisfied with the stories about their husbands' business trips out of town.

But she wasn't sure she could be content with half-truths anymore. Uncle Leo's explanations had sounded credible at the time, but when she lay awake that night, watching the blinds stir at the window, her agitation returned. If it was true that the sheriff had moved on from looking at the Macreadys as suspects, he would not have asked her all those questions about the moonshining business. He probably wouldn't be bothering with her at all.

What had Ben wanted to tell her on the day he died? When her father mentioned that Ben had put the boat up for sale, she'd convinced herself that he'd simply planned to tell her that he was moving to Florida and that their relationship had run its natural course. But he hadn't acted like a man who was about to break up with her. He hadn't been guilty or distant. If anything, his manner that morning had made her worry that he cared more about her than she did about him.

She knew the police had already searched Ben's boat. It must have been the first thing they'd done after they retrieved his body, but Hardy and his evidence techs didn't know Ben or his history with the Macreadys. It was possible that he'd left something important behind that they would overlook.

And she knew something that she was pretty sure the police and maybe even her father didn't know. She knew Ben's secret hiding spot.

Under normal circumstances, people on Lake Monroe didn't lock up their boats, either because they thought it was unlikely that someone would paddle over just to filch their toaster or because they had nothing worth stealing. It seemed probable, however, that the police had decided to lock up Ben's place after the murder, and that meant Natalie would have to find another way in.

She wasn't worried about being seen, at least not from her parents' house. Ben's boat was out of their line of vision. All she really had to worry about was tipsy boaters headed back from the marina or the Lake Monroe Resort, and they were unlikely to be out at this time of year, when the water was far too chilly for a booze cruise.

She remembered the layout well enough to picture the doors and windows, but she had no idea if one of them might be open, or if Ben was the kind of guy who kept an extra key under a flowerpot on the back porch. Still, she was pretty sure that as long as she came at the right time of day, no one would see her casing the joint.

It was late morning when she tied up at the cleats, trying not to think about the last time she'd done this. The body was gone, of course, and so was the blood, though a faint pink stain remained on the pale teak. There was no key under the dingy yellow doormat, and no key under the empty terra-cotta flowerpot, and no key under the legs of the picnic table that she lifted one by one. Breathing hard, she stood with her hands on her hips and surveyed the back of the boat. The windows were high and narrow, except for the kitchen window above the sink, which was the kind that latched at the top and swung outward. Natalie moved closer and stood on her tiptoes to test it, making up her mind that if this didn't work, she'd give up and come back at night with a screwdriver.

The window moved, but it swung in instead of out. Natalie pushed it as far as it would go and then let herself fall back, assessing the possibilities. She had the upper-body strength to clamber up to the ledge, but if she got stuck, she'd be able to go neither backward nor forward. She vowed to herself that in that case, she wouldn't call out and try to flag the attention of a passing boat. She would starve here, hanging half in and half out of her murdered lover's kitchen window, before she would let a stranger see her like that.

It wasn't as much of a squeeze as she feared, and everything would have been fine if she hadn't landed in Ben's sink, her hand splatting right into a half-full cereal bowl as she tried to catch herself. Natalie shrieked and half jumped, half slid to the floor, her heel catching on a pot that had been left on the counter and sending it clattering to the ground. But she couldn't think about the noise; she could only think about her hand, covered in milk and cornflake goo. She tried the faucet, but the water must have been turned off. Out of desperation, she scrubbed her wet hand on her pants, looking in dismay at the spreading white stain on her black leggings.

This was an incredibly stupid idea. She had only wanted to look for information that would help her find Lanny, and now she was sweaty and nervous, wearing stained pants and smelling like rancid milk.

But she could take her time. No one knew she was here, and even if they did, she had as much of a right as anyone to be on her dead boyfriend's houseboat. The dish towel that he'd used to mop up a spill on their last night together was folded on the counter, and she felt a sudden sharp ache in her gut. His presence was so palpable that she could almost smell him, that hickory-and-wood-shavings cologne that she'd loved to inhale from the skin of his neck.

She shook off the sadness and made herself keep going. The kitchen was bare, the cabinets empty except for a couple of boxes of cereal and a large bag of sourdough pretzels secured with a chip clip. The freezer held a bag of ground coffee and a nearly empty tub of butter pecan ice cream. In the bedroom, she started with the dresser drawers, but they held nothing out of the ordinary: socks and underwear in the top drawer, jeans and khakis on the bottom, the middle filled with T-shirts advertising local breweries and 10K races. The small closet was stocked with button-downs and polos, dress pants, a few blazers. The only interesting thing she found was a box with what must have been childhood memorabilia, including a book of rare stamps, a grass-smudged baseball, and a 1985 *Playboy* featuring Goldie Hawn in a human-size champagne glass. She wished she could take the box back to her father. It would mean something to him, even if it didn't mean anything to her.

She took out the bottom drawer of the desk, set it on the bed, and pressed on the wood underneath. On her first try nothing happened, but she felt around until she sprang the latch, a door popping open on a small secret space. It was where Ben had kept the dime bag of weed that he kept replenished with occasional business trips to DC or New York. The bag had worried Natalie at first, given that Ben was in AA, but he seemed to forget about it for months at a time, taking it out only when they had something to celebrate. On the night he'd shown her the secret compartment, he'd blocked her view of what was under the baggie, and she hadn't been interested enough to push. It was only after Ben's death that it occurred to her that the secret drawer was where a man would keep his most sacred possessions.

The bag was just where she'd remembered it, but underneath was something she'd never seen before: a stack of brochures with a Post-it on top, her own name written on it in Ben's handwriting. She pulled off the rubber band and flipped through: advertisements and class schedules for yoga studios in the Florida Keys from Islamorada to Key West.

Natalie wasn't sure how long she sat there. Her hands were shaking, and she dropped the whole stack on the bed, then fumbled them into some order again. She stared at the yellow Post-it with "Natalie" scripted across it in Ben's tight cursive. Perhaps she'd been right to assume that Ben planned to tell her about his move that night, but if so, it wasn't because he was breaking up with her. It was because he wanted her to come with him. Years ago she had daydreamed about Lanny Marsh sweeping her off to a new life, but it was Ben who had actually wanted to do it. It was Ben who loved her, and she'd never even known.

The light had changed, the sky darkening as clouds slid over the sun, and Natalie was so caught up in her own thoughts that it took her a while to realize what she was looking at through the kitchen window. The party boat, she thought. It was an eyesore—still stable enough, but the siding was dingy and battered, the boards of the porch half rotted. Ben and her father had discussed paying a salvage company to tow it away, but it was an expensive and drawn-out process, and they'd had trouble figuring out who held the deed.

But someone had been there, at least according to her father's secretary. If Renée could be believed, lights had been seen on the boat on the night of Ben's murder.

Natalie stuffed the brochures in her coat pocket and opened the door, wrapping her down jacket tight around her throat. She would paddle over and take a look, she told herself. She probably wouldn't find anything, but poking around the party boat would at least be a distraction, a way to get her mind off her own willful blindness and complicity. What else could she do, after all?

27.

As soon as she was back on the lake, with the pock-pock of ice hitting the water all around her, Natalie knew she'd miscalculated. The storm that hadn't been expected to hit until late afternoon had come early, surprising her with freezing rain and a sudden drop in temperature. She pulled the hood up around her face, then patted her side to make sure that the heavy-duty flashlight that her dad had given all his daughters last Christmas was still zipped into the inside pocket. She would just glance inside and then head back to shore, maybe treat herself to a warm-up shot at the Silver Moon.

The front deck of the party boat was badly tilted, as if one of the supports underneath had given way. She tied up at one of the cleats still attached to the rotting wood and clambered on board, landing on her hands and knees. The back of her kayak swung out again into the water, and she tested the cleat to make sure it wouldn't pull away too. The last thing she needed was to come back from her snooping to find that her boat had drifted halfway to the resort.

The freezing rain was coming down faster now, making the deck slick. She'd hoped the sky would be light enough for her to get by without the flashlight, but while she was out on the water it had gone from an overcast pearly gray to dark as evening. She switched the beam on and cast it over a blue tarp that inadequately covered what looked like a pile of moldy furniture.

The layout was the same as most houseboats: a kitchen and a living room, then a bedroom set off by a half wall. People with kids usually built bunk beds into one side of the living room, but here the wall was stacked with crates and boxes. The blankets that draped the furniture were so tattered it looked like an animal had been at them, and the smell was awful, a scent of decay that hadn't dissipated even in the cold season. There would be a bathroom beyond the bedroom, but she wasn't sure she could bring herself to look.

This had been their destination on the night that Croaker, or Lanny, had driven them into the pylon of the Highway 82 bridge. Natalie wondered what they would have done if they'd made it. It was hard to imagine even a bunch of horny teenagers fooling around in this moldering wreck, but maybe the boat had been in better shape back then. She swept a light over the kitchen counter: pots, plates, rusty silverware, as if someone had gotten up and left in the middle of a meal. Natalie's elbow jostled against something on the counter, and when she looked down, she saw a paper to-go cup from a gas station. It was half full, and the coffee inside wasn't gray and scummed over as she'd expected. She touched the cup with her fingertips, and thought she caught a faint hint of warmth.

The whole boat listed suddenly to the right, and Natalie heard herself cry out as the flashlight clattered to the floor and went dark.

For a few moments she stayed crouched, her arms outstretched, trying to reassure herself that she wasn't about to slide into the cold waters of Lake Monroe. The boat hadn't made any more movements, but from the drumming on the metal roof, the freezing rain was only getting worse, and apart from the coffee, she'd seen no sign that anyone had set foot on the boat in at least a decade.

She dropped to her knees and felt around for the lost flashlight, crawling forward into the kitchen, her eyes squeezing shut involuntarily. When her fingers closed around the cold plastic, she sighed with relief, her fingers flicking the switch even as she clambered to her feet.

She was already heading back to the kitchen when something made her turn to take another look at the blankets tossed over the old furniture. She'd been looking for signs that someone had been living here, and when she hadn't found them, she'd assumed that she'd gotten the whole thing wrong. Now, though, with a closer look, she could tell that the blankets had in fact been placed strategically, the corners neatly aligned. She drew one of them aside and saw a stack of metal tubing beneath it; beneath the next, canvas bags of cracked corn and sugar. She pulled up another blanket, and another: more bags, a thin seam of white spilling out of a split corner. She might not know all the family secrets, but she was enough of a Macready to know what that amount of sugar and corn would be used for.

Natalie thought of her grandfather, who had spurred a federal investigation by selling more sugar in one month than their small rural county could possibly use in a year. Someone must have dumped this here, she thought—someone who didn't want to be found with these supplies on his property. Did it have to do with Hardy's election, and the fear that the new regime might view things differently than Sheriff Shifflett? The party boat must have been a last resort while they figured things out. Hauling all this weight up to the stills in the national forest would take time and organization, a boat and ATVs. She put her finger to the spilled sugar and brought it to her lips, hoping, with that sweetness, to clear the bitter taste in her mouth.

28.

Common sense was enough to tell her that someone had been on the boat recently. Even if she'd been wrong about the heat on the coffee cup, no one would store perishables on a rickety houseboat unless they planned to transport them in the near future. Someone had left the corn and sugar there because they didn't want them on their own property, and because they intended to move them soon, probably via the vast trail network of the national forest. Natalie had never actually visited the stills tucked into the hollows above Hazel Creek Baptist, but given all the stories she'd half listened to over the years, she had a pretty good idea where to find them.

But she wasn't going out there tonight. The freezing rain was coming down harder now, striking the side of her face and trickling down her neck, no matter how hard she tried to keep her head down. She was so focused on getting to the shore and back to her car that it wasn't until she'd thrown the paddle on the sand and pulled the kayak halfway up the bank that she tuned in to the feeling that something was off. The quiet felt wrong, the premature twilight pressing down on her like a weighted blanket. Natalie held her breath. Despite the cold, sweat broke out under her arms and between her shoulder blades. Slowly she tried to sink back into the lake, but suddenly she was blinded, eyes dazzled by a bright light from the bank.

An unsteady voice shouted, "Put the paddle down and your hands above your head."

Natalie wasn't holding a paddle, but she obeyed the second part of the command as she turned toward the voice that she was sure she recognized. Her knees went rubbery with relief. It was Deputy Mike Holliday, who had taken the original report after she'd discovered Ben's body. "Mike?" she called, squinting. "Do you seriously have a gun on me?"

"Natalie Macready?" He gave a long, ragged sigh. "What are you doing out here, girl?"

"Can you not shine that light in my eyes?" she said as she resumed pulling the kayak up the slope. "I'm just trying to get this kayak back in the shed. You want to give me a hand?"

He lowered the flashlight to his hip and jogged down the shore. "You know this is private property," he said, lifting the other end of the boat.

"What are you talking about?" she said. "It's part of the national forest."

He shook his head. "This is dam property. Fence is over there."

She remembered now that Mike moonlighted as a guard at the dam. Leave it to him to be out patrolling on a day like this, when any reasonable person would be hunkered down in their truck with a walkie-talkie. He helped her push her kayak into the musty darkness of the boatshed, but when the door closed, he simply stood there, breathing hard with his hands on his hips. "No disrespect, but what the hell are you up to?"

Natalie's mind raced. She couldn't possibly tell him what she'd been looking for on the abandoned boat, much less what she'd actually found. She knew that Mike had done various odd jobs for her father and Uncle Leo over the years, but she had no idea if his loyalty was more to them or to Hardy, his new boss. When she was unable to think of anything better, she said, "I went to Ben's boat. I left some things there—some jewelry." She pointed to her earrings, a pair of cheap studs.

"I heard something about that," he said. "You and Ben." She waited for him to offer his condolences, but instead he looked away, wiping something wet from the bridge of his nose. "Why don't you come back to the office and get warm?" he said. "I've got to fill out my report, and I can give you a cup of coffee."

She didn't want to go, not at all. She wanted to go back to her parents' house, put on her warmest pair of flannel pajamas, and curl up by the fireplace until she fell asleep. She didn't have any particular reason to distrust Mike Holliday, but she'd never really liked him either. He'd been a grade ahead of Cassie in school, and even in high school he'd been known as a mean drunk, the sort of guy who would park too close to somebody's truck or bump against them in line just so he'd have an excuse to start something. Once, she remembered, his girlfriend had showed up to church with a black eye, which she'd sworn she'd gotten from walking into the wall in the middle of the night.

Mike swept his arm out in front of his body, pointing the way to the TVA truck sitting beside her own car in the gravel lot. The engine was chugging, and now that she was closer, she could see steam rising from the tailpipe.

This was how all the bad stories began, she thought—a young woman getting into the vehicle with a man she didn't know as well as she thought she did—and it was as if she could see herself from the outside as she approached the door of the truck. She was there and not there, looking down at the girl who, in spite of everything she knew, reached for the handle and climbed in.

The TVA dam was so old that it looked futuristic, a giant concrete shell the height of a skyscraper separating the lake at the top from Hazel Creek at the bottom. There was a visitors center at the south end, and tucked away at the back of the building was a metal door that led into a small room with a battered desk, a faded yellow recliner, and a phone with several dozen extensions, some of them flashing. "I thought we'd be in the part with the generators and the turbines," Natalie said as she paused inside the door.

"No, it's just me up here," Mike said, gesturing toward the recliner. "Down in the plant, they've got people coming and going all the time. They want me around to keep an eye on the outside, in case somebody ever decides to cut the fence."

Natalie knew the fence he meant, a tall chain-link barrier that blocked off the state road from the concrete spillways that emptied into Hazel Creek when lake levels got too high. "Has that ever happened?"

"Last time was a couple weeks ago," Mike said. "I doubt they were bad guys, though. Probably just teens looking for a thrill."

Natalie took off her coat and hung it over the back of her chair, watching out of the corner of her eye as Mike leaned over a folding table that held a cheap-looking Mr. Coffee. "Did you know I'm an alcoholic?" he asked without looking at her. He shook grounds into the filter, eyeballing rather than measuring.

"What?" She blinked, and then felt her face grow hot as a blush spread from her collarbones to her cheeks. "Do you mean the kind who doesn't drink anymore?"

"Yeah, that kind," he said, filling the reservoir from a jug of filtered water. "I used to see Ben at AA. Not all the time, but two, maybe three times a month. There's a meeting on Tuesdays in the basement of the Methodist church in Marlborough Springs."

Natalie nodded. "When did he stop going?"

"What do you mean?" Mike pressed the button and sank into the chair across from her.

"People said he was drinking again before he died," she said. "I heard he got so bad at the Silver Moon that he had to be taken home a couple times. He was definitely pretty drunk at the Felons' Ball. Do you have any idea why he started up?"

Mike frowned, his thick eyebrows drawing together. "If he was drinking in those last months before he died, he sure hid it well," he said. "None of us had any idea."

They were quiet as the coffee maker spluttered to a stop. Natalie rubbed her palms on her jeans, warming them. It didn't necessarily surprise her that Ben had managed to hide his drinking from his friends at AA, given that she hadn't known he was drinking either.

Even on their last night together, there had been nothing in the fridge but his usual peach seltzers.

Mike rose and took two mugs from hooks on the wall. He handed her the one emblazoned with the snarling logo of the Ewald County Bears, a thin scum of creamer she hadn't asked for floating on the top. "Are you sure about that?" Mike asked. "I'm surprised, that's all. People fall off the wagon all the time, but Ben didn't seem like the type."

Natalie took a long sip of coffee, barely noticing the cloying taste. "I saw him drinking at the Felons' Ball," she said.

But where, she wondered now, had she first heard that Ben was drinking before the day of the party? She was pretty sure it was from Hardy, when he interviewed her at her parents' house shortly after the murder. Then Uncle Leo had told her that Ben got so drunk at the Silver Moon that he had to ferry him home. But Gus, the bartender at the resort, said Ben had never stopped in there. And Natalie hadn't seen a single bottle in her search of his boat.

"I have to go," she said to Mike, setting her mug on the floor. It wasn't just that she'd been lied to, she thought bitterly. It was that she'd been lied to for so long, so relentlessly, that she couldn't even tell the truth when she saw it anymore.

29.

When Natalie left the dam, she fully intended to drive home, but when she reached the intersection with Southridge Road, she turned left instead of right and kept going. The freezing rain had stopped, and the roads were wet but not slick. A deer peered out at her from the shadow of the trees, their eyes meeting as Natalie passed by.

She'd wanted to know all the secrets, and now she couldn't unhear them. If Ben hadn't been drinking before the Felons' Ball, that meant that Uncle Leo had lied—to her, and to the sheriff. And it meant that whatever had happened to upset Ben enough to fall off the wagon after twelve years of sobriety, it had happened right there, at her parents' house.

She stopped for gas on the other side of Ewald, close to where the bottomland pitched up into the mountains. She was sure she knew the gray-haired, crotchety-looking woman at the register, though she couldn't think of her name. "Getting cold out there," she said, looking up from her crossword as Natalie placed a pack of Twizzlers on the counter. "Going to be Christmas before you know it."

Natalie looked back toward the door. How had it turned from day to night in the thirty seconds she'd spent inside the gas station? A pyramid of six-packs draped in tinsel sat beside the rack of newspapers, and she grabbed one before she could change her mind. "I'll take one of these too."

The old woman rang it up without asking for her ID. "You're Trey Macready's girl, ain't you?"

Natalie nodded and then, realizing that the woman hadn't looked up, cleared her throat and said, "Yes."

She couldn't explain the fear that gripped her then. The old woman met her eyes, and Natalie felt sure that she was going to tell her something she didn't want to know, something awful, but all she said was "You be safe out there." Her attention was back on her crossword before Natalie even made it to the door.

Hardy Underwood lived on the gravel road that curved around the back side of Burns Mountain, in a white clapboard house that looked dingy and run-down in the glow of the safety lights that switched on as soon as Natalie pulled into the driveway. For a minute she stayed in the car, breathing slowly to calm her racing heart. By the time she stepped out onto the gravel, he'd opened the door and was leaning against the doorframe, dressed in his brown sheriff's uniform with the stripe down the side of the pants. "Well now," he said. "To what do I owe this pleasure?"

She held up the six-pack. "Surprise. Can I come in?"

He stood back and ushered her inside. "Hate for you to see the place like this, but I wasn't expecting guests."

Clothes hung from the backs of chairs; ties had been looped around doorknobs. Another uniform was laid out on the back of the couch, and she wondered if he slept there. He'd taken the six-pack from her hands, and when she turned around, he'd popped the tops on two cans and held one out to her. "I'm not complaining, but how did you know where I live?" he asked.

"Luke mentioned it one time," she said, taking a seat on the couch. "I knew there was only one house on this road, so I figured I'd take my chances."

Hardy took a seat beside her, but the couch was so low that his knees came almost to his ears, and after a moment he jumped to his feet again. Natalie glanced around the room, taking in the stuffed bookshelves, the cardboard box full of wrapped presents, the big screen that had probably cost more than all of his furniture combined. "Are you going to see your daughters for Christmas?"

Hardy shook his head, leaning against the frame of the pass-through separating the kitchen from the living room. "Their mother's taking them to Aruba. I'm hoping I can get down to Atlanta for a three-day weekend in January. Depends on the workload around here." He cleared his throat. "So is this a social call, or was there something in particular you wanted to talk about?"

Natalie tried to take a swig of her beer, but it went down wrong and she fell into a coughing fit. Hardy moved beside her again. "Hey, are you okay?" he asked, patting her back clumsily, as if he were burping a baby. "Need some water?"

She shook her head, and then, before she could lose her nerve, she put her head down on his shoulder. He hesitated only a moment before his arms came around her, hands clasping behind her back. She knew she had to do something to stop herself from crying, so she raised her head and kissed him, first on the underside of his chin and then on his mouth.

He drew his head back to look at her. "Natalie, do you know what you're doing?"

"I just can't go home right now," she said, but as soon as the words were out of her mouth, she knew that it was the wrong thing to say. "No, I didn't mean it like that," she insisted as he drew back even farther. "Not like I'm scared to go home. I just need some space. I can sleep on the couch tonight, and I'll be out of here before you wake up in the morning."

"You've been through a lot," Hardy said, patting her shoulder again cautiously. "You don't have to tell me anything you don't want to, but you should probably talk to somebody. Why don't you let me call one of your sisters?"

Natalie shook her head. She leaned forward to kiss him again, on the mouth and then the neck as she straddled his lap. Hardy sighed, his hands moving up under the back of her shirt. "But I don't think we should have sex tonight," she said, pulling away just far enough to look him in the eye. "Not because I don't want to. It's just with every-thing that's been going on . . ."

"I understand," Hardy said, reaching up to tuck a strand of hair behind her ear. "I don't have any expectations."

"And I don't mean we can't do other stuff," she clarified. "Just not sex. I'm not ready for that yet."

He kissed her again, harder this time. "Can I touch you?" he asked, and she nodded as he snaked a hand up under her shirt to run his thumb along the underside of her breast. He moved his hand inside her pants, pushing aside her underwear, and then she could feel his smile widen against her neck when he felt that she was wet. "I knew it," he whispered. "I always knew."

30.

The next morning she slept in until nearly ten, when Hardy woke her with a kiss on the cheek. "You want breakfast?" he asked, sitting so heavily on the side of the bed that she slid across the tilted mattress.

She let herself roll against his hip and smiled up at him. He hadn't pushed for sex last night, but they'd done everything else, and she felt sore in all the right ways. "I think my clothes are still in the living room," she said. "I'm glad you woke me, though. I have to teach in a couple hours."

He didn't smile back. "Your dad called me."

"What the fuck?" Natalie sprang up, clutching the sheet to her chest. "Just now?"

"Last night, after you went to sleep. He said you weren't answering, so your mom checked your location. They just wanted to make sure you were okay."

"Oh my God," she moaned, falling back against the pillows with an angry sigh. "That's so humiliating." Not only did Hardy now know that she still shared her location with her parents—something her mother had insisted on as long as Natalie lived at home—but he also knew that her father felt perfectly free to go over her head and discuss his daughter's private business with any man who happened to be in the vicinity.

Suddenly she noticed the seriousness of Hardy's expression, and her stomach dropped. "Could you get in trouble for this?" she asked.

"I can lie if you want me to. I can say that I showed up drunk, and you had to let me sleep on the couch, and leave out the part about . . ." She gestured at the unmade bed.

Hardy shook his head, reaching out to trace the curve of her face. "I'm not worried about that," he said. "But if we do this again, I want you to know that I have to keep my work and my private life separate. I'm not going to ask you any questions, and I'm not going to answer any questions either. Okay?"

The hard line of his mouth worried her. "Of course we're going to do it again," she said, letting the sheet slip down to her waist.

Hardy exhaled and pulled her toward him, kissing her neck while he reached between her legs. "You're going to make me late," he said, and she smiled as she kissed him back, because that was exactly what she was going to do.

On the way to Kaitlyn's for dinner that evening, Natalie got a feeling on the back of her neck. It wasn't fear exactly. It was the kind of feeling that she used to get in high school and college when she realized that a guy was watching her from across the room. Even before she looked his way, she could feel herself adjusting to his gaze, straightening her spine and moving her shoulders back. It didn't matter if she found him attractive or not. It was the fact of being looked at that made the change in her.

On the shoulder, a digital sign blinked out a warning about flash floods. She should have been paying attention to the road, but she couldn't help glancing back at the white SUV that had been behind her ever since she turned onto the state highway. It looked just like the county-issued vehicle that Sheriff Shifflett had driven, but with the rain obscuring her vision, the figure in the driver's seat was only a dark blur, and she couldn't see the panel on the side where the logo would have been. Of course it could have been any local who happened to drive a Ford Explorer, but there was something both frustrating and titillating about the way it stayed right behind her, refusing to pass even when she slowed to let another driver merge at an intersection. She wasn't sure if it was Hardy driving, but she did feel a little disappointed when the SUV kept straight instead of following her onto the rutted dirt two-track called Bible Camp Road.

Kaitlyn had been campaigning for years to move into town, but Luke said he liked the privacy of living in the country. He liked not having neighbors, and he liked being able to set up targets on the hay bale in the back pasture and shoot his AR-10 at targets he labeled with the names of the guys he didn't like at work. Natalie joined him from time to time, though he always made fun of the little Glock her father had given her for her twenty-first birthday, which Luke called her Barbie gun. "If you ever get in real trouble, you call me," he said. "I'll come take care of it." At the time, Natalie had rolled her eyes, but now she wondered if she'd fallen right back into the familiar family patterns without even meaning to. Here she was, falling for another big tough guy who promised her safety instead of even trying to handle her problems herself.

Kaitlyn answered the door with Anjali in her arms. "Come on in," she said, raising her voice to be heard over the rain pounding on the tin roof. "It's like a damn hurricane out there." Belatedly she covered one of Anjali's ears, and the baby snatched at her fingers.

Cassie was on a blanket on the floor, arranging a set of foam letters to spell Anjali's name. She looked up and flashed Natalie a lips-only half smile. On social media Cassie had perfected a dewy no-makeup look that Natalie knew from experience actually demanded a great deal of time, but today her face was bare, cheeks hollow and pale lips so dry that Natalie could see flakes of skin in the corners. When they'd walked along the lake together, Cassie had been angry, but now she was sad, and it made Natalie try to remember the last time she'd seen her oldest sister like this, shorn of the self-control she wore like armor. It must have been the day after the boat crash, when Cassie had visited her in the hospital and sat on the side of the bed, sobbing into her hands.

Before she could second-guess herself, Natalie got on her knees and wrapped her arms around Cassie. For a second Cassie's arms stayed by her sides, but then she hugged Natalie back. Kaitlyn lowered herself onto the blanket beside them, and Cassie and Natalie disentangled just long enough to incorporate her and Anjali into their embrace. The baby cooed, placing a hand on Natalie's face as if to palm away the tears that streaked her cheeks.

"I'm sorry," Natalie said into Cassie's hair. She paused, knowing that the moment demanded more than those two words but unsure how to go on.

"Me too," Cassie said, wiping her eyes with her knuckles. "I know I've been distant. I was just so unhappy. Now Anj and I are supposed to go back to LA in a week, and I don't know what to do. People keep texting me, asking why Jay isn't showing up for his private sessions."

"Give me your phone," Kaitlyn said, and when Cassie handed it over, she stuck it in the dirt of the potted plant at the end of the couch. "And you're not going back to LA. Fuck that."

"Did I tell you that Uncle Leo said he could get me a job at the Silver Moon?" Cassie said, half laughing. "He said a waitress just quit and they need someone to fill in. It might not be a bad idea, actually. I could definitely use the money." When Kaitlyn wasn't looking, she grabbed the phone and slid it back into her pocket.

"I made out with Hardy Underwood," Natalie blurted. "We didn't have sex, though."

Kaitlyn shrieked and fell on top of her, knocking Natalie to the ground. "I knew it," she gasped. "I knew it as soon as I saw you. Why didn't you do the dirty deed?"

Before Natalie could answer, Kaitlyn peppered her with more questions: was he a good kisser; did he wax his chest and his shaft; how big was his dick, both length and width-wise. Natalie was laughing so hard that tears trickled from her eyes, but the closeness between them still felt fragile, something that might disappear as quickly as it had come. For this moment at least, she felt that she didn't mind being the spoiled brat of the family if she could keep her sisters together like this. "Oh my God, you know I'm not going to tell you about his dick," she said, swatting at her sister's shoulder as their laughter subsided. "But let's just say I have no complaints."

"I knew it. You can just tell by looking at him that he'd be good in bed." Kaitlyn extricated herself from the pile and rose to her feet, grabbing the back of a chair for support. "Sometimes I forget how damn top-heavy I am now," she said. "Come on, I want to show off the nursery. I put the crib together today."

Cassie glanced around the room as she stood, Anjali on her hip. "Did Luke go out to get pizza or something?"

"He's not here," Kaitlyn said over her shoulder as she walked toward the stairs. "I got Thai. We can heat it up after I show you upstairs."

He's not here could have meant *He had to take an extra shift* or *He had to help his mom get her car out of a ditch*, but the fact that Kaitlyn offered no further details made Natalie think it meant something more like *He's driving around drinking a forty and aiming a finger gun at every deer on the shoulder*. Natalie looked back at Cassie to see if she'd caught Kaitlyn's tone too, but she was fixing the strap on Anjali's shoe and didn't look up.

Though the farmhouse was at least a hundred years old, with rough-hewn pine boards and glass knobs on the doors, Kaitlyn had decorated it like a standard starter home, with Target throw pillows decorating hand-me-down couches and overstuffed chairs. On the wall were pictures of windswept sea oats on the Outer Banks that Kaitlyn had taken herself and set in distressed frames that looked like driftwood. An accent wall across from the fireplace was painted light blue, a color that the sisters had chosen together and that Natalie remembered was called Silken Peacock. At least Kaitlyn wasn't the type to mount LIVE LAUGH LOVE plaques or line her puffy-painted wineglasses from sorority mixers along the mantel.

Upstairs, Kaitlyn led them past the closed door to her bedroom to what Natalie knew was the biggest of the three spare bedrooms. As soon as she pushed open the door, Anjali, in her mother's arms, gave a happy shriek. The walls were painted the pale yellow of a baby chick, the furniture white with soft padded bumpers along the rails. A rug in the shape of a rainbow spanned the space between the dresser and the changing table. Even the rain driving through the winter-bare trees outside the window couldn't tarnish the room's brightness, so soothing and peaceful that Natalie felt a sudden urge to curl up on the rainbow and take a nap.

"You did this all by yourself?" Cassie asked, tightening her grip on Anjali, who was trying to throw herself toward the basket of stuffed animals in the corner.

Kaitlyn shrugged. "Mama wanted to take it over, but I didn't want everything top-to-bottom Pottery Barn." She stooped and picked an elephant from the basket to hand to Anjali, who promptly inserted it into her mouth. "There's something else I wanted to show you, though," Kaitlyn said, opening the door again and ushering them across the hall to the little room she used as a study. "I noticed something the other day when I was entering some stuff in QuickBooks. Something that doesn't look right."

QuickBooks was the accounting software they used at the studio. "What do you mean?" Natalie asked, but Kaitlyn had already sat down at the desk and opened her laptop. Natalie and Cassie peered over her shoulder, Anjali happily gumming the elephant's trunk.

"You remember those checks Ben gave you, that he never asked to be repaid?" Kaitlyn turned the laptop so the screen was facing Natalie. "They're all for nine thousand nine hundred and ninety-nine dollars. Every single one. Do you know what that means?"

Natalie shook her head impatiently. "Any gift over ten thousand dollars has to be reported to the government," Kaitlyn explained. "So if you don't want them to look at what you're doing, you keep payments under that amount. It's called structuring."

"Fuck," Natalie said, wishing she'd grabbed a beer from downstairs. She thought back to her conversation with Uncle Leo at Macready's, when he'd told her that Ben had been setting up shady equipment sales and pocketing the profits. Was it possible that Ben had diverted at least some of that money into her studio?

But that story had never really made sense to her. Ben made plenty of money through legitimate means, and he wasn't a particularly flashy guy. She could think of no reason why he would have wanted to steal from Macready's, and if he did, why on earth would he give the money to her?

And there was another possibility, one that made more intuitive sense. Hardy had already suggested that her father and Uncle Leo might be making liquor again. What if they had given Ben the cash and directed him to pass it on to Natalie? She knew her father, and she knew he would have felt no compunction about gifting her dirty money. It might have seemed poetical to him, to see the business that had made their family wealthy in the first place repurposed for this new generation.

"What are you going to do?" Cassie asked, swaying from side to side with Anjali in her arms.

Natalie knew what Cassie expected her to say: she would do nothing. She would look the other way, as their mother had been doing for thirty years. "I'll tell Hardy," she said instead.

Neither of her sisters seemed satisfied with her answer. Cassie changed the subject, asking where Kaitlyn had found her cute shoes, and after a minute or two, they went downstairs and heated up the pad Thai that Kaitlyn had ordered. They talked about holiday plans, and what they would get their parents for Christmas, and the rain. Natalie spoke as little as she could get away with. She'd decided to keep the plan that was coming together in the back of her mind to herself for the time being. It was clear that Cassie believed that Natalie would never stand up to their father, and there was no point in challenging her until Natalie determined whether her dad and Uncle Leo really were making moonshine again.

There was still a slight chance, she thought, that the sugar and corn on the party boat belonged to someone besides her dad and

Uncle Leo. If that was the case, there was nothing to worry about, and she could roll around with Hardy to her heart's content without worrying about what he might be digging up on her family. But before she saw him again, she had to see for herself what was going on in the national forest. Tomorrow, she would go back to Hazel Creek.

31.

The name for it was money laundering. When she was a child, Natalie thought it had to do with putting money through the washing machine to get marks off the bills, and even now the image lingered in her mind of twenties and fifties rushing through the spin cycle, Benjamin Franklin staring damply out through the window in the door. It had never sounded all that bad, especially compared to the crimes that were rumored against her family years ago—the midnight executions, the bodies in the lake wrapped in wire mesh and weighted down with concrete blocks.

If her father and Uncle Leo had started up again, firing the old stills and reconnecting with their old partners at the nip joints in Richmond and Norfolk, that was their business. On the other hand, if they'd had been routing the profits of that business through her studio without telling her, they'd made it *her* business. When Natalie's father told her that rednecks didn't do yoga, she'd quoted back the slogan of the local tourism commission: "Bringing the World to Ewald County and Ewald County to the World." That was what she was going to do, she'd told him. She was going to take the town she grew up in and shake it out of its self-satisfied rural inertia. She was going to bring some goddamn amenities to the county's two thousand, two hundred and twenty-six residents, whether they liked it or not. The thought that he might have helped her not because he believed in what she was doing but because he needed to hide the profits from his bootleg liquor filled her with a near-homicidal rage.

It was three-quarters of a mile from the landing at the Old Creek Road up to the graveyard. Natalie knew the distance because she had hiked up here with her mother at least a dozen times, usually in the spring, when Rosemary roped her into helping out with Decoration Day. Though she never would have admitted it to her parents, Natalie had sort of enjoyed those May walks through a forest just waking up after the long mountain winter—the slight chill in the air, the trillium and pitcher plants peeking up from beneath the carpet of fallen maple leaves. She liked helping the old ladies who came from the resort over the slick rocks in Hazel Creek, and when her mother got caught up in a conversation, she liked taking over Rosemary's spiel, relating the history of the Hazel Creek community and its displacement at the hands of the TVA during World War II. "Isn't your family angry?" the old people sometimes asked, but Natalie always said no, not anymore. The lake had taken from them, she said, parroting her mother, but it had given them just as much. The county's current prosperity was directly traceable to the tourists who came from Charlotte and Knoxville to spend their leisure time on the shores of Lake Monroe, and she was not about to look a gift horse in the mouth.

Today seemed like the inverse of those sunny May afternoons. Everything was wrong—the bare trees and cold gray sky, the smell of snow that would probably fall before night—and over and over she had to persuade herself not to turn around. Would she even be able to find the stills? From years of listening to her father's stories, she had a vague sense of where they were in relation to her great-grandfather's cabin, but it wasn't like he'd drawn her a map.

By the time she passed the old church and reached the clearing that held the cabin, dusk was falling, faster here in the mountains than down by the lake. The dingy gray clapboard siding nearly blended in with the background, but the sharp line of the roof stood out against the sky, a squirrel chittering along the ridgeline. Natalie chided herself for not coming earlier in the day. The last thing she needed was to get stuck out here in the dark.

She passed the springhouse, now little more than a heap of stones.

When she and her sisters were little, they'd made it into a playhouse, she and Kaitlyn taking turns being the teacher and the student while their mother and Cassie tended the graves. The dirt path turned squelchy here, and suddenly, looking down, she went still, her knees bent in a half crouch.

A large footprint in the cold mud. Just one, perfectly preserved from heel to toe.

Natalie looked around sharply, but the clearing was still empty. The footprint could have been days or weeks old, she told herself. It could have belonged to her father, or her uncle, or someone else entirely. The men in her family had big feet that would have fit the print, but so did a lot of other people. The only sure way to know whether her father and Uncle Leo had been coming back to Hazel Creek was to hike up to the stills and see if they were operational, but Natalie glanced again at the sky and decided to revise her plan. If they'd been to the clearing, she reasoned, they'd probably ducked inside the cabin at some point, to drink or get out of the rain. If she found evidence of their presence inside, she'd have the proof she needed to confront them without the nuisance of spending another hour hiking through the freezing woods.

As a child, she'd seen pictures of the couple who had built this cabin—her great-grandfather tall, gaunt, pale-eyed, with the look of a backwoods John Brown; her great-grandmother spare and equally severe, with Rosemary's hard line to her mouth. They'd raised seven children in this cabin, three of whom had died before their eighteenth birthdays. Her great-grandfather had disappeared before the TVA dam was complete, and though some people said he'd gone back to Tennessee to visit his mother, others said that he'd thrown himself into the floodwaters from one of the rocky outcroppings along the shore. It wasn't just that she came from holy rollers, as she'd told Jay; she came from a line of zealots, men who were willing to kill or die if they couldn't make the world what they wanted it to be. The women in their lives must have learned to get along or get out of the way.

She moved closer. If there had ever been a path to the kitchen door, it had grown over long ago. The grass around the front steps had gotten so tall that it had fallen from its own weight. If someone had been visiting the house, they must have gone around to the front door. As she paused, trying to talk herself out of a sudden urge to turn around and go back the way she'd come, she heard it—a crackle from the other side of the house. A beat of quiet, and then it came again.

It didn't sound like an animal. It was too measured, too considered. It had sounded like footsteps, circling the house just beyond the line of the trees. She switched on her flashlight, but the beam caught only the eyes of some small creature that stared back for a split second and then skittered away.

She listened again for the crackle of leaves, but the quiet was so absolute that she began to wonder if she'd ever heard anything at all.

It wasn't Trey or Leo Macready, she knew that for sure. They'd left early that morning in her father's car, heading over to Bristol to check out a deal on a cement mixer. She had nothing to be afraid of. She would stick her head inside, take some pictures on her phone, and then she could leave.

But the front door was padlocked. The lock looked relatively new, unrusted, and she tried to remember if her mother might have snapped it on after the Virginia Board of Historical Preservation denied her request to preserve the old cabin as a tourist attraction. Natalie thought again about bypassing the cabin and following one of the deer paths out of the clearing to hunt for the still, but when she walked around the side of the house, she found that one of the windows in what her mother had called the front room was stuck open. She grabbed the windowsill and pulled herself up until she could brace her elbows on the frame, her feet suspended a few inches above the ground.

What had her life come to, she'd thought, that she'd found herself crawling through windows twice in as many weeks? At first she thought the room was bare, but as her eyes adjusted, she made out a couple of beer bottles on the dusty surface of the desk and a pair of shoes kicked off in the opposite corner. Natalie sucked in her breath. The bottles and shoes weren't historical artifacts, and neither were they detritus left behind by some careless poacher. Someone had been living here, and now she was Goldilocks, the silly girl traipsing in where she had no business.

Then she heard it again—the cautious crackle of leaves behind her in the clearing.

She leveraged her body forward and tumbled into the cabin, jumping up immediately and turning to scan the trees outside the window. She could feel herself sweating now, her breath coming in gasps.

Whoever it was, he knew now that she was here, and she needed a place to hide. Natalie wrenched open the cellar door and gazed down into the black space. The stone cellar steps descended into nothing, the stench of dead animal strong enough to make her retch. She couldn't imagine stepping off into that darkness. She could hear him on the porch now: the hollow sound of boots knocking against the top step, and then a key sliding into the padlock.

She told herself to try the doors to the bedrooms at the end of the hall, but her body felt loose and ungovernable. Maybe, she thought desperately, he'd be surprised at the sight of her, and she could rush past him through the open door. The thought of having a plan made her feel better, and she crouched behind the basement door, poising herself to hit, to run right through him like wind through a screen.

She heard a click, and then his voice. "The safety's off," he said. "I'm not fooling."

Natalie made a dash for the window, but he was on her now, his body forcing hers to the ground. She clawed and struck out wildly, and he pinned both her arms to the floor, the smell of him thick in her nostrils. "Stop fighting me," he said through clenched teeth. "Stop fighting, goddammit, and I'll let you go."

When she ceased struggling, she could hear the breath in her throat, the loud rasp of it. He waited a minute, and then he released her arms and crawled backward, bracing his body against the wall. She closed her eyes until the black spots receded from the corners of her vision. "Croaker," she said.

It had been him from the beginning. He'd smashed her car window, and he'd killed Ben. She could think of no other earthly reason why he'd be hiding out like this, away from everything.

But if he'd come back to get revenge on the Macreadys—the people he believed had ruined his life—he couldn't have meant it when he said he'd let her go. He'd been terrorizing her, and now she'd done the very stupidest thing possible and come straight to him.

He seemed to see on her face what she was thinking, and he huffed out a laugh. "Jesus," he said. "I'm not an ax murderer, no matter what your daddy told you." He looked down at the pistol in his hand, and she could tell just by the way he held it that he wasn't comfortable with guns. "Or any kind of murderer, for that matter."

Her breathing had slowed to a shudder now. There was no possibility of running; he was between her and the door. She was still shaking, her teeth chattering so hard she had to clench her jaw to make them stop. "How long have you been living up here?"

He shrugged. "A couple weeks? I haven't really kept track of time. I camped out near the graveyard at first. Only moved in here when it got cold. I don't mean to be disrespectful or anything—I know this is y'all's family place. I just didn't have anywhere else to go."

She wanted to ask more questions. Curiosity seemed out of place at that moment, when she was still at least a little worried for her life, but it was the uncomfortable feeling of having missed something that was nagging her. The shivering small man across from her in his damp clothes didn't look much like the vengeful killer she'd made him out to be. "Why are you wet?" she asked.

He sighed heavily as he looked down at his wrinkled T-shirt and dirty jeans. "I hiked down to Bluestem Creek to try to catch some trout, and I fell in," he said. "Then I had to walk all the way back. I never was much of a fisherman, but for some reason I thought I'd be better at it now that I really needed to be."

Her eyes fell on the groceries stacked on the table: cans of beans, bagged apples, packets of tuna. No wonder he'd needed some variety, if this was what he'd been living on for weeks. She was about to turn back to him and ask how he'd managed to carry all this up to the cabin when she noticed a light-blue carton half hidden behind a box of Rice Krispies.

Oat milk. Not the generic Kroger brand, but the kind you could only buy at the Harris Teeter in Tyndall. Either he'd broken into their house, or someone had brought it to him.

Natalie could scarcely make a place for the thought in her mind, let alone put it into words. "Has Cassie . . ." She stopped, made herself swallow before she could go on. "Has she been—helping you?"

Croaker's eyes followed hers, and seemed to understand what she'd seen and what it meant. "I was working at the Silver Moon, busing tables and taking out the trash, when she came in for lunch. I thought, *Oh shit, this is it,* but she was real friendly, and then when I got fired, she asked around until she figured out where I was. I came back one day and she was just sitting on one of the gravestones, waiting for me. She said she'd thought about me a lot and she just wanted to see how I was getting on."

"Luke told me you came up to him at Tractor Supply," Natalie said. "When you first got back to town. He said you acted drunk and crazy, like you were out to get us."

Croaker sighed and let his head fall back against the wall. "Yeah, I did see Luke in the parking lot, and he came up to me with his mirrored sunglasses on and poked me in the chest. I don't know what I did that sounded crazy, but I definitely wasn't drunk. It was nine o'clock in the damn morning."

Of course Luke had exaggerated, she thought. Croaker showing up out of the blue must have reinforced his sense that the family was under threat, and that he was the only one who could protect them. "If you're angry at us, I understand," she said. "We all loved Lanny, but it bothered me a lot that you got blamed for what he did." She stopped, unable to explain that the vengeful, desperate Croaker Farber who had been described to her now seemed to be a figment of her family's collective imagination, a bogeyman invented to haunt her teenage nightmares. The man sitting in front of her clearly had no intention of hurting her, and she found it hard to believe that he ever had.

Croaker's face was seamed with dirt, his eyes tired as an old man's. "I just wanted to come home," he said. "After so much time had gone by, I thought it would be okay. But first the police start harassing me for smashing your windshield, and then your uncle got me fired from the Silver Moon. I understand that I fucked up, but I paid my debt to society. I don't know why they won't just leave me alone."

"What do you mean, you paid your debt?" Natalie said, but her voice was so small and weak that she was surprised when Croaker answered. "What do *you* mean, I got blamed for what Lanny did?"

She made herself say it. "He was driving the boat," she said. "Wasn't he? But Daddy and Ben made it look like you did it, because they didn't want Lanny to get in trouble."

Croaker shook his head, but Natalie couldn't look at him, couldn't hear the words he was saying through the blood pounding in her ears. She scanned her memories of that night, blurred and fragmented by the liquor she'd sucked down before they left the resort. She remembered Lanny standing up, telling Croaker he was going to drive, but she'd filled the blanks that followed that moment with assumptions, made up of bits of overheard conversations and her own assessment of probabilities. Lanny had always been the golden child; naturally it followed that he'd been the one behind the wheel, and her father had forced Croaker to take the fall. But what if, as always, she'd seen only what she wanted to see?

32.

It was a relief to find that her mother was the only one home when Natalie returned to the house. Before Rosemary could speak to her, Natalie called out that she needed to change and ran up the stairs, where she peeled off her muddy jeans and sweatshirt and threw them in the hamper. She'd been wrong, again. She'd manufactured a conspiracy out of thin air and convinced herself of its validity. For a moment she allowed herself to hope that the other loose ends she'd been chasing would be explained away just as easily—that Jay would surface again in California or Amsterdam or Madagascar, and Ben's killer would turn out to be a stranger looking to grab money or valuables from a boat he'd assumed was uninhabited. Maybe her father was right about leaving things to the professionals. Maybe, in trying to protect her family, Natalie was only making things worse.

Downstairs, she tried to sneak past the glass-walled study, but Rosemary appeared suddenly in the hall, wiping her hands on her jeans. "I didn't expect you so early," she said. "Don't you teach this afternoon?"

"It's my day off." As Natalie turned to pass, she looked at her mother more closely. "You've got something in your hair," she said, reaching out to pluck the curl of silver ribbon from behind her ear.

Her mother took the ribbon from Natalie's fingers and shook her head. "Remember those cookies I ordered for the reception after the baptism? I thought they were going to come already packaged, but she sent the cookies and the cellophane bags separately. I've been bagging and tying for hours."

All Natalie wanted was to get to her room, but she knew a thinly veiled hint when she heard one. "Maybe we should cancel the baptism," she said. "I don't think Cassie really wants to do it, especially with Jay missing."

"We can't cancel," her mother said in a tone that precluded argument. "It's been in the church program for the past month. Besides, he's not *missing*. Cassie said he just needed a break from all the troubles they'd been dealing with at work."

Natalie shrugged and gave in. "Do you need help?" she asked. "I have a few minutes."

Rosemary had set up an assembly line on her desk: bags on the left, cookies in the middle, rolls of pink and silver ribbon on the right. As always, Natalie found it surprisingly restful to share a task with her mother, the two of them working together in perfect concerted rhythm.

"I'm sorry about the other night," her mother said, deftly winding a strand of ribbon around her little finger and tying it off. "I told your dad not to call Hardy. I knew you'd be mortified, but he didn't listen."

The next cellophane bag was impossible to open, and Natalie picked at the flap with her fingernail, relieved that she didn't have to look at her mother. "I think he's a good man," Rosemary continued. "Make sure you know what you want before you let things go too far. I can tell he'd like to settle down."

"Can you?" Natalie said, reaching for a cookie. "Are you worried that I'll scare him away or that I'll take him for granted?"

Her mother shrugged. "Either," she said. "Both. I just want to see you taken care of, Natalie. That's all a mother wants."

"I know, Mom. Have you actually tried one of these cookies?" Natalie ran her thumb along the scalloped doves set in bas-relief inside a frosted heart. "They don't look like they'd taste very good."

Rosemary made a face. "I imagine they'd taste like toothpaste," she said, in a hushed tone that suggested this was the making of a minor scandal. "Can you believe that I just realized I forgot to mail the Vergottis' invitation? I found it under my datebook when I cleared off the desk. I was afraid there wasn't time to put it in the mail, so I'll go over after we finish and stick it in their box."

Natalie reached for the scissors. "Why do you have to invite the Vergottis? Amanda's just one of our students."

"Yes, but she and Kaitlyn were such good friends in high school, and it seems like they've reconnected. I ran into them last month having lunch at the resort. Now that Amanda and Matt bought that house in Maplewood, I think we should be neighborly."

Natalie laid the bag she'd just finished on the edge of the desk. "Where's the invitation?" she asked. "I don't mind running it over while you finish up here."

"Suit yourself," her mother said. She ran the edge of the scissors along the length of ribbon, the sound like something tearing at the seams.

Natalie parked on the narrow apron of blacktop at the bottom of Amanda's driveway and followed the wide flagstone steps to the front door. Like all the houses on the lake, it was low-roofed and shaded in the front, with garden beds where azaleas and lilies would bloom in the spring. Even before Amanda opened the door, Natalie knew that the living room would open up to a wall of floor-to-ceiling windows. The Vergottis probably had all-white furniture too, the kind that people bought when they had other people to clean up after them.

"Natalie," Amanda said, sounding pleased and embarrassed at the same time. She wore workout clothes, and her long blond hair was piled on top of her head in a messy bun. "Do you want to come in?"

Natalie felt her face grow hot. Of course she wanted to come in, but now it felt as if Amanda's awkwardness had somehow transferred to her. "I just came to give you this," she said, thrusting the envelope in Amanda's direction. "It's for Anjali's baptism. My mom forgot to put it in the mail on time, so I offered to bring it to you."

She was pretty sure she was overexplaining, but Amanda was nodding. "Just let me put this down and I can get us some tea. I was on my Peloton," she continued over her shoulder as she led the way into the living room. "But the class just finished. I've been using it more lately, so I don't have to go outside when it's cold."

Belatedly, Natalie realized that Amanda was apologizing for using her Peloton instead of coming to yoga. She set her purse on one of the chairs at the marble bar. The room was exactly what she'd expected, like an issue of *Southern Living* come to life—a white couch, of course, and a glass-walled coffee table; lots of plants; exposed beams, dark against the white ceiling. In the room to the left, she could see the Peloton, a pink towel monogrammed with the initials *AMV* draped over the handlebars.

Amanda gave her a quick smile as she filled the kettle. "I'm so glad you stopped by," she said. "I admire what you're doing so much. Matt and I were living in Richmond when he got the job down here, and I thought, *God, what am I going to do with myself back in Ewald?* I was still picturing downtown the way it was when we were kids, with nothing but a Family Dollar and the IGA."

"It's changed a lot," Natalie agreed. "How are you feeling these days? I've been thinking about you after what happened in class," she said.

It wasn't really true, of course. With everything that had happened in the past few weeks, she'd given hardly a thought to Amanda Vergotti, but the sympathy seemed to do the job and thaw Amanda's polite reticence. "Ugh, I'm still so embarrassed," she said, her shoulders slumping. "I know it's just a medical issue. It's not anything I have control over. But what a mess." She waved her hand through the air, erasing the words as if she'd used up her allowance of self-pity. "Anyway, it's not important. I know what your family is going through right now."

"It's been a hard couple of weeks," Natalie admitted, but she didn't know where to go from there. She wondered if Cassie might be right after all about her neglecting the self-reflective side of yoga, the part that might have taught her to confide in people and get them to confide in her.

The door to the Peloton room was open, and Natalie found herself drawing closer, admiring the sleek curves of the twenty-five-hundred-dollar bike. On the screen, a guy with his arms raised above his head was frozen mid–fist pump. The blackout shades were drawn, obscuring the sunny day outside. "That's not really why I came, though," Natalie said, turning to face Amanda again. "Kaitlyn mentioned to me that y'all had been hanging out again, and I thought that was so great, because she definitely needs more friends around here. Luke is fine, but he's not the kind of guy who's going to sit around and have deep conversations."

Amanda was pouring hot water into two large handcrafted mugs, but now she took a deep breath and placed the kettle back on the stove. "Kaitlyn told you that we're hanging out?"

She sounded skeptical, even suspicious. "She told me you were playing tennis," Natalie said, trying to infuse her voice with certainty, wondering at the same time if she might have gotten the details wrong.

Amanda picked up the kettle again and filled the mugs, pouring the water so high that it almost overflowed. It seemed that for some reason even the mention of Kaitlyn had put her on her guard, and Natalie felt a line of sweat beading between her shoulder blades.

"If you're worried about Kaitlyn, you should probably talk to her directly," Amanda said. "I don't want to be a go-between."

"That's fair," Natalie said, wishing she could run out the door without another word. "I'm sorry if I said something that offended you. It's just that I heard this rumor that was so crazy. I know it's none of my business and you can tell me to fuck off, but are you and Kaitlyn . . ."

Amanda leaned against the counter and crossed her arms over her chest, as if she'd changed her mind about offering Natalie tea. "Are me and Kaitlyn what?"

Natalie exhaled. "On the night of the boat crash, I remember seeing you rolling in the sand. You were always whispering and touching each other. Then recently some people said that maybe you were in a relationship or something."

She wanted to make it clear from her tone that it didn't bother her. If Kaitlyn left her husband for Amanda Vergotti, it would certainly be a scandal, but Natalie would back them all the way. She knew as well as anybody how easy it might be to stumble into a kiss, and then into bed, with someone who was supposed to be off-limits. But Amanda was looking at her as if she had two heads.

"Who . . . ," she began, and then waved it away with that familiar flick of the hand. "Never mind, I don't want to know." She handed Natalie her mug after all, and gestured toward the living room. "Do you want to sit down?"

Natalie perched on the edge of the white couch and looked around for a coaster. She was afraid to put the hot mug on the glass table without one, so she held it on her knee, letting it scald her skin through her jeans. The mild pain felt good.

"Did you know that I'm an only child?" Amanda cupped her own mug in her palm. "I used to look at y'all and wish I was the fourth Macready sister. I thought it would be so great, staying up eating popcorn and telling secrets. The three of you look so pretty when you're together, so much alike. But you're really not that close, are you?"

"Sometimes," Natalie said. "We used to be." She had never tried to tie down the point in time when her relationship with Cassie and Kaitlyn had changed, but looking back now, it seemed obvious. It was the boat crash. Before that, they didn't always get along, but they were a unit. The differences between them were symbiotic, drawing them closer rather than detaching them from each other. It wasn't like that anymore. Their embrace at Kaitlyn's house had been only an echo, a pale reminder of what they'd lost back then.

Amanda looped the string of her tea bag around her finger. "I know you care about Kaitlyn," she said, her voice kinder than Natalie had expected. "But Natalie, you can't just show up at somebody's house and ask if they're cheating on their husband. Seriously, what is wrong with you?"

33.

Maybe that was the real question that should have compelled Natalie's search through her family's past—not *Who killed Ben Marsh?* but *What is wrong with me?* In the aftermath of her visit to the Vergottis, humiliation moved through her, flushing every part of her body with scalding heat as she remembered how Amanda had looked at her. Natalie had gotten everything wrong. She had tried to prove to her family, and most of all to herself, that she was no longer the naive child they took her for, but she'd ended up proving the opposite.

She tried not to think about it. She slept over at Hardy's house for the next two nights, and that Saturday her mother invited him over for dinner. It was unusually warm, in the high sixties, and they sat out on the deck, where the catering tables had been set up on the day of the Felons' Ball. Her mother made roast beef and chess pie, and her father was at his most charming, his childhood stories about smoking rolled-up tobacco leaves and the one time he'd tried to drive a stock car punctuated by Hardy's rumbling laugh. Hardy kept his left arm hooked around Natalie's shoulders while he ate, and she caught her mother smiling with approval.

She didn't tell Hardy about what she'd seen on the party boat, or the evidence of money laundering that Kaitlyn had found while going through their accounts, or her conversation with Croaker Farber. For his part, Hardy kept his pledge not to talk about the investigations into Ben's death and Jay's disappearance, and she didn't ask. Jay's social media stayed dormant. Natalie heard from Luke that they'd gotten access to Jay's bank records, and his debit and credit cards hadn't been used since the day he went missing. She had a dream where she went back to Hazel Creek, and he was living in the cabin with Croaker, roasting trout in a cast-iron pan over a hobo fire. When Natalie asked what in the world he was doing, Jay shrugged and said, "I can see the stars out here."

She drank most of a bottle of wine at the dinner with her parents, and she didn't feel it when Hardy got out of bed the next morning. When she woke, the space beside her was empty, and when she called out his name, it came back with that peculiar echo that denotes an empty house.

Her phone buzzed on the bedside table, and she jumped, remembering the morning she'd woken on Ben's houseboat to find that Luke had texted to tell her that Croaker was back in town. She no longer believed that Croaker had played any role in Ben's murder, but it still seemed that that text had been the start of something.

But it wasn't her phone. It was Hardy's—his personal phone rather than the department-issued cell that, if he was anything like Luke, he kept on him at all times. The notification on the screen read *Mike Holliday*: one text, one missed call. She picked up the phone and tried to open it, but of course he had a passcode.

Natalie had never even tried to snoop through Hardy's things—in the weeks they'd been seeing each other, she hadn't so much as peeked in the medicine cabinet—but then again, Hardy had never left her alone before. She knew his birthday, she realized, and before she could second-guess herself, typed in *111984*. To her surprise, the screen rolled up and the apps appeared. Holding her breath, she clicked on the text icon.

The text from Mike simply read, *Hey call me back*. The next two threads were with Bella and Christina, who must have been the daughters. Buried farther down was the ex-wife, Angie. They communicated about child support and Bella's horse-riding lessons. Luke was on there; unsurprisingly, they seemed to talk mostly about football and microbrews. There were no texts from her father or Uncle Leo, and none from other women. She was about to close it out, both disappointed and relieved, when the phone buzzed again, and a second text came through from Mike. *Boss you on your way to the marina?* she read. *The divers are here.* Immediately, three dots appeared below the message. *Make sure you got your mittens, it's a cold one out there.*

She had no idea what Mike was talking about, or why he'd want Hardy to wear mittens, but the three odd texts in quick succession had unnerved her in a way she couldn't explain. On the way to the studio, she turned on Jay and Cassie's podcast, hoping that the relaxed tones of Jay's familiar voice would calm her. She kept it turned on while she dialed her father's number.

"Domino's Pizza," he said—his accustomed greeting, which usually made Natalie sigh and roll her eyes, but she didn't have time for that today.

"Daddy," she said, and told him what she'd seen on Hardy's phone.

"The marina?" he repeated, his voice sharp now, businesslike. "He didn't say what they're doing?"

"No," she said. "Don't let him know I told you."

"I've got to call Luke." He hung up before she could say more, and Natalie bit her lip in frustration.

She didn't realize that she'd accidentally pressed fast-forward on the podcast until the audio kicked in on Cassie in the middle of a sentence. ". . . trauma response because of what happened when I was seventeen. My sympathetic nervous system was completely dysregulated, and yoga helped me learn to . . ."

Natalie hit pause and looked down at her phone, reading the title of the episode. *Episode 86: On the Vagus Nerve and How Yoga Can Help Us Heal from Emotional Trauma.* She clicked back thirty seconds and listened to the whole sentence. *I was in a constant state of trauma response because of what happened when I was seventeen.* She went back even farther, but no context was provided, and they went on to talk about the nerve centers and how yoga and breathwork helped the body unlearn conditioned responses—something she might have been interested in under other circumstances but couldn't begin to pay attention to now.

Natalie didn't realize she'd put on the brakes until the car came to a stop, a driver passing in the southbound lane turning to flip her the middle finger. Her hands were trembling on the steering wheel as she shifted into gear again. Cassie was talking about the fascia and the psoas muscle, and Natalie slammed the palm of her hand against the volume button until she stopped midsentence. At the bottom of the mountain, Natalie turned left instead of right, heading for the Silver Moon.

34.

'm here to see my sister," she told the hostess, who looked confused until Natalie pointed at Cassie keying in an order by the bar. At that moment Cassie looked up, one of her rare, sweet smiles illuminating her face, and Natalie wished she was there for any reason in the world—to talk about Anjali's baptism, or what they were going to do for Christmas, or even Jay's untouched bank account—rather than what she had really come for.

Natalie crossed to the bar, and Cassie gave her a side hug, leaning her head briefly on her sister's shoulder. "I'm just about to go on break," she said. "Let me take this order by the window, and then we can head out to the deck. Do you want anything? Coffee?"

"Coffee would be great," Natalie said, and Cassie filled a white ceramic mug from the pot behind the counter before bustling over to the window, where a gray-haired couple she didn't recognize was bent over the menu as if it were the Dead Sea Scrolls. As Cassie approached, their faces lit up with a wintry sunshine that Natalie knew was really her sister's reflected glow.

At ten thirty, the place was empty except for the older couple and a single man on the deck, nursing a Bloody Mary and peering out at the lake through a set of binoculars. Natalie sipped at her coffee and wondered if there was still time for her to sneak out the side door.

She didn't realize that Cassie had come up behind her until her sister tugged on her ponytail. "So where have you been for the last few days?" she asked, leaning her elbows on the bar beside Natalie.

"What?" Cassie's words were so far from what had been on Natalie's mind that for a moment she couldn't make sense of the difference.

"Oh, come on." Cassie bumped Natalie's chair with her hip. "I've never been into cops personally, but you could do worse. Hey, could you pick Anj up from day care today? My shift's until four, and I can't get ahold of Mama."

"Of course." Natalie took a long sip of coffee. "Can you go outside?" she asked, nodding to the double push doors that led out to the deck. She knew that Cassie probably assumed that she wanted privacy, and that was true enough, even if it was for a different reason than she ever would have suspected.

"Let me grab my coat," Cassie said, turning toward the office. "I've got a scarf for you if you want it. I think it's snowing a little bit out there."

On the deck, Cassie sketched a wave at the lone man with the binoculars, who called, "Hey Cass, can I get another one of these?" as he shook the ice in his glass.

"I'm on break, Ray," Cassie yelled over her shoulder as she led Natalie around the side. "You'll have to wait fifteen minutes or go in there and make it yourself."

They leaned against the wall by the kitchen door. The deck was narrow here, barely wide enough for two people to pass, and clearly frequented by the kitchen staff, with a full ashtray balanced on the rail beside a few empty bottles of Peroni. "Feel free," Cassie said, gesturing to the ashtray. "I won't judge."

To Natalie's surprise, she believed her. It didn't really make sense, but Cassie seemed to have relaxed since Jay went missing. Her accent was back, the faintly nasal mountain twang she'd always seemed to be repressing when Natalie visited her in California, and she seemed more at ease in her body, abandoning the rigid ballerina poise she'd maintained in and out of the studio. "What's the deal with the guy back there?" Natalie asked as she pulled her cigarettes from the pocket of her coat. "I didn't see any birds. Is he a peeping Tom or something?"

"Ray?" Cassie said. "He heard over the police radio that there's something going on at the lake today. That's why he has the binoculars."

"What do you mean, something's going on?"

Cassie shrugged. "I thought maybe it was a training thing."

That would explain Hardy's absence that morning, though not why he hadn't warned her ahead of time. "Do you think you're going to stay in this job?" Natalie said, studying the cigarette in her hands without taking a drag. "You could always come back to the studio."

But Cassie shook her head. "I'm done with that," she said. "I mean, I'm not going to waitress forever. I had that job at the magazine in LA before I met Jay. I'd like to look for something like that again."

"I'm really glad you're happier now," Natalie said, ignoring Cassie's skeptical look at the unexpected sentimentality. "Are you still mad at me? I was telling the truth when I said nothing happened between me and Jay, but I know we were probably spending too much time together. I was so confused after what happened to Ben."

"I know." Cassie plucked the cigarette from Natalie's hand and took a long drag. "I realized I didn't have any right to be mad about it," she said on an exhale, "because I'd done the same thing."

For a moment, Natalie didn't get it. "Luke," she said finally. "Wait, really? Did you sleep with him?"

Cassie made a face. "It was a onetime thing, when I came home a couple of summers ago."

"Are you *serious*?" Natalie yelped, her voice rising in spite of her best intentions. "Jesus, Cassie. Does Kaitlyn know?"

"No," Cassie insisted. "There's no reason she has to know. It was literally just a dumb drunken mistake. But Luke's been a real asshole since I came home. He keeps threatening to tell her."

How the past stayed with them, Natalie thought. Even Luke, the most practical and hardheaded of any of them, had stayed so laser-focused on getting the girl he'd mooned over back in high school that he'd been unable to adjust to the real life he'd built with Kaitlyn. Maybe for him, as for her, it had all started with the boat crash, the trauma of that night and Lanny's subsequent flight from Lake

Monroe keeping them stuck in their adolescence like mice in a glue trap.

At least, Natalie thought, she knew now that she wasn't the only terrible person in the family. She might have thought about sleeping with her sister's husband, but Cassie had actually done it.

And that wasn't all Cassie had done. "I ran into Croaker up at the cabin," Natalie said. "I'm sorry I didn't tell you earlier, but I didn't know what to do. He told me you've been helping him."

Cassie said nothing, letting her head fall back against the wall. She looked stunned, and Natalie could see that it had never occurred to her that her family might find out. "Did you tell Mama and Daddy?"

"No, of course not." Natalie felt a pricking between her fingers, as if she'd been stuck with a tiny needle, and looked down to see that her cigarette had burned all the way down to the filter. She tossed it into the lake and turned back to Cassie. "I thought all this time that it was really Lanny driving. That everyone had lied so he wouldn't get into trouble. If it really was Croaker who was driving, why were you always so uncomfortable when Lanny's name came up? Did something happen between the two of you?"

Cassie put her hands over her face, digging her thumbs into her eyelids. "Do you remember at the bonfire at the resort, when I sat down with you? I put my drink down while we were talking. Lanny had given it to me, but it had a weird taste, so I didn't finish it." She lowered her hands. "I didn't realize it until later, but you must have thought that it was yours."

Natalie felt as if something cold and heavy had settled in her gut. She could see the red Solo cup in her hand, feel her throat moving as she chugged it down, hoping to get drunk enough to forget about Lanny and her abandoned plans for the night. It had tasted strange to her too, but she'd chalked it up to the moonshine, which she'd always expected to taste horrible.

"At the hospital, they did blood tests," Cassie said. "He'd drugged you. Mama made me promise not to tell."

Natalie grabbed her sister and hugged her so tight that she could feel her lungs constrict. "It's okay," she whispered. They had been raised to keep secrets, and how could Cassie—as broken as Natalie herself by the events of that night—deliberately defy their parents? "But what happened to Lanny?" she asked, pulling back. "Did they do something to him?"

Cassie shook her head. "He was there for Thanksgiving, and then the next day, he just wasn't. I honestly didn't question it when they said he'd left town. He'd talked about leaving for years, and then I never heard Daddy say a bad word about him. It was like Lanny was the son he'd never had. When I was older, I did a couple Google searches for his name and could never come up with anything, and that made me wonder. But I didn't have any proof." She checked her watch and sighed. "Shit. I better get back to work. Can we talk about this later?"

"Of course," Natalie said. "I'm not going anywhere."

Cassie grabbed her hand and squeezed, and they kept their fingers laced as they came around the corner to the outside seating area. Ray was still there, watching a fleet of Virginia Marine Police boats that had appeared in the middle distance. Even without binoculars, Natalie could make out Hardy standing up in one of the first boats, directing a man who had just dropped a long hook into the water. "What are they doing?" Cassie asked, forehead creasing as she frowned into the sun.

Natalie had to swallow before she could speak. "I think they're dragging the lake."

35.

She had seen the same thing once over by the marina. That time a tourist had hit the dock on his Jet Ski, catapulting himself into the air and then into the water. He didn't come up, and within an hour, both the Virginia Marine Police and a group of local boaters were on the water, pulling grappling hooks along the lake bottom. Natalie and Kaitlyn had happened to be eating lunch at the resort that afternoon, and they'd ordered another round of drinks so they'd have an excuse to linger on the deck, watching the boats move methodically back and forth until one of the men gave a shout and raised his arms above his head. He'd found something, and it was heavy enough that he couldn't pull it up by himself.

This was different. Natalie knew that dragging the full expanse of a lake as big as Monroe wasn't feasible. The process only made sense if you had a pretty good idea of where the body was, and if the water was shallow enough to sound the bottom.

"Thanks for the heads-up this morning," her father said. "I still can't believe they didn't even ask. I'm not going to say no to the sheriff, but just as a matter of courtesy, you'd think they'd call me up and tell me they were on their way."

Natalie had expected to find him in the house, glowering out through the plateglass windows in her mother's room, but he was down at the dock, getting his boat on the lift. He put the boat in dry dock every year on the second Sunday in December, and he wasn't going to change his plans just because the police had decided to drag the lake. "You staying for dinner?" he asked, not looking at her. "Run inside and tell your mama so she'll set enough plates."

"I don't think so," she said. She sat down and swung her legs over the side of the dock, watching as he winched the carabiners to the pulleys. How many times had she watched her father take a boat out of the water for the winter? It was as much a part of their routine as Christmas shopping and decorating the tree.

A quarter of a mile away, she could see Hardy in a VMP boat, directing the dragging operation. They had started at the mouth of the cove and would move in toward the Macreadys' place until the water got too shallow. In different circumstances, her father would have been right out there with him, but she could tell that he resented Hardy's lack of deference too much to acknowledge their presence, much less participate.

"Daddy, I need to know what's going on," she said. "Have you and Uncle Leo been brewing again? Does that have something to do with Ben's murder?"

Her father was still looking out at the lake, and from his expression, she couldn't even tell if he was listening anymore. "Honey, you don't need to worry about anything like that."

She felt more frustrated than ever. "Tell me the truth, and I'll believe you, but don't keep putting me off with bullshit. Why is Uncle Leo always traveling? Is he trying to build up your network again?"

"That's a nice little conspiracy you've worked out," her father said, pulling a cigar from his pocket. "Uncle Leo leaves town to meet people. People he couldn't meet here. Do I have to spell it out for you?"

"What do you mean?" she asked, but then, suddenly, she thought she understood. "Do you mean *men*?" Uncle Leo's secretiveness, his evasiveness—could it really have such a simple explanation? "But Uncle Leo always dated women," she said. "I've seen the pictures."

"Lord Jesus, he sure did," her father said. "I used to be so jealous of the girls he brought home. He'd meet them at cocktail bars and offer them a hundred dollars to come for dinner with our parents. I don't think he ever fooled anybody, though."

She should have apologized then. She could tell that it was what he wanted, but she couldn't bring herself to give up the righteous anger that filled her then. "Why do you have to keep secrets from us?" she said, crossing her arms. "Even about Uncle Leo—why did you think you couldn't tell me something like that? It's like you think I need to be protected from every part of grown-up life."

She'd passed up the opportunity to make things easy between them, and now he was angry. "For Christ's sake, look at the decisions you make, Natalie," he said. "Do you even know how much money I paid out to keep your studio afloat?"

The wind was full in their faces now, and for a moment she wondered if she'd heard him correctly. "It was you?" she said, her voice barely audible even to her own ears. "But it looked like money laundering," she said. "Kaitlyn went back through the accounts, and all the checks were just under ten thousand dollars. Why would you do that?"

Her father rubbed at his chin. "If it had been over ten thousand dollars, I would have had to fill out a gift letter, and you would have found out where it came from," he said. "It never occurred to me that someone would be going through this stuff with a fine-tooth comb. Believe me, I've had more than my share of conversations with Hardy Underwood over the past few months."

Natalie could feel a headache coming on. She'd proved her loyalty to him in every way she could, and it still wasn't enough. "I saw his body, Daddy," she said, her voice cracking in spite of her best efforts. "I walked through his blood. I just want to know who did it."

"I don't know," her father said, but there was something in his eyes—a flicker that she recognized. They were so much alike, he'd always said, in both their good points and their flaws. She'd always been able to read him, and what she saw now was that he was afraid.

36.

She stayed out after her father left, fetching the binoculars from the boathouse and walking far down the beach to get a better look at the operation down by the marina. A crowd had gathered at the Silver Moon, watching a group of men in orange vests waiting on the lakeshore, some of them mumbling into radios. A truck rumbled on the sand, and chains ran from the trailer on the back down to below the surface of the lake. A reporter stood at the edge of the beach, holding a microphone close to her lips as she gestured to the scene behind her.

The snow had stopped and the sun had come out, but the air stayed cold. The bartender served sandwiches on a buffet table. People rotated in and out, sitting for a few minutes over a sandwich or a cup of coffee and then going back to the bar. Natalie watched Cassie come out every fifteen minutes or so, taking drink orders and emptying ashtrays, and even from a distance, she could tell that Cassie was trying not to look toward the lake.

Then two divers emerged from the water and swam toward the Virginia Marine Police boat at the mouth of the cove. One of them gave a thumbs-up to the men on the shore.

With a loud grinding noise, the chains grew taut. The truck roared, and now she could see something moving under the surface of the water, bubbles rising from the disturbance below. The people at the marina were cheering. It was like a party, Natalie thought—like the Felons' Ball in miniature. All they needed was Trey Macready standing at the forefront of the crowd. But her father was nowhere to be found.

Natalie moved all the way to the end of the dock. Her heart was in her throat. She had never understood what that expression meant, but now she got it; it felt as if her esophagus was blocked, a solid muscle filling up that space where her breath should have been. Her hands tightened on the wooden rail. It felt flimsier than it should have, and suddenly she found herself imagining the whole deck giving way, plunging into the dark, frigid water.

The hood appeared, like the head of a sea monster surfacing. At first so much water streamed from the grille and under the hood that it was hard to even make out the color, but Natalie could tell that it was dark, black or navy blue. It wasn't Jay's silver Honda, and she gave a sigh of relief before closing her eyes and praying that it belonged to some long-ago bootlegger who had driven into the lake back in the days when Ewald County was the moonshine capital of the world. The more of it emerged, the more confident she felt: this car had been underwater for years, if not longer.

She could see the whole shape now. The style was at least thirty years old, with a spoiler and a long, low hood clearly modeled on a sports car. The crowd on the deck had gone nearly silent, but none of them were as rapt as she was, watching with single-pointed attention as the car was hauled onto the trailer. She stared hard at the driver's side, searching for any signs of shifting weight behind the glass, but the curtain of underwater plants covering the windows made it impossible to see anything inside.

For a moment, Natalie felt as if her knees were going to buckle. As the car settled onto the bed of the trailer, water still streaming from every seam in its body, she felt certain that despite the grime and rust, she knew its shape, its outline and color. She had seen it not too long ago in photos, with a grinning Lanny Marsh leaning against the driver's door.

37.

She had to know. Later she might be willing to listen to explanations, but before she talked to either of her parents, she had to know for sure if she'd guessed right.

She let herself in the side door, relieved to find that the living room and kitchen were empty, as was her mother's glass-sided study. A white cashmere throw lay folded on the chaise longue, a cozy mystery splayed in the middle.

Natalie went to the ornate chest of drawers and opened the first drawer, then the second, rummaging for the photo album they'd given her father for his birthday. It wasn't where she remembered it, on top of the box of thank-you cards printed with Monet water lilies that her mother had ordered from the Metropolitan Museum of Art. She slammed the second drawer shut with the heel of her hand and opened the third one, kneeling now on the cold floor, her hands starting to sweat.

"Back from your love nest?"

Her mother leaned against the doorway, impeccably dressed in a pale-pink angora sweater and winter-white wool slacks over ankle boots. She was wearing her jewelry too, the diamond earrings and pendant that she only took off to sleep. Her voice was cold, but Natalie thought she detected a note of uncertainty, perhaps even of fear.

The red photo album rested on top of a pile of books in the bottom drawer. Natalie took it out and opened to the pages where Rosemary had replaced the pictures of Lanny with baby pictures of Natalie and her sisters. "I saw the look on Ben's face when Daddy was showing him the album," she said. "I didn't know what to make of it at first, but then I realized that he'd seen something. Something that had to do with Lanny."

Her mother crossed her arms over her chest. "Ben stole the pictures," he said. "The night of the Felons' Ball. He sneaked in here and took them right out of the album while we were all at the tournament. I didn't know a thing about it until he called me later that night. He was still drunk as Cooter Brown. The only thing I could make out was that he'd found the picture of Lanny on Thanksgiving."

"But why was he so upset?" Natalie said, already afraid she might not want to know the answer. "What did that matter?"

Rosemary sighed and perched on the edge of the chaise longue. "Ben was in rehab when Lanny left town," she said. "It was his third or fourth stay at this facility down in North Carolina, and when he was gone, Lanny would make do on his own. Since it was Thanksgiving, your father invited him to stay with us, and he couldn't figure out why Cassie was so upset about it. Then we got the blood tests. I wanted to go to the police, but your daddy told me he had a plan, to just leave the whole thing to him, so I did. When Ben came back from wherever it is he'd been, your daddy told him that we woke up on Thanksgiving morning and Lanny was gone. I forgot all about those old pictures. I threw them in the box with a million other old photos, and I never dreamed that Kaitlyn would pull them out."

"I don't understand." Natalie's face felt numb, with cold or shock. "Why didn't you just say he left the day after Thanksgiving?"

"Do you remember the rain that week?" her mother said. "You were in the hospital, so you might not have been paying attention, but we got nearly twelve inches in twenty-four hours. Lanny couldn't have left on the day after Thanksgiving, because the roads were bottomed out. His little car never would have made it."

Her mother looked up, their eyes meeting, and Natalie wondered how it was possible she'd never noticed how clear they were—a pure unadulterated blue, like snowmelt.

"What about the postcards?" Natalie said. "Ben got those from Lanny for years. I saw them."

Rosemary shrugged, as if small details like these hardly mattered. "Well, Leo could have written those," she said. "He's wonderful with imitating handwriting. Back in high school, he was always forging your grandfather's signature on notes to get out of class. But I'm only guessing—I don't really know what happened to Lanny. That's the honest truth, Natalie. I never asked."

"You're lying."

For the first time, her mother looked surprised. "Did I assume that your father had killed Lanny? Of course I did, but I didn't know the details. I just knew that we had to get those pictures back from Ben. Your father was already sleeping, so I had to go myself. And he was very upset," she said, her voice measured. "He kept saying that he had to do the right thing once in his life, for Lanny. When I told him what Lanny had done to you that night, it was as if he didn't hear me. He went on and on about setting things right. He said he was going to go straight down to the sheriff's department the next day and show him the photos that proved we'd lied."

"But it was twelve years ago," Natalie protested. "He didn't have any real proof. Daddy could have said he'd gotten the date wrong, or blamed the cop who took the report."

Her mother's eyes flashed in a way that made her want to back quietly out of the room. "For goodness's sake, Natalie, I wasn't playing the goddamn lottery," she snapped. "For all I knew, Hardy Underwood would have at least taken him seriously enough to open an investigation, and then what? I just couldn't risk it."

Natalie looked away. The longer she listened to her mother, the more likely she'd be to see her point of view, and she couldn't let herself do that. She'd been the one to find Ben lying there, soaked in his own blood; she'd taken his hand, clammy and rubbery at the same time.

"They found Lanny's car," she said. "They just pulled it out of the lake. Is his body inside?"

Her mother sighed. "I don't think so," she said. "I truly don't know the details, but your father told me once that Lanny would never be found. I don't think he would have said that if he'd put the body in the lake." She stood up, rolling her shoulders back. "Excuse me, sweetheart. I have to call your father, and then I'll have to talk to Mr. Singletary."

"Why do you need to talk to a lawyer?"

"Well, I don't know what your father will want to do," her mother said. "What happened to Ben has been weighing on him quite a bit. He may decide that the best thing to do is for us to come clean."

"What?" Natalie leaped to her feet. "Mama, he can't make that kind of decision for you."

Her mother smiled bleakly. "It doesn't sit lightly on a person, killing someone you've known for forty years. Besides, prison didn't seem so bad for Martha Stewart."

"How can you sit here and make jokes at a time like this?" Natalie could hear her voice cracking, and to keep herself from breaking into tears, she made herself talk louder. "For fuck's sake. You killed someone. Martha Stewart was in jail for insider trading, not murder."

"Don't you cuss at me, Natalie Rose." The veins in her mother's neck appeared, tight as violin strings. "And lower your voice, please."

"Jesus, Mama—" Natalie began again, but then her watch beeped. It was three fifteen, and the You Are My Sunshine day care closed at three thirty. "You don't know what you're talking about," she said. "You only did what you did to protect Daddy. You don't need to martyr yourself just to ease his conscience."

Her mother shook her head, smiling. "Your father gave me everything," she said. "What kind of person would I be if I wasn't willing to give everything in return?"

38.

Natalie parked at the curb in front of the day care, pausing a minute to draw on her gloves and cinch her hood tight around her face. She hadn't been able to reach Kaitlyn or Cassie on the phone, but she'd left messages that she hoped underlined the urgency of the situation. She needed her sisters to help her make sense of this. Their mother had bowed her head while her husband said a prayer for the repose of Ben Marsh's soul, all the time having the vision in her mind of blood blooming from Ben's chest, blood on the floor of the boat, blood on her smooth white hands. Someone had once given Rosemary a novelty tea towel that read "Love Is Knowing Where the Bodies Are Buried," and apparently, in their family, that was more than a joke.

Cindy had gone all out decorating for Christmas, and between the plastic holly wreath and the paper bells taped to the door, it was hard to find a place to knock. Natalie waited a minute and then rapped again, smiling in spite of herself as she listened to the babble of voices inside. She could already feel Anjali's warm, solid weight in her arms. She craved her niece's presence, which would remind her that the Macreadys had produced at least one good thing.

The door was opened by a teenage girl Natalie had never seen before, wearing a men's burgundy sweater and carrying a toddler in her arms. The toddler, a round-faced little boy in overalls and a knit hat with bear ears, wrapped his fist in the girl's sweater and stared up at Natalie with his mouth open. Natalie tried to put on a pleasant face for his sake. "Hi, I'm Natalie Macready," she said. "I'm here to pick up my niece, Anjali."

The girl looked hesitant. "Come in," she said, stepping back from the doorway. "I'll go get Cindy."

Natalie stamped her cold feet on the mat. In what had originally been the living room, a group of four preschool-age children sat on a rag rug, looking up at her as if they'd been interrupted in the middle of a business meeting.

The girl had disappeared, but she was back with Cindy before Natalie had shaken the numbness from her hands. Cindy wore a belligerent expression that Natalie didn't know how to interpret. "Hi," Natalie said, plastering on the same thin facsimile of a smile that her mother would have used in this situation. "How are you?"

Cindy gave a huffy laugh. "Imagine that," she said. "Every other day she's the last child to be picked up, and then today you're early."

Natalie checked her watch: she *was* early, but only by five minutes. She wondered if Cassie might owe Cindy money—could that be the reason for her attitude? "Well, I'm here now," she said, widening her smile.

Cindy scoffed again, hands on her hips. "Lord, anybody could tell where you came from," she said. "You're your daddy's girl through and through."

Natalie felt the pressure of angry tears rising behind her eyes. After the day she'd had, it seemed so unfair that now she had to stand here and listen to Cindy Caldwell, who'd always hated her for no particular reason. "Where is she?" she asked. "I'll just grab her and get out of your hair."

"I know about you," Cindy said, waving a finger in her face. "I know all about your family. The night he died, I told Ben he ought to know better than to mess with a little slut like you. And look what happened to him." The kids on the rag rug were all staring now, and one little girl in a pink sweatshirt had started crying.

Natalie took a step closer, thinking how good it would feel to connect her palm to that smooth cheek. How satisfying it would be to yank those curls, to wrap Cindy's red wig around her wrist and snap her head back. She had tried to take the principles of yoga seriously, but she was still a Macready.

But after everything that had happened today, she was not going to waste her time on a catfight with Cindy Caldwell. "I don't know what was between you and Ben," she said wearily. "And honestly, I don't care anymore. Would you just go get Anjali, please?"

Cindy exchanged a look with the pale girl, and Natalie expected her to bustle away to the back room, but she didn't move. "What?" Natalie said. "What's wrong?" Surely Cindy had not hurt the baby, she thought. She might be crazy, but she wasn't that kind of crazy.

Cindy crossed her arms over her chest. "She's not here." There was defiance in her voice, but also something that sounded a lot like fear.

"What?" Natalie's voice rose. "Cindy, you tell me right fucking now what you've done with my niece." The pale girl gasped, and the boy in her arms imitated her, his mouth a perfect O.

Cindy's eyes were still hard, but her chin trembled, and now Natalie could see the fear in her eyes. "She's with Luke," she said.

39.

From the driveway, Natalie called Luke, but it went immediately to voicemail. Cindy wouldn't tell her anything else—where Luke had taken Anjali, or why—and Natalie hadn't wanted to waste time arguing with her. It didn't make sense that Luke had picked up Anjali, unless maybe Cassie had asked both of them, and simply forgotten that she'd double-booked. The curtains twitched, and Natalie could see Cindy's pinched, frowny face glaring out at her, so she hurriedly put the car in reverse and backed out.

She could drive up to the farmhouse on Bible Camp Road, but what would she say when she arrived? If Luke was simply doing a favor for Cassie, he wouldn't react well to the idea that Natalie felt the need to check up on him. If she got there and found Anjali napping in her car seat on the kitchen floor while he fixed a broken cabinet, she would need an excuse. Maybe she could say she wanted to borrow something of Kaitlyn's—a book, a casserole dish, a yoga top. It was lame, but he would buy it; Natalie and Kaitlyn had been the same size before Kaitlyn's pregnancy, and traded clothes so often that they sometimes forgot what belonged to whom.

Her thoughts returned to Lanny, that old car rising to the surface like some primitive creature of the deep. She couldn't bring herself to be sorry he was dead, but she felt a little sick when she thought about how her father and Leo had talked about him all these years, as if he'd been the golden boy, their heir apparent. If she saw her father at Rotary or a church picnic, chances were good that he'd end up telling a story about Lanny—the time he'd sweet-talked the old principal out of suspending him after he was caught with weed in his locker, or the time, age twelve, he'd towed Kaitlyn's unicorn float all the way across the lake on a dare, swimming with the rope between his teeth. If the Macreadys and Ben were the Duke boys, then Lanny was supposed to be the second generation, raising hell from one end of the county to the other, and his flight from home had been, she'd believed, the great sadness of her father's life.

Except it had all been theater. All of it—the fond stories, the nostalgia—was meant to distract the audience from the fact that Lanny Marsh was not wandering around the Pacific on a merchant ship, but dead and gone for twelve years now. Until Ben had found out, and proved that his loyalty was not to the Macreadys, after all.

If Natalie had turned her head the other way, she never would have seen it. If, when she came to the intersection of Goshen Street and Highway 82, she'd been looking at the Texaco station rather than at the studio, she wouldn't have glimpsed the back end of the truck, just visible behind the corner of the building. But she did see it, and braked suddenly, making the Chevy that had been riding her ass through downtown squeal around her, the Skoal-hat-wearing driver leaning out the window to point her way and lick the V between his fingers. She sat for a moment, heart pounding, and then turned in the middle of the road and pulled into the studio lot.

Visitors to the studio rarely left their cars in the back. Unless you had the code to the rear door, it was easier to park in the side lot by the main entrance. Somehow, though, before she even rounded the corner, she knew that she would find that back door open and that the truck would turn out to be Luke's, the tricked-out F-150 that he'd insisted on leasing even when Kaitlyn barely had enough money for groceries.

Natalie was already halfway to the door when she turned around, went to the passenger side of her car, and reached into the glove compartment for the pink-skinned Glock 19. The magazine was in a pink camo pouch under the car's owner manual, but it felt lighter than it should have, and when she checked it, her stomach sank: she'd forgotten to load it after the last time her dad took her to the range. Her hands were shaking as she reached for the paper box of ammo— her dad had always said to keep it separate, but thank God she'd never bothered to listen—and shook the bullets into her palm. The magazine took fifteen, but she loaded only five, wincing as the hard metal edges pressed into the skin of her thumbs. She clicked the magazine into place, then checked the safety and slipped the Glock into her purse.

It wasn't as if she was going to actually use it, she told herself. She couldn't even put her finger on what she was afraid of, but just knowing the gun was there made her feel better, the sick feeling in her gut dissipating slightly.

Natalie moved through the doorway, and as she paused, she realized that she could hear Anjali babbling from inside one of the studios. She sounded neither hurt nor scared, and Natalie's knees went weak with relief. She walked forward cautiously and looked through the open door into Studio A, where her niece was sitting on a half mat in her puffy winter coat, eating a pouch of pureed apples.

"Time to get going, honeybunch," Luke called from the hallway. When he caught sight of Natalie, he looked surprised, but not as if her presence worried or upset him. "Hey there," he said. "You forget something?"

He was wearing a duffel bag over his shoulder, and the shape of his jacket kept her from seeing if there was a holster at his waist. But of course there was, Natalie thought; Luke didn't even go to the grocery store without a gun.

"Hey," she said. "I'm just here to pick up Anjali. Cassie asked me to bring her back to the lake."

"No can do," Luke said, still in the same chillingly upbeat tone. "She's coming with me, right, pumpkin?" Anjali looked up and gave him a fleeting smile. "I just stopped by to relieve you of some of that extra cash in the register. I know you don't even pay Kaitlyn for half the time she spends in here."

"You can't do that." Natalie gauged the distance between Anjali and Luke. The baby was closer to him than she was to Natalie,
which meant she couldn't risk a sudden move. "I don't care about the
cash," she added, in case he'd misunderstood her. "But you can't take
Anjali."

"She's my daughter," he said.

Natalie's mouth was dry as sand, and she made herself swallow
before she could speak. "Did Cassie tell you that?"

"She didn't have to tell me. Look at her."

They both looked, but from Natalie's perspective, Anjali didn't
look any more like Luke than she did like Jay. Her skin, eyes, and hair
were the same color as Cassie's. She might as well have been born by
osmosis, like a paramecium.

"Cassie said it only happened once," Natalie said.

Luke had that familiar cocky look that she used to think was sort
of cute, head tilted back and to the side. He'd been longing to tell
someone how he'd finally gotten the girl he'd been pining after for
years, and so he was even willing to tell Natalie about it now, when it
should have been clear that she was trying her best to stall him. "Once
is all it takes, Natalie. I did the math."

"But do you know for sure?"

Luke scoffed. "I don't need a damn paternity test, if that's what
you're asking. I knew as soon as I saw her at the Felons' Ball, and I
went straight to Cassie and confronted her. She thought she could buy
me off." There was contempt in his voice. "As if I would sell my child."

"But you can't just take her," she said. "You need Cassie's permission. Otherwise it's parental kidnapping." She had no idea how
she knew this term, or whether what she'd said was even true, but it
seemed to give Luke pause. "What about Kaitlyn?" she tried. "What
about your wife and her baby? You're just going to leave them and
disappear?"

His mouth twisted. "She's been planning to leave me, did you
know that? That bitch Amanda wrote her a check for five thousand

dollars. The only reason she isn't already gone is that she can't find a car."

Natalie thought of the little convertible that she'd been planning to get rid of before someone shattered the windshield at the Felons' Ball. Shortly before that night, she'd promised to sell that car to Kaitlyn—the car that would have made it possible for her to leave her husband.

"Jesus, Luke," she said, shaking her head. "You smashed my windshield, didn't you? I bet it was your idea to put the roofies in Cassie's drink on the night of the boat crash. You gave Lanny that cup to give to her, so you could rape her on the party boat."

For a moment he looked taken aback, and she realized that he hadn't expected her to put it together. Still, he had nothing to lose by admitting it now. "It wouldn't have been *rape*," Luke said in a disgusted tone. "Cassie wanted it all right. She made that pretty clear when we made this one." He smiled at Anjali, who cut her eyes in his direction without looking up from her applesauce.

Natalie could feel her knees shaking, and she willed her body to keep still. She could imagine how he would kill her, as if it were a movie she was watching—her body slumping to the floor of the studio, Luke throwing her into the bed of his truck and spreading a tarp over her limp form. If he and Anjali were heading into the mountains, he could pull into any backcountry campsite and dump her body down a ravine. Hunters might find her next deer season, but by then, he would be long gone.

Luke would have a good plan, because that was the kind of man he was. He would have money, and a new ID, and a cover story that would pass muster with strangers in restaurants and motor courts. He would have a destination in mind and a plan to get there. She had read stories about men who took their children to Mexico and never resurfaced.

Anjali, who had turned to look at Natalie, now threw her empty pouch on the floor and began crawling toward her aunt. Natalie lunged forward and scooped the baby into her arms, retreating against the wall. When she looked back to Luke, he was out of the doorway in a tactical crouch, his Sig Sauer pointed at her head.

"That was cute," he conceded. "And if it was your daddy standing here, or your boyfriend Hardy, I'd say you'd be pretty safe making a run for it. But you know I could shoot both your eyes out right now without harming a hair on that little girl's head."

Whether it was something in Luke's tone, or whether Natalie was holding her too tightly, Anjali picked that moment to start bawling. Natalie let out a low moan of fear. "Give her to me," Luke coaxed as he moved closer, still with the gun trained on her head. "Hand her over, and you can walk right out of here. You think I want to hurt you, Natalie? You're like a sister to me."

But she didn't believe him. Whether or not she gave up Anjali, there was no way that Luke was letting her walk out alive. Natalie jiggled the baby frantically, which only made her cry harder. "I think I have a pacifier in my purse," she said, raising her voice to be heard over Anjali's cries. "I'm going to reach for it, okay?"

Luke said something, but she couldn't hear him. Anjali's screams were so earsplittingly loud that Natalie wondered if someone passing by might hear and call the police, but it was five o'clock, and this side of town never saw much foot traffic.

He was close enough now that he could probably shoot her and grab Anjali before she fell. Natalie balanced her niece with her left arm and reached into her purse with her right. In two seconds, she racked the slide with one hand and brought the Glock up to aim at his chest.

Luke laughed. "I remember that thing," he said. "Didn't that come with your Barbie Dream House?" He took a step back, still grinning.

Natalie switched on the laser, and Luke looked startled when the green light appeared on his chest and then moved to his forehead. The sound was something she felt more than heard, a hand on her shoulder pushing her heavily to the floor as she clutched the baby to her chest.

She looked up, and there was a blank spot where Luke's head should have been. As if on a time delay, his body fell backward, hitting the floor with a thump that seemed to shake the walls.

"You stupid shit," she said to the soles of his boots, forcing the words out through chattering teeth. All this could have been avoided, if only he'd been the kind of man who was willing to take no for an answer.

40.

EIGHTEEN MONTHS LATER

When she saw the forecast, Natalie wanted to call the whole thing off. Six inches of rain had been forecast for the next twelve hours—not enough for the creeks to overflow their banks, but enough to make the trails in the national forest slick as if they'd been greased. But neither she nor Hardy could find the number of the ranger who was supposed to meet them at the marina at seven thirty the next morning, and finally she set her alarm and went to sleep, comforting herself with the thought that no tourists could possibly care enough about Appalachian folk traditions to take a ferry out to the Hazel Creek graveyard on a day damp enough to make you wring out your underwear.

But she was wrong about that. Three people had shown up, a vigorous elderly couple from New Jersey on a scenic tour of the Blue Ridge and a woman from Richmond who thought she might have family buried in Hazel Creek, although the names she mentioned didn't sound right. The ranger had brought yellow rain slickers for everyone, and Natalie played her part, narrating the history of the town and the arrival of the TVA as the boat flew across the lake. Hardy, who had shaken hands with the ranger but hadn't bothered to introduce himself to the tourists, kept a protective hand on the small of her back, as if half afraid she might do a backflip off the side of the boat.

"Natalie's mother has been doing these tours for twenty-five years," the ranger announced as they came in sight of the landing. "I think this is the first Decoration Day she's missed in all that time."

He looked to Natalie, and she nodded in confirmation. The wife from New Jersey looked concerned. "She's fine," Natalie assured her. "My dad caught a bad cold this spring and hasn't been able to shake it, so she wanted to stay home with him."

"Oh," the wife said sympathetically, putting her hand to her chest. "Well, you have to watch those things when you get to be our age."

They were pulling up to the landing now, but when Natalie jumped down and held out her hand to help the woman from Richmond onto the sand, Hardy shook his head and moved her gently to the side. "You're doing plenty," he murmured, too low for the others to hear. "Let me take over now."

That was what she loved about him, Natalie thought. He knew what she needed, and found a way to give it to her without ever making her feel like she was being condescended or talked down to. Lately he was even more solicitous than usual of her energy and her moods, but with Hardy this concern, which surely would have irritated her from another man, made her feel safe and protected. They were two halves of a whole now, linked not only by love but by the secrets they shared.

She knew that Hardy was probably not a wholly good man. After they'd been together a month or two, she'd finally gotten around to googling him and found that, as she suspected, he hadn't told her the whole truth about his reasons for leaving Atlanta. He'd been one of the officers present at the shooting of an unarmed homeless man outside a downtown hotel, and had been disciplined for lying to internal affairs during the investigation. She never told him that she knew, just like she'd never told him about what she'd found on the party boat. She and Hardy had their shared secrets, but that didn't mean she couldn't keep a few secrets of her own too.

The wet leaves on the trail were slippery, but not as bad as she'd feared, and even with the husband from New Jersey's bad knees it took them less than half an hour to make it up to the graveyard. Natalie related the history of the congregation, pointed out some of the more notable graves, and then gave them each a bunch of flowers from the insulated bag she'd carried up the mountain. While the tourists poked around, she and Hardy went to work on her family's graves, heaping daisies and carnations beneath the headstones of James and Helen Sinclair, Robert and Patience Mason, and Otto, her grandmother's uncle, who'd been cut in half by a train.

She wondered if they'd have time to hike to the old cabin. She'd never told anyone about seeing Croaker Farber up there, but by the time she went back, months after Luke's death, he'd cleared out. She didn't know what had happened to him, but probably nothing good.

"Could we be buried up here?" Hardy asked as he laid a bouquet of daisies on the headstone of Elizabeth Mary Sinclair, Beloved Wife and Mother.

Natalie sat back, rubbing her dirty hands on her thighs. "Would you want to?"

He shrugged. "Maybe. I don't have any idea where the Underwoods are buried. I like the idea of being part of something."

Natalie took a handkerchief from her bag and rubbed at the black smudges obscuring Robert Mason's birth and death dates. She worked on, forgetting the damp soaking through the knees of her leggings, until she felt Hardy tucking his jacket around her shoulders. "You're shivering," he said tenderly. "Shaking like a little mouse."

She turned sideways to kiss his hand, but then she stopped. A brown-haired woman with a baby carrier strolled down the next aisle of graves, doing that side-to-side jiggle that mothers did when carrying sleeping children. Natalie almost fell backward onto her butt, grabbing Hardy's arm just in time.

It was June now, and she hadn't seen Kaitlyn since Christmas, when they'd all met at their parents' house for a dinner that seemed more like an exercise in willful denial than a celebration. As always, there had been two trees, a big messy one with the ornaments they'd made as children, and one on the glass porch decorated only with white candles and magnolia petals coated in resin. Friends dropped by with fruitcakes and divinity, and no one said a word about Jay, or Lanny, or even Luke, who had been buried only the week before.

By then it had been determined that Natalie would not be charged with murder. Hardy had recused himself from the investigation, but the sheriff of Tyndall County concluded that Natalie had shot Luke in self-defense, and the Commonwealth's attorney agreed. Cindy Caldwell kicked up a fuss, naturally, but once she was reminded that she was lucky not to be charged as an accessory to a kidnapping, her outrage seemed to die down. Months later, Hardy told Natalie that Cindy was the one who'd called a tip in to the department that Jay Desai's body could be found in Macready Cove—a tip based, as far as Natalie could ever tell, on wishful thinking alone.

Jay's body had been found, though not in Macready Cove. The car was located first, in a gravel lot not far from the dam offices. The lot was used by the TVA employees, but not in the winter, when they preferred the paved lot closer to the main road, where you were less likely to bottom out on a muddy day. Natalie went out there after the car had been towed and saw that the Toyota hadn't really been in the lot at all, but pulled off into a clear space in the trees that was obscured by brush on three sides.

Several weeks later Jay's body washed up, and some months after, they found a tripod. Though his phone was never located, the police said the gash on the back of his head must have come from a rock he'd hit on the way down, after capturing a pic of some impossible pose executed on the lip of the Lake Monroe Dam.

Or maybe, Natalie thought, that was simply what they wanted to think. She had no reason to connect her parents to Jay's death, and yet the coincidence of timing was difficult to overlook. Their oldest daughter and granddaughter had been living on the opposite side of the country, and now they were back, safely within the Macreadys' circle of influence. All it had taken was the swift excision of Jay Desai from their lives, and the truth was that no one seemed to miss him all that much.

After Jay's body was recovered, Cassie found an apartment, a new day care for Anjali, and a job at an environmental nonprofit in Tyndall County. She commuted there three days a week, and Natalie picked up Anjali and gave her dinner on the nights that Cassie worked late. Still, the sisters didn't talk much, and Natalie understood that the closeness they'd shared on the deck at the Silver Moon had been a fragile, conditional thing. Cassie didn't know how to thank Natalie for rescuing her daughter at the studio that day; her gratitude was too complex, too inflected by the nuances of their family's past, to put into words. Anjali looked more and more like her mother as she grew, and Natalie wondered sometimes if Luke had been right about her paternity. Though no one ever mentioned it in her presence, she knew there had been plenty of rumors going around town after she'd shot her brother-in-law.

Natalie appreciated that it was difficult for Cassie, ending up back in their hometown after she'd fought so hard to leave it. Right now she was still trying to have it both ways, as if she could be part of their family while still maintaining her independence. That was impossible, but Natalie would let her come to that in her own time, knowing that eventually Cassie would leave her silly hippie job and find a man who fit in with the rest of them. Falling in line with their family might cause her sister some pangs of conscience, but Natalie didn't have much sympathy for that. Cassie had made her own bed.

Kaitlyn would have nothing to do with the studio now, not that Natalie could blame her. The week after Luke's death, she'd moved into a rented house near downtown. She hadn't called to give Natalie the address, and Natalie had only figured out where it was when she happened to drive by and saw Kaitlyn hauling trash to the curb. Natalie wanted to stop and take the trash can out of her sister's hand, but when their eyes met, Kaitlyn cut her eyes in a way that clearly meant *Keep moving.*

Now, a year and a half later, Natalie almost didn't recognize the woman standing in front of the grave of Zipporah Miller, b. 1818, d. 1861. Kaitlyn had gained enough weight to change the outline of her face and body, and she'd dyed her hair a muddy brown that seemed like the last color anyone would choose from the boxes in the drugstore aisle. When Natalie approached, she looked up and pasted on a smile, and at least that was familiar—the same bright but hesitant smile she'd used to greet their yoga students.

"How did you get here?" Natalie asked.

"Parked on the side of the road and walked in," Kaitlyn said, still jiggling the baby, whose eyes were open now. The hike from the state road was nearly two miles, and Natalie could hardly believe that Kaitlyn, who'd been afraid to go to the Walmart down in Tyndall by herself, had done it alone with a baby strapped to her chest.

"Mama's not here," Natalie went on. "Daddy's sick. I don't know if you heard."

Kaitlyn nodded, and Natalie wondered now if she'd come precisely because she knew Rosemary wouldn't be here. "Is he going to be okay?" Kaitlyn asked.

"Of course," Natalie said, trying to speak firmly enough to dissipate the anxiety she always felt when she talked about her father now. The cold that had lingered through the spring had hollowed him out. He'd lost twenty pounds and let his beard grow out, a dingy gray. "I keep telling him to go to the doctor, but you know how he is."

Kaitlyn looked away, her lips tightening. When she turned, the baby met Natalie's gaze and suddenly thrust out her little arms, squirming in the carrier. "Oh my God," Natalie said, her voice catching. "Can I hold her, please? Just for a minute?"

"Of course." Kaitlyn unbuckled one strap and held the baby by the armpits as she lifted her into Natalie's arms. "I call her Emmy," Kaitlyn said, hanging the carrier from the arm of Patience Mason's stony-eyed angel.

"Emmy girl," Natalie whispered into her niece's ear, trying to swallow the pang she felt. She wondered if Kaitlyn had gotten the smocked dress she'd sent with *EMC* embroidered on the collar, for

Emmeline Macready Caldwell. Their father would have made a joke about Einstein's formula, but he, like Rosemary, had never seen the baby in real life.

"We're moving," Kaitlyn said, pulling out her Marlboro Lights and taking a few steps away from her daughter. "I found a job in Charlotte. Cindy is helping me out with money."

"*Charlotte?*" Natalie repeated in disbelief. She couldn't picture her sister in a city. Kaitlyn had always refused to attend out-of-town yoga trainings, claiming that interstate traffic made her anxious. "Do you really think you'll like it there?"

"I want something new," Kaitlyn said, shaking a cigarette into her palm. "I'd offer you one of these, by the way, but I heard you're pregnant."

Natalie found herself blushing, repositioning Emmy atop the small mound of her belly.

"Are you living with him now?" Kaitlyn gestured to Hardy, who'd been pretending to read the names on the same two graves for the past five minutes.

"We're engaged," she said. "We just closed on a house." She wouldn't tell Kaitlyn that her father had insisted on providing the down payment on the house, or that she and Hardy had dinner with her parents every Friday night. She wouldn't tell her that with the money they'd saved, they'd invested in a small distillery that would make legal liquor labeled as moonshine, for the benefit of the tourists who were flocking to Lake Monroe in greater numbers every summer. There was even talk of a moonshine festival, which her father said was the stupidest thing he'd ever heard. She knew that her father and Uncle Leo were probably still brewing up in the mountains, and she knew that Hardy had probably agreed to look the other way. Natalie had held on to Jay's yoga retreat idea too, and she'd done a little research into what it would cost to build rental cabins on her parents' property, though of course she hadn't told her father about that part.

"I wish we could spend time together before you leave," Natalie said, pressing her lips to the top of Emmy's head. "I wish we could put all of this behind us."

"People are dead, Natalie," Kaitlyn said. "I'm not blaming you for Luke—I'm not saying he didn't deserve it, but he's not the only one. I don't want my daughter growing up around people who think there's nothing more important than saving their own skins."

But was there any difference, Natalie thought, between her parents' skins and her own? She knew that Kaitlyn believed she'd given her body in exchange for Hardy dropping his investigations into the Macreadys, but that wasn't how it had felt to her. Everything Natalie had done, she'd done willingly, to protect what was theirs. "I don't think it's as simple as you're making it out to be."

"Interesting to see you turning into such a team player," Kaitlyn scoffed. "When you were always happy to be the spoiled brat."

That stung, but Natalie understood. She had wasted a lot of time purposefully ducking every kind of responsibility. Why would her sister believe that now she was ready to take on the burden of being her parents' daughter, in full knowledge of what it meant?

Just as suddenly as she'd thrust out her arms to Natalie, Emmy threw herself toward her mother, Natalie barely pulling her back in time to keep her from smashing her head on a gravestone. Natalie sucked in a breath, but Kaitlyn didn't seem fazed. She screwed her cigarette out on the bottom of her hiking boot and took her daughter, buckling her back into the carrier.

"I hope you're happy," Kaitlyn said. "I really mean that. I hope you get everything you want."

It was an odd kind of goodbye, but Natalie understood what Kaitlyn was saying. Two roads had diverged, and Natalie had chosen the broad and familiar one, whose end she could see perfectly well without moving a single inch from where she stood. She was a Macready, and she would stay a Macready even when she married Hardy Underwood. Kaitlyn would have said that Natalie had given up her integrity to remain their father's favorite, but Natalie knew the truth was that she'd finally grown up. It wasn't her job to worry about the people her family had hurt. She could only save herself.

It made her nervous to think of Kaitlyn leaving town in possession of their secrets, but there was one secret, the most important one, that Natalie was pretty sure Kaitlyn would never guess. If her great-grandfather had been right and everyone buried in Hazel Creek Baptist's cemetery was going to heaven, then there would be one unexpected angelic form rising from the graves on Judgment Day. In the midst of all the Millers and Powells would be Lanny Marsh, forever eighteen years old, with the round hole of a 9mm in the back of his head. In a way, it was better than thinking of him in an unmarked grave in some faraway country on the shores of the Pacific. Lanny should rest here, among their own people. No matter what he'd done, he deserved that much.

Trey had told her the truth about Lanny last week when his cough was especially bad. "I shot him," he said, looking at her with pleading eyes, as if he'd mistaken her for his confessor. "I drove the car into the lake, and then I took the die-cast and threw it in at the same spot. I did it for you, baby. So he could never hurt you like that again." When he was done, he made her put her hand on the family Bible to swear that she would never repeat it to anyone, not even Hardy.

Natalie understood now what her mother had meant when she said she was prepared to give everything for her husband. That was what family meant in the end. All this time Natalie had tried to imagine what she could have done if she'd been on Ben's boat the night of his murder—how she would have stepped in, thrown herself forward, put herself in jeopardy to save him. Now, when she pictured that moment, she could only see her mother turning to her, bloody as a birthing sow, and placing the knife in her hand.

Acknowledgments

Writing a book is never easy, and I couldn't have written this one without the support of my family, especially my husband, Keith, and our incredible children. Most of them aren't allowed to read my books yet, but they still think it's kind of cool that I write them.

Thanks to my wonderful agent, Denise Shannon, whose opinion I trust more than just about anybody I know. She'd read only a few pages of *The Felons' Ball* when she told me that I was on the right track and should keep going. It turned out she was right, as usual. Sarah Stein is my ideal editor, and I'm still pinching myself that I get to work with her. Thanks to Claire Dee at the Denise Shannon Literary Agency, and to everyone at Harper Books, especially Heather Drucker, Katie O'Callaghan, Jackie Quaranto, and David Howe. My UK agent, Judith Murray, is a dream to work with. Thank you for supporting my books on the other side of the pond.

Bill Boyle read the first chapter and told me it was good before I was ready to believe it. Vanessa Cuti and Charlie Cline read drafts when I was feeling stuck and gave comments that made the whole book significantly better. Thanks to all of you, and to the rest of Bill's class at the Center for Fiction, especially Ariel Ramchandani.

I've been lucky to get to visit so many great independent bookstores in the past couple of years, and I'd like to give a special shoutout to ones here in Virginia: Downtown Books in Lexington, Fountain

Bookstore in Richmond, Birch Tree Bookstore in Leesburg, Book No Further in Roanoke, and Blacksburg Books. Farther afield, I've loved getting to know the readers at Carmichael's Bookstore in Louisville, Kentucky; Novel in Memphis, Tennessee; WordsWorth Books in Little Rock, Arkansas; Square Books in Oxford, Mississippi; Foxtale Book Shoppe in Atlanta, Georgia; Left Bank Books in St. Louis, Missouri; Murder by the Book in Houston, Texas; Malaprop's Bookstore in Asheville, North Carolina; and the Pat Conroy Literary Center in Beaufort, South Carolina. My friend Jen Murvin at Pagination Bookshop in Springfield, Missouri, is a fierce champion for books and a gift to the literary community. Flannery Buchanan and Chelsea Powers at my beloved Bluebird Bookstop are building an incredible group of readers in central Virginia, and I am so grateful to have been taken under their wings. (Get it?) Thanks to the Ladies Who Libro for the laughter and the encouragement, especially the fabulous Elle Cosimano.

My editor at *CrimeReads*, Dwyer Murphy, has given me an amazing opportunity to interview and learn from writers I admire. It's my favorite job I've ever had, and I can't believe I get to do it once a month. Thanks to all the writers I've had the opportunity to talk to for the Backlist, and the many other friends I've made in the writing community over the past few years.

I've been practicing yoga for twenty-three years, and it's changed my life for the better in about a million different ways. Thanks to the teachers, especially Carroll Ann Friedmann and Liam Buckley at Ashtanga Yoga Charlottesville, Ross Stambaugh, and Segovia Pagan.

Thanks to my colleagues and students at VMI, especially Henry Wise and my spring 2024 fiction students, who read one particular scene and made a few suggestions so I'd sound like I knew what I was talking about. Thanks to James McLaughlin and Jim Brown for taking me out to Maxwelton and teaching me how to shoot, sort of.

I've been surrounded my whole life by strong women who live by their principles, stand up for others, and have taught me to do the same. This book is dedicated to my mother, Mary Welek Atwell, my best friend and forever role model, and to my chosen sisters: Sarah John, Diane Brookreson, Sabrina Rose-Smith, and Norm Ash. Here's to the next twenty-five years.

About the Author

POLLY STEWART is the author of *The Good Ones*. She grew up in the
Blue Ridge Mountains of Virginia, where she still lives. Her short
fiction has appeared in *The Best American Mystery Stories*, and her
nonfiction has appeared in the *New York Times, Good Housekeeping,*
and other publications. She writes the monthly Backlist column for
CrimeReads.